The Perfect Dad

Francie's List

☺ Won't mind tap dancing in the hallway

☺ Will take me to the Dairy Queen

☺ Reminds me to buckle my seatbelt

☺ Likes dogs and meatloaf

☺ Will love us

Mom's List

♡ Likes the opera

♡ Will buy me new muffler for my car

♡ Strong enough to carry me upstairs

♡ Will send me flowers

♡ Will love us

Please address questions and book requests to: Harlequin Reader Service
U.S.: 3010 Walden Ave., P.O. Box 1325, Buffalo, NY 14269
CAN.: P.O. Box 609, Fort Erie, Ont. L2A 5X3

Born in the USA

NEW HAMPSHIRE

MURIEL JENSEN

Racing with the Moon

Harlequin Books

TORONTO • NEW YORK • LONDON
AMSTERDAM • PARIS • SYDNEY • HAMBURG
STOCKHOLM • ATHENS • TOKYO • MILAN
MADRID • WARSAW • BUDAPEST • AUCKLAND

HARLEQUIN BOOKS
225 Duncan Mill Road, Don Mills,
Ontario, Canada M3B 3K9

ISBN 0-373-47179-3

RACING WITH THE MOON

Dear Reader,

It's so exciting for me to reconnect with characters from earlier in my career and to think that they're still alive, even if it's just in publishing.

Genny Scott was inspired by a woman I knew in Los Angeles who'd been through an earthquake experience similar to the one in Genny's past, and Jack is the result of knowing the world is filled with wonderful men and simply putting their best qualities into one neat package in a three-piece suit.

I set their story in New Hampshire because my husband and I spent "Leaf Peeper" weekend in North Conway with my family and I couldn't get enough of the color, the fragrance of the wind and the sound of it in the birches, and the wonderful feeling of coming home that I get anywhere in New England.

I hope you'll find all those things in this reprise of *Racing with the Moon*.

Muriel Jensen

P.O. Box 1168
Astoria, Oregon 97103

To all the beautiful young ladies of
Maddox Dance Studio

Chapter One

"It's like being a padiddle."

Genevieve Scott gave her patient a quick, vague glance, then looked back at her watch and continued to count. Satisfied that Emily McGovern's pulse was normal, Genny freed her wrist and stood to push the glass-paneled doors open. Sunlight flooded into the opulent French country-style bedroom.

"Your pulse is good, Emily," Genny said, moving back to the bed to smile over her. "But I wonder if there's enough blood getting to your brain. A padiddle?"

Emily, amid her Laura Ashley sheets and pillow covers, heaved a tragic sigh. "One headlight," she explained. "You remember, riding with your boyfriend and spotting an oncoming car with only one headlight. Whoever shouted 'Paddidle!' first earned a kiss." Emily turned her face to look out at the blue sky and evergreen treetops visible beyond the terrace. "Now all it'll earn me are looks of pity or disgust."

"Well, maybe that's your own fault," Genny said gently, sitting on the edge of the bed. "You pity yourself."

"I've lost a breast."

"You're alive and healthy."

"I'm deformed."

"You're beautiful," Genny said sincerely. She picked up a mirror from the bedside table and held it up. When Emily turned her face away, Genny followed with the mirror. "Look at yourself. At sixty-three you're as beautiful as you were on your album covers. You don't even have to go through chemotherapy. I'd say you've got it made."

"Ha!" Emily scoffed. But she took the mirror from Genny and looked at her own reflection. She gave the soft curls of her graying red hair a desultory pat.

Genny watched her, feeling affection mingled with helplessness. When Nursecare had assigned her to Emily three weeks before, she'd wondered if her patient could be the same Emily McGovern who'd risen as a young woman to the top of the music charts with her sultry, romantic sounds, and remained popular as musical trends came and went. Genny remembered reading that she'd retired six years previously after the death of her daughter.

The moment she'd seen Emily, she recognized the still-beautiful face. A warm, witty nature had drawn Genny's friendship immediately. Though Emily was recovering beautifully from the surgery, she was finding the emotional trauma of a mastectomy more difficult to overcome.

Emily put the mirror down and fixed bright but weary gray eyes on her nurse. "I suppose I shouldn't care at my age," she said grimly. "But I do."

"You should care," Genny corrected, squeezing her hand, "but you shouldn't regret. Let's get you out onto the terrace for some sun."

Genny fitted cotton slippers on Emily's feet and helped her up. She moved slowly toward the balcony. "You have to get some sun and exercise instead of hiding in your room. You don't want your family going back to New Hampshire in August without you, do you?"

"Jack and the girls would never leave without me."

"Well, you wouldn't want to prevent their going, would you?" Genny stepped onto the patio, waiting to steady Emily as she made the small step down. "Judging by what you've told me, you must have the most generous son-in-law in the world."

Genny moved behind Emily to support her weight as she eased onto a thickly cushioned chaise. The woman settled with a groan of effort. "I know. Almost makes up for my worthless daughter, rest her soul. We shouldn't speak ill of the dead, particularly those in your own family, but a worthless woman remains a worthless woman after she's gone."

Genny placed a red Pendleton blanket over Emily's knees, and a glass of water on the floor beside her. "But she left you with two beautiful granddaughters and a man who adores you. And if you take good care of yourself, you should live another thirty or forty years. You're a rich woman, Emily.''

Emily said, with a trace of a smile this time, "I'm a padiddle.''

Genny leaned against the railing and shook her head at her. "Where did you ever get that metaphor? Makes you sound like a truck driver or a biker.''

"It just came to me one night," she replied. "Something important to me is missing.''

"Replace it with a prosthesis," Genny encouraged. "Or better yet, have reconstructive surgery.''

"That's fake.''

Genny smiled. "Growing a real one is out of the question.''

Emily acknowledged that truth with the first genuine smile Genny had seen on her since she'd begun her daily visits two weeks ago. "You really are a tyrant," Emily said. "You coat it all with sweet kindness, but underneath you're just a big bully. So what's a prosthesis or surgery going to do for me?''

Encouraged by her interest, Genny came to sit on the Adirondack chair that matched the lounge. "It'll stop that feeling of being a 'padiddle,' for one thing," she said, repeating Emily's word with a note of disapproval. "It'll give you confidence, make you look great in your clothes, maybe even get you some second looks from gentlemen of culture and style." She simulated those qualities with a waggle of her eyebrow and an upward tilt of her nose.

Emily laughed, but sobered quickly. "And when the gentleman of style discovers what I really look like?''

Genny shrugged as though that should be of no concern. "Then you run the same chance every woman does. We all attract men by how we appear, but hold them by how we *are*.''

Emily fought against the truth of that statement but finally capitulated with a sigh and a maternal pat on Genny's hand. "Why hasn't some brilliant man taken you out of circulation?''

Genny laughed. "Mostly because I'm not *in* circulation, I guess. Between my work and my daughter, there isn't much time for a social life.''

Emily shook her head. "I can't believe you've been single nine years. What's wrong with the doctors in this town? Are they blind?''

"I don't see much of doctors in home health care," Genny

replied, leaning down to retrieve Emily's water glass and hand it to her. "Mostly I see geriatric gentlemen who *do* have big ideas for me one moment, but usually forget what they were the next."

"I'd fix you up with my son-in-law," Emily said, "but he works so hard you'd never see him. And you should have a man who'll feed you peeled grapes and tell you how beautiful you are."

Genny considered that life-style and nodded her approval. "If you find a man like that, you know how to reach me." She stood and patted Emily's shoulder. "I'll be right back. I brought you a present, but I left it downstairs with my purse."

Genny ran lightly down the curved staircase, meeting a tall, portly man wearing black slacks and a long-sleeved white shirt. He paused on the landing, carrying a silver tray bearing a steaming china teapot and two cups.

"Are you leaving, Miss Genevieve?" he asked in surprise.

She smiled. "No, Cavendish. I brought something for Mrs. McGovern but I left it in the kitchen. I'll be right up. I wouldn't miss your scones for anything."

He nodded formally, the glint in his eye betraying his affection. "Very good, Miss. Don't run on the stairs, please. We wouldn't want to lose you now that Mrs. McGovern is doing so well."

"I'll be careful," she promised. "And Cavendish? Don't call me 'Miss.' It makes me feel as though I'm in line for the throne or something."

He shrugged a shoulder, careful of the tray. "Perhaps that's where you belong, Miss Genevieve."

"This is America, Dishy." Genny whispered as though she were sharing a confidence. "There is no throne."

Cavendish whispered back. "That never bothered Sarajane."

Genny looked at him blankly for a moment.

"Miss Emily's daughter," he explained. "Mr. Jack's wife."

"Ah." Genny nodded, noting he'd failed to put a title of any kind before Sarajane's name. They were slipping onto personal ground she had no right to discuss. She smiled at the man who was every inch the gentleman's gentleman. "Run up with Mrs. McGovern's tea, and I'll be right behind you."

Genny continued down the stairs and into the big, comfortable kitchen where she'd left her purse and the unorthodox gift she'd purchased just that morning for Emily.

JACK FLEMING PUT his briefcase under the small hall table and glanced at the stack of mail. Seeing nothing of interest in it, he picked up the *Oregonian* and frowned over the lead story as he climbed the carpeted stairs, pulling at his tie.

"Mr. Jack!" Cavendish's surprised greeting brought his head up. "What are you doing home?"

Jack grinned at him. "Gave myself the afternoon off. Why? Entertaining your bookie in the kitchen?"

Cavendish sighed. "I should be. Over the rump roast of the last horse he suggested I...support."

Laughing, Jack slapped his shoulder. "I'd suggest you try the stock market instead, but it's just a horse race of another sort." He sobered, asking seriously. "How's Mrs. McGovern today? Any more cheerful than yesterday?"

"Considerably," Cavendish replied. "I've just brought her tea on the balcony."

Jack continued up the stairs. "Thank you, Cavendish."

He was pleased to see Emily lying in the sun. He walked through her room and onto the balcony, then leaned over her and planted a kiss on her forehead.

"How's my favorite old lady?" he asked, sinking onto the foot of her chaise. "Plotting your nightclub comeback yet?"

"Hardly." Emily kicked his hip, but gave him a warm smile. "Just soaking up the sun. Why are you home?"

"I was worried about you."

"What will the bank do without you all afternoon?"

"Probably slip into the red and fold," he said, smiling as he took her hand. "But I have my priorities." He tried to read her eyes, but she always revealed so little. Unlike Sarajane, whose every displeasure had been made public knowledge. "So, how are you...really? You worried me yesterday. I've never seen you so down."

Emily squeezed his hand. "I'm sorry, Jack. I didn't mean to add to your burden, but it's hard for a man to understand how I feel."

He nodded. "Yes, it is, but as a man, I can only reassure you that you're still gorgeous." He grinned. "And some other man, who doesn't know what a pill you can be, would probably find you exciting, even fascinating."

"That's what Genny said."

"Did she?" He had yet to meet the redoubtable nurse, but she'd said a lot of things Emily and the girls were always repeating to him. Even Cavendish dosed himself a week before with a hot toddy made from her recipe. Until that moment, Jack had never seen him trust a word of advice that hadn't come directly from the Court of St. James—and he'd known Cavendish over twenty years.

Emily, carefully casual, studied her nails and said, "She's trying to talk me into a prosthesis."

He nodded just as casually, though he'd have liked to hug her. He knew how dangerously sensitive Emily was, and he didn't want her to think he attached that much importance to the move. "Good," he said. Her attitude this afternoon was definite progress over the alternate bouts of private sobbing and almost catatonic silence.

"Genny's still here," Emily said. "You'll finally get to meet her. She's usually gone by the time you come home." She looked over her shoulder. "She ran downstairs to get something. I wonder what's keeping her?"

Jack shrugged. "I didn't see her on my way up. I'll get another chair." He went to the corner of the balcony where they stood folded and leaning against the house.

"Okay, Em, here I come! Close your eyes."

Jack heard the high melodic voice and turned. He saw a fair-featured young woman in a white blouse and skirt leap onto the patio without noticing him. She carried a...he put the chair down and looked again. It definitely was. And to think he'd almost stayed at the bank for a staff meeting.

"Don't peek, Emily!" she ordered, slipping the straps of a silky, smoky-blue lace bra up her arms and onto her shoulders. The formidable cups lay on her considerably smaller chest, sadly concave, as she tucked the flapping ends with hooks and eyes under her arms. "Ready?"

Emily giggled. "Ready."

Jack, almost afraid of what could be coming next, said under his breath, "I'm sure as hell ready."

"Ta-da!" the young woman announced, going into an impressive shimmy when Emily opened her eyes. With arms held out, she paraded in front of her like some unusually lithe Valkyrie. Emily doubled over in convulsive laughter.

"Look at me!" the young woman demanded, continuing to parade. "Don't you want to be able to wear this? Isn't this the prettiest thing you ever saw? If you get the prosthesis, you'll look so sensational..."

And then—as she thrust her chest out dramatically to drive home her message—she saw him. She went instantly still, arms gracefully extended as though she'd been paralyzed on the brink of a *grande jetée*. Her eyes widened, then closed. They were the same smoky shade as the bra, he noted. Emily's laughter grew more uproarious. Cavendish, standing in the doorway with a tray balanced on the fingers of one hand, gaped.

Biting hard on the inside of his lip, Jack set up the chair beside Emily's chaise, then extended his hand. "Brunnehilde of the Valkyries, I presume," he said. "I'm Jack Fleming."

Her cheeks were pink but she met his eyes. He had to admire that. "Genevieve Scott," she said, reaching out to shake his hand. Then she realized she was still wearing the bra. She slipped it off and, her blush deepening, handed it to Emily. She took his hand. "Shall I go to the railing and jump?" she asked ruefully, "or can you forgive and forget a little foolishness in the interest of...driving home a point?"

He laughed. "There's nothing to forgive, and I doubt that I'll forget that performance for some time. Please, sit down." He indicated a chair and looked up at the butler. "Yes, Cavendish?"

Cavendish seemed to have to concentrate on speaking. He cleared his throat, regaining his air of decorum. "I wondered if you'd be joining the ladies in a cup..." The word seemed to make him hesitate. His eyes darted to the object Emily held, and he clarified, quickly but regally, on the chance there might be a question, "A cup of tea, sir. Tea."

Enjoying the moment, but mindful of the man's dignity, Jack nodded soberly and took the cup and saucer from the tray. "Thank you, Cavendish."

The man started to leave, then turned back and cleared his throat once again. "There's a telephone call for you, Miss Emily. It...slipped my mind."

"Thank you, Dishy." Emily smiled at Genny as she rose to help her to her feet. "You sit and have tea with Jack. I can manage if I go slowly."

She began a careful, steady trek into her bedroom. "Tell them I'm on my way," she called to Cavendish's retreating back.

Alone on the balcony with Jack Fleming, Genny thought how seldom the physical features she attributed to people she'd heard about matched their actual appearance. Emily made her son-in-law sound like a warm and generous teddy bear. Genny had entertained the image of a short, thick, cuddly man with glasses, a wide smile and a bald spot.

In fact, Jack Fleming was tall and lean in a subtly elegant gray suit. He looked at her with clear eyes the same deep green one would expect to find in the jungle, and his rich brown hair was thick with a scattering of gray visible at a side part and at his temples. His jaw was square and solid. He did have a beautiful smile, but it was less like a teddy bear's than a wolf's. After her performance, she couldn't blame him. At least his reference to the warrior queen of the Valkyries and her breast armor revealed a sense of humor.

"I apologize," she said seriously. "That wasn't very professional."

He handed her a delicate china cup filled with steaming tea, a scone tucked on the saucer. "No, it wasn't," he said, pouring his own. "But I understand what you were doing. It seems to have worked far better than the doctor's prodding and my lectures. Emily was just telling me she's agreed to think about it."

Jack dropped his jacket on the back of the chair on the other side of Emily's chaise. He sat and reached to the table for his cup. "In fact, you've done wonders for her in general. Physically she's in much better shape than when you first started coming. Her attitude worries me, though."

Genny broke the point off her scone. "She's finding it hard to believe that the surgery will only affect her life if she allows it to."

"Has she told you we'll be spending the month of August in New Hampshire?"

Genny nodded, chewing. "I don't foresee a problem. As long as she takes things slowly, she should be fine. Are you flying or driving?"

"Flying." He grinned before taking a sip. "The thought of a week on the road with my daughters alternately giggling and fighting in the back seat has as much appeal as oral surgery."

Genny laughed. "I suppose that's one advantage to having an only child. You don't have to listen to bickering."

He raised an eyebrow in surprise. "You have a child?"

"Yes." She nodded enthusiastically. "A nine-year-old girl."

His eyebrows rose a little higher. His eyes went swiftly over her, the gesture apparently innocent, but slowly executed. It was the same look he'd given her when she'd stopped her silly shimmy and noticed him standing there. She fought the blush that threatened again. "Obviously an only child doesn't age a parent like having two children does," he said.

She sipped her tea and met his eyes, determined to remain professional. "I was a young mother."

He gave her that look again. "Eleven?" he guessed.

She laughed. He was prying, but she didn't seem to mind. She'd have to think that through later. "Eighteen."

He winced and put his cup aside. "I don't even remember eighteen. I think I was somewhere between Patriot High School and Harvard."

"Daddy!" A leggy, dark-haired girl in neon-green tights, green-and-black leotards and scuffed ballet shoes leapt onto the balcony and landed unceremoniously in his lap. "How come you're home so early? Hi, Genny." Without waiting for an answer, she gave him a resounding kiss on the cheek. "I bet you missed us and decided to take us out to dinner."

Jack grinned indulgently at his youngest daughter. "Nice try, Lees. I came home to check on Grandma. How was ballet class?"

With the eagle eye of youth, Lisette frowned at the chaise, ignoring his question as she leaned out of her father's lap to snare the bra with one finger in a strap. She held it up. "What's this?"

Genny closed her eyes and pretended to be invisible.

"It's Grandma's," Jack replied calmly.

Lisette frowned and shook her head. "No. Grandma wears these ugly white—"

"Hi." Danielle, fifteen, stepped onto the patio in bright pink spandex tights and leotard and aerobic shoes. She leaned down to hug her father and noticed the bra in Lisette's hands. "Dream on, Lees. I'd start with something smaller."

Lisette crossed her eyes and stuck her tongue out at her. "It wouldn't fit you, either," she taunted, leaning against her father.

Dani made herself comfortable on the chaise. "Not yet," she replied with a smile for Genny. "But I have aspirations. What're you doing home, Dad?"

"I do live here," he said, his tone mildly acerbic.

"Only at night. During the day, you live at the bank."

"He came home early to take us to dinner," Lisette said.

"You did?" Emily appeared in the doorway.

Jack looked over his shoulder, ready to capitulate if going to dinner meant Emily would leave the house. "Sure. What are you hungry for?"

"Whatever you can bring me back in a doggy bag."

Jack shook his head. "You come with us, or you make do with leftovers."

"Come on, Grandma," Lisette wheedled.

"No, I—"

"If you don't come," Dani said, her expression deliberately pitiful, "Dad won't take us, either."

Emily appeared to consider for a moment. Genny held her breath. She knew Emily hadn't left the house since her surgery, except to see her doctor.

"Cavendish is stuffing pork chops right now," she said finally, looking away from the girls to turn back into the room. "It wouldn't be fair to let him go to all that trouble for nothing."

"We'll put them in the freezer!" Lisette said as her grandmother disappeared inside.

"That's enough, Lees," Jack said quietly.

"She's not any fun anymore," she pouted.

"You're not a lot of fun when you don't feel well, either. And," he added when she opened her mouth to argue further, "I said that was enough."

Lisette dragged herself off his lap and turned toward the house with a groaning sigh. "I'll go change my clothes," she said listlessly. "Just in case someone wants to take me for ice cream later."

Jack smiled at Genny, silently sharing a wry acknowledgment

of the tenacity of children. "You never know what the next moment might bring," he said to Lisette.

With another sigh, she disappeared into the house.

"We should have given her to a movie studio when she was born," Dani said, swinging her legs over the side of the chaise. "She thinks she's another Molly Ringwald."

Jack looked puzzled. "Who?"

Dani stood, shaking her head at him. "You've got to catch up, Dad. She's an actress."

"Sorry. I just figured out that Guns and Roses isn't a security operation for florists."

Dani leaned down to hug him. "Good thing you're cute, Daddy. You'd never make it on style."

As Dani left them, Jack frowned at Genny. "There you have it. Condemned as a heartless nerd by my own children. Do you know who Molly Ringwald is?"

She nodded apologetically. "But only because I also have a dramatic actress at home. Francie does a victim-of-abuse act that would make Patton cry."

From Emily's room came the deep, slightly tinny sound of Vaughan Monroe's voice singing "Racing With the Moon."

"Uh-oh," Jack said. "I know what that record means. She's in a funk."

Genny nodded. Emily had a formidable record library from her years as a music legend. When she played Vaughn Monroe on her old 78 turntable, it meant she was feeling down.

Jack sighed. "She considers him the very pulse of forties soul."

"Try not to worry," Genny advised. "That's the nature of recovery from such a grave insult to the body—one day up, the other down. Sometimes emotions can change even moment to moment. And it's a little worse for Emily. By the nature of her work, always on stage, her face and body admired by a vast audience, she's more sensitive to the change in her body. She'll come around."

Jack nodded consideringly, then smiled. "Why don't you go home to your daughter. We're all here now to look after Emily." He stood, making her realize he wasn't giving her a choice.

"If you're sure..." she said hesitantly. Two free hours would be precious to her, and the family would probably enjoy an afternoon without an intruder in their midst.

"I'll see you out," he said, leading her through the library that also led onto the balcony.

They walked down the stairs side by side. Jack waited at the threshold of the kitchen while she went in to get her purse. Cavendish was putting a pan of fat, herb-covered, stuffed pork chops in the oven.

"See you tomorrow, Dishy," she said.

He closed the oven door and frowned at her. "Perhaps we could come to some sort of agreement about Dishy and *Miss* Genevieve. I'll drop the Miss if you'll erase Dishy from your vocabulary."

"Deal." Genny held out her hand. "What's your first name, Cavendish?"

He looked taken aback for a moment. "Why, Roger, Miss Genny..."

"Ah—ah," Genny reminded.

He sighed. "My name is Roger, Genevieve."

"Good. Good afternoon, Roger."

He bowed. "Good afternoon, Genevieve."

Jack raised an eyebrow at Cavendish, who looked back at him blandly.

"I think my butler's considering leaving my household for yours," Jack observed at the front door.

Genny laughed at the thought. "I think he'd be a little much in a two-bedroom apartment in Beaverton." She offered her hand. "It was nice to meet you at last, Mr. Fleming. I apologize again for—"

"Please," he interrupted. "No more apologies. You'll be back tomorrow?" He sounded vaguely anxious.

"Yes, of course," she replied.

"Good." He smiled and opened the door for her. "I'm leaving for Seattle for two days, and I'd like to know someone will be around for Emily to talk to. There're Cavendish and the girls, but that's not the same."

"Of course," she said again. "Goodbye, Mr. Fleming."

Jack waved as she drove off in an old clunker. He wandered back into the kitchen, snatching a green onion from a platter of vegetables Cavendish was preparing. He leaned a hip on the counter and watched his long-time friend make roses out of radishes.

"How did she earn the privilege of calling you Roger?" Jack asked, dipping the onion in a little pot of dill dressing in the center of the platter. "I've known you since you went to work for my father, and I've paid your salary for the past sixteen years, yet I have to call you Cavendish."

Cavendish concentrated on the radishes. "It was preferable to being called Dishy, Mr. Fleming."

Jack took a healthy bite of the onion. "How long have I been trying to get you to call me Jack?"

Cavendish gave him a quick, horrified glance. "That wouldn't be proper, Mr. Fleming. This is America, but you run a civilized household."

"Maybe I should start calling you Dishy."

Cavendish dropped the knife and radish and dried his hands on a towel. "Sir..."

"Fell victim to the lady's charm, didn't you, Cavendish?"

Cavendish turned to his employer with a sigh, straightening under his blue-and-white-striped *cordon bleu* apron. "I'm afraid I did, sir," he admitted.

Jack popped the rest of the onion into his mouth and chewed. "Dangerous thing for a man to do, Cavendish."

"I know that's been your experience, Mr. Fleming," Cavendish replied noncommittally, retrieving a block of cheese and a carton of cream from the refrigerator. He turned to Jack with a rare expression of personal concern. "You forget I was married for eleven years before I went to work for your father. I wouldn't trade those years for the kitchens at Balmoral Castle. All women are not like Sarajane."

Jack nodded thoughtfully. "I know that. But it's virtually impossible to tell those who are from those who aren't until it's too late. A man can be destroyed in the process."

Cavendish reached into the high, glass-fronted cupboard for a mixing bowl. "Or a man can decide he learned something and apply it to the next encounter."

Cavendish closed the cupboard and turned to face him. "That's as chancy as betting on horses, Cavendish," Jack said.

Cavendish smiled, placing the bowl on the chopping block in the center of the kitchen. "True, sir. But you've no chance of winning if you never put your money down."

Chapter Two

"This is called a hanger." Genny held up a bright plastic hanger and made a production of placing a pair of jeans over its cross piece. Francie giggled from the floor of the closet where she rooted through debris.

"It's a wonderful invention," Genny went on. "You should try it. Then you'd have room to lie on your bed, or sit on your chair..." She indicated the clothes strewn on both surfaces. Then she kicked gingerly at a patent leather tap shoe with silk ribbons that was sitting in the middle of the carpet. "You could even walk across the floor without tripping."

Triumphantly Francie held up the other shoe for which she'd been searching. "Here it is." Emerging from the closet, her thick blond ponytail disheveled, her cheeks flushed, she giggled again. "You're such a case, Mom. You can't put shoes on a hanger, anyway."

Genny hung the hanger on the almost-empty rod. "That's true," she said with a smile. "But if you hung up everything that's on the floor, you'd then have a place to put your shoes."

Francie nodded grudgingly. "You're right. Maybe we could get a butler to clean up after me like the one where your patient lives."

"Cavendish?" Genny passed Francie a handful of hangers and pointed to the bed. "Hang those up and I'll work on the bottom of the closet. I'm afraid a butler's a little out of the budget right now. You'll just have to get used to cleaning up after yourself."

"Would we have more money if we had a father?" Francie asked.

"If he worked. All father's don't work."

"The man who has the butler must work really hard to be able to pay for him." Francie walked to the closet and hung up a jean jacket. "Maybe we could get one like that."

Genny hung a plaid shirt beside the jacket, grinning at her daughter. "When we decide to look for one, we'll definitely get one like him." For a moment she let herself remember Jack Fleming's kindness to his mother-in-law, his easy affection for his children, Cavendish's quiet respect when he spoke to him. Every woman's dream man—loving, successful and sweet—with an edge of danger in his smile.

"What are you laughing at?" Francie asked, handing her a folded sweater. "Will you put this on the shelf, please?"

Genny shook her head to dispel the mental image. Life as a single-parent nurse with more bills than money did not allow for dreams. She took the sweater and placed it on the shelf her daughter couldn't reach.

"Are you smiling because you're thinking about *my* father?" Francie persisted.

Genny tried not to look guilty. It was odd to realize that she'd hardly thought about him since Francie was born. Francie bore so little resemblance to him, there was nothing to remind her of that part of her life.

"It was so long ago, Francie," she said carefully. "And we were together such a short while. It was like another lifetime."

Francie smiled up at her, dark blue eyes wide and questioning. "Don't you want another husband? You can't have another little girl if you don't have a husband, can you?"

Wondering how this conversation had come about, Genny urged Francie to a clear corner of the bed and sat down with her. "I don't need another little girl," she said, hugging her, "because I did such a good job making you!" As Francie giggled, Genny added, "And if I had a husband, I'd have to share you, and I'm too selfish."

Francie leaned heavily against her and sighed. "I'd like to have a father that was here, though. I mean, I know he ran away from you, and it's not your fault, but Lucinda Wilson's father always picks her up from tap class and takes her to Dairy Queen afterward. I'd like a father who would do that."

Genny kissed her hair. "I take you to Dairy Queen sometimes."

"I know." Francie sighed again. "It's not the going for ice cream. It's that he always gives her a kiss when she gets in the car and makes her put on her seat belt. Then he says, 'How'd it go, Duchess?' like she's so special. And she can't even do kick-ball-change without getting all mixed up." She said with a self-deprecating grimace, "I guess I'm jealous. I should just be glad I have a fun mom. Stephanie Gordon lives with her grandparents, and they don't let her do anything!"

Genny's heart ached for Francie's wistful admission. Genny had loved her own father desperately, though she'd seen so little of him before he passed away. Marriage would never work for her; she'd proved that with a two-week try at seventeen. She carried too much baggage from long ago, but how did one explain that to a nine-year-old child who felt something was missing in her life.

"Nice men who can afford a butler are hard to find, you know," she said, giving Francie a quick hug. "But if you come across one you'd like, we can check him out."

Francie's eyes and demeanor brightened. "Really?"

Genny nodded. "Of course, there's a lot more to it than that. He'd have to like you, he'd have to like me, he'd have to not get upset by the sound of tap dancing in the hallway every morning and evening."

Obviously enthused by the prospect of such a man, Francie added, "And he should like dogs."

"We don't have a dog."

Francie dismissed that detail. "But we should. And he should like meatloaf, and macaroni and cheese."

"The man or the dog?"

Francie elbowed her ribs. "Mo-om. What else?" She grinned up at her. "What do you want him to be like?"

She sounded too hopeful about the possibility of a man entering their lives, but Francie was so uncomplaining. Genny couldn't deprive her of this small fantasy. She gave the matter thought. "He should like the opera," she said.

"No!" Francie complained.

"Why not?"

Francie rolled her eyes. "Mom, in opera there's no dancing! How about the ballet?"

Genny made a face at her. "You listed your qualifications. These are mine."

"Okay, okay, the opera," Francie conceded. "What else?"

Genny let herself launch into serious fantasy. "He should be strong enough to carry me up a huge staircase."

Francie giggled. "Why? Are you gonna sprain your ankle or something?"

"Just because it's romantic."

"Should he buy you stuff? You know, diamonds? A porch?"

Genny frowned. "A porch?"

"You know. The fancy car."

Genny laughed. "That's a Porsche," she pronounced carefully. "And, no, I don't need a Porsche. But a new muffler for the car would be nice."

"What about flowers?"

"Oh, definitely flowers. Daisies and tiger lilies."

"What do you want him to look like?"

Genny shrugged. "Looks don't matter that much. He could be chubby and cuddly like a teddy bear."

Francie laughed and fell backward on the bed. "But a teddy bear would look funny in one of those black suits you wear to the opera."

"A tuxedo," Genny said. "Yes, he would. Or he could be tall and handsome. Either way. As long as he loved you and he loved me."

"All right, Mom." Francie got to her feet and pulled Genny to hers. "Now we know exactly what kind of a father we're looking for. Where'll we go to find him?"

Genny picked up the plastic basket filled with clothes at the foot of Francie's bed. "The Laundromat," she announced.

Francie frowned seriously. "Would we find a man who can afford a butler at a place where people go because they don't have their own washer and dryer?"

Genny shrugged. "You never know what the next moment will bring." As she walked out of the room in search of her box of quarters, Francie following, she wondered with a preoccupied frown where she'd heard that before.

"I AM NOT GOING." Emily turned a page of her *Vogue* without looking up.

Jack pulled the magazine out of her hands and tossed it aside. "Yes, you are," he said firmly. "It's a beautiful Sunday afternoon, the girls are at the neighbors' pool party, and it's Cavendish's day off. I have to run to the store, and I'm not leaving you here alone."

She glowered at him. "You haven't been inside a store in ten years. What do you need?" She folded her arms, thinking she had him trapped.

"Aspirin," he replied. "You're giving me a headache. Do you want a sweater?"

"No. Because I'm not going out."

"Emily," he said patiently, "you're going out if I have to lower you into the convertible with a rope. You haven't been out of this house in weeks, except to see the doctor."

The stubbornness in her eyes changed suddenly to pathetic vulnerability. Knowing how indomitable she was, he braced himself for a change in tactics.

"You're a perfect specimen," she said quietly, looking away from him. "You don't understand how I feel."

"Your doctor understands how you feel," he insisted, "and she says you should get out of the house."

"I'm lopsided."

"Then you should do as the nurse suggests and you'd be even again."

"Her name is Genevieve."

"I know. Don't try to change the subject."

"Jack," she pleaded, "I feel conspicuous."

"As well you should," he said, deliberately pulling an outdated orange sweater out of the back of her closet. "You're going to be very conspicuous while you're being lowered out the window wearing this sweater."

"God, you're thickheaded!" she exclaimed in frustration. "Put that monstrosity back and get the white jacket that matches these pants."

Gently he pulled her out of the chair and steadied her while helping her with the jacket, taking special care of the still-painful muscles on her left side. When he finished, she was smiling sadly into his face.

"What makes you such a treasure?" she asked.

With masculine artlessness, he adjusted her collar and grinned at her. "Greed," he answered. "You're leaving me your fortune, aren't you?"

She studied him evenly. "I could have used your investment advice years ago. What I have left, except for living expenses, is in the girls' names."

He rolled his eyes and pretended disgust. "Now you tell me. Now that I've employed a nurse so you'd be looked after, spent half an hour arguing with you, played around in all that frilly stuff in your closet..."

She pulled him toward her to kiss his cheek. "Thank you. When I was well, I was a help to you with the girls, but now I'm just a burden. My own flesh and blood would have dropped me on the doorstep of the nearest hospital and walked away." Tears welled in her eyes.

Jack pulled her gently toward him and hugged her. "Stop it," he scolded. "You're the one who came to help us when Sara left—who helped me tell the kids when she died—who's been like my own mother to me rather than my mother-in-law. Let's not talk about debts, okay? Let's just be happy we all have one another."

She drew away and smiled winningly. "We could do that in the house."

"We're going out," he said, putting an arm around her and guiding her slowly toward the hallway. "We're going to have lunch by the water, then we're going to buy a Sunday paper and come back and read it on the patio while we drink cappuccino and eat shortbread."

She smiled in surprise. "We have shortbread?"

"Cavendish made it last night. He knows how much you love it."

Emily leaned trustingly against Jack as they started slowly down the stairs. "To think some women haven't even one dream man in their lives, and I have two."

IT HAD BEEN A LONG DAY. Genny sat in her car in front of the office complex that housed Nursecare, Inc. She considered what to do with her free afternoon and evening. Francie was staying overnight with a friend, the laundry was caught up, she had laid in a few groceries, and whatever remained undone could wait another day.

The apartment would be quiet without her daughter, but it had been months since she'd had an evening to herself. She could buy fast food at a drive-thru, she considered as she locked her car and walked into the building. She could rent a movie, read a book, or just work on her quilt. The possibilities wouldn't seem exciting to some, but she'd never been a party girl. She thought seriously about stopping for bubble bath and chocolate on the way home.

Laurie Holmes, Nursecare's receptionist, handed Genny a message. "Mr. Fleming wants you to come over right now," she said, repeating the contents of the note.

Genny looked up from the posh riverfront address written in Laurie's graceful script.

"But it's five o'clock."

Laurie nodded. "He apologized for asking you to come to him, but said he had meetings all afternoon."

"But, I just left Emily." Genny frowned curiously, wondering if he had a complaint of some kind he didn't want to make in front of his mother-in-law. Her mind ran over the events of the past week and found nothing that could be considered a problem. He probably wanted to discuss Emily's progress with her—it had been six days since they'd talked. That thought relaxed her. And it certainly wouldn't be hard to look at him again.

She smiled at the receptionist as she passed her weekly time report across the desk. "Well, anything for Emily. How does my schedule look for the next week, Laurie?"

Laurie consulted the thick book with its many colored notes, cross-outs and additions in the margins. "I think it's your last week with Mrs. McGovern. You have Mr. Henry Monday, Wednesday, and Fri...oops." She looked more closely at the book, then shook her head. "I don't understand this. You've been crossed out."

"Crossed out?" Genny grabbed a corner of the book and turned it toward her. She *was* crossed out. With a thick red *X*. She looked up at Laurie in alarm. "What does this mean?"

Laurie reached for the phone. "I don't know. Keep your appointment with Mr. Fleming, and I'll try to reach Mrs. Parker and find out what's going on.''

Elaine Parker, director of Nursecare, was always cool and distant with her, Genny thought, but she was that way with everyone. She wouldn't have fired her without notice. Would she?

Genny drove to Jack Fleming's work address in a mild panic, all thoughts of bubble bath, chocolate and a quiet evening effectively squashed. She was a good nurse. She could get a job anywhere. But Nursecare allowed her to work her schedule around Francie, and for a working mother that kind of perk was worth more than a bigger salary.

Miraculously Genny found a parking place in the late-afternoon crush of cars. She stepped into the lobby of the ten-story building and consulted the wall directory for Mr. Fleming's office. First Westward Bank's offices were on the sixth floor. It figured, luck wasn't with her today. She glanced defensively at the elevators, found the door marked Stairs, and started climbing.

"I'm going to have the most gorgeous legs and bottom in the State of Oregon," she muttered to herself as she cleared the fourth floor, breathing hard. "People will come from miles around to see me in my French-cut swimsuit. They'll probably make me Mrs. America and offer me a spot turning letters on *Wheel of Fortune.*"

She reached the sixth floor, gasping noisily. "Or they might just give me oxygen and move me in with Mr. Henry, and he can have his way with me at last."

Her grim humor did not dispel the consuming worry over her job, but it did give her a certain perspective. She could tease herself about her marginal physical attributes, but professionally, she did her absolute best.

She had a sudden image of the thick red X on her schedule superimposed on a picture of herself wearing a teal blue C-cup bra over her clothes and doing a shimmy on the balcony of a patient's home. She closed her eyes and bumped her forehead against the sixth-floor door. "Stupid, Genevieve," she told herself. "Stupid."

That had always been her problem. She was open and fairly uninhibited, with a wicked sense of humor and usually little fear of making a fool of herself. A psychologist might say she was trying to shake off the past, pretend that a lead-weighted chunk of it hadn't followed her into the present. She liked to think she was fun-loving. Remembering the *X*, she wondered if Jack Fleming had sided with the fictional psychologist.

Well, if he had, she decided, walking onto the sixth floor, she would make every effort to change his mind. A receptionist directed her to an office at the end of a blue-carpeted room thick with cluttered but vacant desks. The large round clock on the wall read five-thirty.

In the office, Genny found another vacant desk. She studied the poster-size vintage photos on the walls. They showed employees at work in different operations of the bank. When no one returned to the desk after a few moments, she concluded that its resident had probably gone home. She approached the door behind it. Brass letters proclaimed the office to belong to Jack Fleming.

If she knocked, she thought, it would announce her presence. If she simply went in, politely but with confidence, she would gain the advantage. That was a good plan.

Turning the knob firmly, Genny walked into the office. A dozen men sitting at a long conference table littered with papers and coffee cups turned to stare at her. A meeting in progress was a possibility she hadn't considered.

"Excuse me," she said thinly, taking several discreet steps backward. "I..."

A man at the head of the table stood. "It's all right, Mrs. Scott." Jack Fleming nodded to the men around the table. "That's it, gentlemen. Have a nice weekend."

There was the silent movement of chairs on the thick carpet and subdued conversation as eleven men in suits filed past her, some ignoring her, some glancing her way speculatively. One lingered a moment to study her slim white pants and tailored shirt with wicked appreciation. He looked over his shoulder at Jack Fleming, who was coming toward them. "Playing doctor this weekend, Jack?" he asked. "About time."

"Bye, David," Jack said. When the man didn't move immediately, he opened the door a little wider. "It's almost Friday night. I'm sure the David Welsh alert has sounded in all the singles bars in Portland. Time's wasting."

David shook his head at Genny. "Curious sense of humor, but an okay dude as bankers go."

Jack pushed him through the door and closed it, then pulled out the closest chair and gestured Genny into it. He took a carafe of coffee and two paper cups off the top of a stack in the center of the table and brought it to the end where she sat. He sat in the chair next to her and poured.

"I apologize for bursting in," she said, reaching for the cup. "There was no one at the desk outside and I..."

Jack pulled the cup back then placed it in front of her. "It's hot," he said. "Handle it by the rim. We don't use foam cups anymore." He grinned and leaned back in his chair. "Dani's very conscious of preserving the environment and threatened to have her science class picket us if we didn't do our bit."

Genny smiled, her defenses slipping. He was as gorgeous as she remembered. And as nice. She reverted to type and asked directly, "Does your summons have anything to do with my being crossed off Nursecare's schedule for next week?"

"Yes," he replied.

She felt the color drain from her face and leaned back in her chair. Her resolution to change his mind knew instant death at his unqualified affirmative. She sighed. "It was the bra, wasn't it?"

He paused, the coffee halfway to his lips, and blinked. "Pardon me?"

"You fired me because of the bra," she said. Anger stirred to replace shock. She moved her cup out of harm's way and leaned toward him. "I thought you understood. When it happened, you said there was no need to apologize."

"Mrs. Scott—"

"I just wanted Emily to see that nothing really has to change," she went on, talking over him, "that she can still feel feminine and seductive. Because she is, you know, despite her age. She's still got that—"

"Mrs. Scott—"

"—that torch singer sizzle that—"

He caught the hand with which she gestured. That stopped her as effectively as if he'd covered her mouth. His hand was warm and firm, and hers was completely lost in it. She was submerged in the sensation long enough for him to interrupt a third time.

"You haven't been fired," he said quietly. His eyes were steady and faintly amused.

She remained suspicious. "I haven't?"

He put her hand in her lap and moved her coffee back toward her. She took a sip, quickly. "No. You were simply removed from the schedule until I could talk to you. Mrs. Parker wasn't sure I'd be able to catch up with you before Monday."

Genny waited for him to explain, covering her tingling hand with her other one.

"I'd like you to come to work for us full-time," he said, relaxing in his chair, "until the end of the summer."

Genny was confused. "But I'm there several hours a day, five days a week."

"I mean live with us," he clarified. "Come to New Hampshire with us. Mrs. Parker had no objections. You'd retain your status at Nursecare and return to your regular schedule September first."

Genny stared at him. "Go to New Hampshire?" She'd always wanted to go to New England. But as part of the comfortably connected Fleming household? No. This was real life. She called herself back to reality. "Mr. Fleming, I'm flattered by the offer, but Emily is doing very well physically. I'm not sure you really need me."

"I think I do," he corrected politely. "Her emotional recovery has me worried. My trip to my father's summerhouse is an annual thing, but this time it also has to do with business, with a change in the administrative structure of the company, and with a party my father's planning for a longtime friend who's retiring from the bank. Although I'll be around, I'll be tied up much of the time. I'd like to know Emily will have someone around in whom she can confide, and who'll also be able to see to her physical needs." When Genny continued to stare at him, he added, "The girls like you, Cavendish even lets you call him Roger, and I..."

I'm fascinated, he thought. *I don't like it, but I'm intrigued. You're pretty, calm, funny, and a good nurse. Perfection. But experience has taught me that doesn't exist in a woman. I'm not sure if I want you to prove me right or prove me wrong.*

"I'd feel much more comfortable about the trip," he said calmly, "if you'll come with us."

Genny tried to say something intelligent. It was like being offered a paid vacation. Francie would be ecstatic. Francie...

"Mr. Fleming," she said, "I have a daughter…"

He nodded. "I remember you mentioned her. That's not a problem. I'm not sure what the sleeping situation will be in New Hampshire, because my brother and his family will be visiting, too, but I'm confident we can make you both comfortable. Between my girls and Cavendish, there'll always be someone to look after her when you're busy."

"She loves to tap dance," Genny said, realizing as the words came out how absurd they sounded. When he raised his eyebrow as though wondering what her point was in telling him, she added hastily, "I mean, she could drive you crazy if you don't love her. She finds every patch of linoleum or hardwood floor." She shrugged wryly. "And I don't discourage her because I hope she'll be able to support me with it in my old age. Can you tolerate that for a month?"

"While Lisette's doing pirouettes, Dani's doing aerobics, and Emily's listening to Vaughan Monroe?" He smiled. "I think so. Any other questions?"

There had to be a score of them, but Genny couldn't think of one, except, "When are you going?"

"A week from today. If you decide to come, I'd like you to spend a little extra time with us helping Emily get everything together for the trip. If you don't mind, you might lend the girls a hand, too." His expression sobered. "I know you're hiring on as a nurse and not a nanny, but since Emily's been ill, the girls have been a little adrift for female companionship and advice. If you could help a little there, I'd appreciate it."

"Of course," she agreed easily. Half of nursing was hand-holding. She laughed a little nervously. "We'll come, if you're sure that's what you want."

"Good." He stood, went to the big desk at the far end of the room and picked up the briefcase that was on it. "That relieves my mind." He ushered her to the door, through the small outer office, then through the big room beyond. He waved to the receptionist, who was shrugging into a suit jacket.

Her mind awhirl with the surprising offer, Genny smiled at him as he stopped in front of the elevators then waved as she started for the stairs. "Thank you, Mr. Fleming. I'll see you Mon—"

"Oh, wait!" He called, catching her hand. The elevator doors opened and he pulled her into the small car. "Ride down with me. I forgot to mention..." The elevator doors closed, and the car began moving downward.

Genny had no idea what he said. She saw him smiling down at her in that easy, relaxed way that made her feel both comfortable and strangely agitated. She saw his lips move, but all her ears picked up was the ringing in her brain.

The walls inched toward her. Instantly her breathing grew shallow. She tried desperately to remember the therapy. Breathe deeply. Think of open spaces. Imagine expanses of water and sky and land. See beyond the confinement. See beyond the fear.

She always knew when it was going to work. This time it wasn't. As the walls began to crush her, she saw Jack Fleming's expression change, heard him ask her as though from far away if something was wrong.

She couldn't reply, but she had little doubt that the scream ringing from her throat would give him his answer.

Chapter Three

Jack reached for her, afraid she was going to collapse. With surprising strength, she slapped his hands away. She was no longer screaming, but she was gasping for air, and her eyes were wide and terrified.

His instinct was to get her to the bottom floor and out of the building to a doctor, but she didn't look as though she'd last that long. A quick glance at the floor indicator told him they were between four and three. He jabbed the third-floor button. The car stopped smoothly, and the doors opened.

She sped out past him and stopped in the middle of the plush, empty hallway, both hands over her face. As two men came around the corner, laughing over weekend plans, Jack put an arm around her shoulders and led her to the far end of the hall.

She breathed deeply as he leaned her against the wall, holding her arms to steady her. Her face was white and her hands were trembling. She put them on the front of his jacket and pushed against him. He felt their chill through his shirt. "Please," she whispered. "I have to breathe."

He took several steps back and put his hands in his pockets, fighting an inclination to hold her. He'd never seen a woman look so desperate.

After a moment, she lowered her hands and crossed her arms over her chest. She glanced at him quickly, her eyes filled with distress before she lowered them. "I'm sorry," she said. Her voice was raspy from the scream.

"I don't understand what just happened," he replied gently.

"But it didn't seem to be something you had a lot of control over."

She looked at him again, surprise and gratitude in her glance. She sighed and wiped a hand across her eyes. "Claustrophobia. If I'm prepared for it, I can usually control it. When I'm surprised..." It was unnecessary to say anymore. He'd seen the result.

He handed her a handkerchief, carefully maintaining his distance. "When you started to leave, it occurred to me that we hadn't talked about salary. I'm sorry. In my business, deals are often made between floors. I didn't think twice about pulling you into the elevator."

She dabbed at her eyes, then put the handkerchief to her mouth and drew a deep breath. Jack was relieved to see that it was even and that her color was coming back. She gave him a faint smile. "It's all right. I was excited about the job. Sometimes cheer offsets my control more than stress. Because I indulge it more, I guess." She brushed her bangs off her forehead and looked him in the eye. "I'll understand if you'd prefer to withdraw the offer."

He shook his head. "There aren't too many elevators in the woods of New Hampshire."

She wanted so much to go, but she forced herself to be honest. "No, but I'm sure there are closets, phone booths, small cars..."

Genny paused. He remained quiet, and she wondered if honesty had cost her the job. When he glanced at his watch, she realized that a woman's hysterics was probably the last thing a man in his position wanted to deal with.

"Is your daughter waiting for you?" he asked.

The question startled her. "No. She's spending the night with a friend."

"Then let's have dinner and talk about this." He reached for her arm, then remembering that she had pushed him away the last time he'd touched her, stopped short. "I'll make a phone call at the restaurant to get myself out of a dinner meeting." He pointed to the stairway door.

"You don't have to," she began to protest, but he was walking toward the door, leaving her to follow. She did.

At the door she tried again. "Mr. Fleming, I..."

He opened it, instinctively reaching for her arm to guide her through. Remembering again, he dropped his hand. "Sorry," he said ruefully.

"I won't get hysterical if you take my arm," she said, trying hard to get herself back on an even emotional keel. "I...pushed you away because I was backed against the wall and you were squarely in front of me." She smiled hesitantly. "Sometimes people can make me feel as closed in as elevators. Are you sure you wouldn't prefer another nurse?"

He wouldn't, although he was probably asking for trouble. "Emily likes you," he insisted, taking her elbow. He guided her through the door, retaining his hold on her as they walked down the stairs. "I want you to come with us, but I'd like a better understanding of what you're up against."

She laughed softly, relaxing. "So would I, Mr. Fleming."

IN THE POSH dining room of a turn-of-the-century hotel, the maître d' led them across a thick burgundy carpet, through a cluster of small tables, to a bank of booths along oak-shuttered windows.

Jack took one look at the high backs of the booths and wondered if they were up against another problem. He asked the maître d' to wait a moment and turned to Genny. She nodded, reading his mind. "This is fine. Open at the top and on one side."

The maître d' handed out menus, giving them one doubtful glance before walking away. Genny couldn't restrain the laugh. "I think he's wondering what we're going to do with our food that requires a booth open at the top and on one side."

Jack gave her a wicked glance over the top of his menu. "Or with each other."

Genny had to look away. Her pulse felt unsteady. Must be residual shock from the elevator incident.

"Their prime rib's excellent." Jack put his menu aside. "And you look as though you could use some red meat. I'll bet all you eat is yogurt and broiled fish."

His easy, teasing expression was back. That she could deal with. She put her menu on top of his. "Because I'm a nurse and know the dangers of cholesterol? You're presuming I'm a person of strong character and self-discipline."

"Aren't you?"

She thought about that, leaning into the soft booth, relaxing her tense shoulders and back. "Fiscally, professionally, maternally—yes. But I have a passion for rich food and corny jokes."

He grinned. "At least the rich food doesn't show. High metabolism?"

"Jazzercise class."

He said nothing, but his eyes went lazily over that part of her visible above the table. She shifted nervously, sitting a little straighter. He looked up into her face, his eyes quiet and unreadable. "Tell me a corny joke," he said.

"I don't remember any," she confessed. "Francie does though, and I laugh every time she tells them."

"She'll find a willing audience in my father. He loves dumb jokes."

That reminded Genny that they'd come to dinner to discuss the trip. She prepared to bring up the subject, but she was thwarted by the arrival of the waiter to take their order. When he left, Genny tried to assume a professional air. Something about this man seemed to have short-circuited her ability to do that. "You wanted to talk about my...suitability for the job," she reminded.

He raised an eyebrow. They were lighter than his hair, she noticed, and only softly defined so that she noticed the brightness of his eyes—the warmth and the intelligence there. The direct look in them called her back to business.

"No," he corrected. "I'm convinced you're suitable. I wanted to know more about *you*, so I don't inadvertently put you in that position again." He grinned disarmingly. "You scared the hell out of me."

She laughed, half embarrassed, half amused. "I'm sorry. Actually you reacted very well. Usually people trapped with me start screaming, too, and try to get away from me. When it's over, they're afraid to touch me."

He couldn't imagine that. In fact, he often found himself wanting to touch her. Not in a sexual way, but as an offer of comfort or support. He read people well; it was one of his strengths as an administrator. And for all Genevieve Scott's confidence and honesty, he sensed a fragile quality beneath her competent presence. She was afraid, or she'd lost something or someone she needed.

Not that he could be the one to fill the space. Except for his family, he'd dismissed life on a personal level in favor of business. It was so much more predictable. But he cared about those he employed.

The waiter brought a bottle of wine. After the tasting ritual, he poured Beaujolais into Genny's glass, then Jack's. He put on the table a basket of white flatbread broken into irregular pieces, and disappeared.

"I forget was this is called," Jack said, buttering a wedge and handing it to her. "It's Romanian. I like it, but it's only fair to warn you Lisette thinks it tastes like cardboard."

Genny took a careful bite. It was bland with just a suggestion of sweetness. "I like it, too," she said.

Jack held his glass up. "To wide open spaces," he said.

"I'll drink to that." She touched her glass to the rim of his and drank. The rich flavor awakened her palate, and she closed her eyes to enjoy it. She was more accustomed to the grocery store's cheaper type vintage.

"After we got off the elevator..." Jack buttered a piece of bread for himself. "You started to explain that people can make you feel confined."

"Yes." She hated trying to explain her reactions, particularly to a man. She'd always unconsciously chosen social solitude rather than have to deal with it. But he was her employer, and she did owe him an explanation for the elevator fiasco.

With a sigh, she decided that he may as well know the real woman behind the nurse. If this didn't kill his willingness to include her in his trip to New Hampshire, nothing would.

"Men are often the problem." She smiled apologetically. "Because of their size, particularly. The attentions other women love...being hovered over, backed into a corner at a cocktail party, sheltered by a man's embrace in a rainstorm..." She sighed again, having difficulty admitting the truth, accepting the deprivation of it. "They're things that make me scream because I feel my air's been cut off, that I'm being crushed."

Jack saw the enormity of her burden in her eyes. "I'm sorry," he said.

She shrugged a shoulder, not unconcerned, but powerless to correct the problem. "So am I. It's very hard to explain to someone that hugs terrify you."

"I don't know much about phobias," he admitted. "Were you born with it?"

"No." She took another sip of wine. To fortify herself, he realized. It occurred to him that her past was none of his business, however much he wanted to understand her.

"Don't go on," he said, covering her hand on the table. He felt its coldness and closed his fingers around it. He smiled into her look of concern. "The question came out instinctively, but if it hurts to talk about it, forget I asked."

She wanted to turn her hand and clasp his, because it was so large and warm, and it had been a long time since she'd felt cozy and protected. Simultaneously she was tempted to withdraw her hand, change her mind about his offer and run from the restaurant. Afraid of either course of action, she remained still.

"I can talk about it. It's just that there isn't a lot to tell." She smiled hesitantly when he withdrew his hand. She wasn't certain if that made her feel better or worse. She joined her fingers in her lap and said calmly, "I was buried in earthquake debris when I was six. It was two days before they found me." She lifted a shoulder. "That's all, really."

Jack stopped, the wineglass half way to his lips. He replaced it slowly on the table. He stared at her, aghast that such a thing could have happened to her. A hundred grizzly images crowded his mind. A dozen questions demanded attention. He selected one carefully.

"Where did this happen?"

"Southern California," she replied.

He considered her age and calculated the year. "The Sylmar earthquake." He frowned. "A freeway overpass was damaged and a wing of a Veteran's Hospital collapsed. I was only a teenager but the story dominated the news for a week."

She nodded. "My mother was a nurse there. She'd brought me to work with her."

"But it happened at six in the morning."

"Yes. She was called in to replace a nurse who'd gone home ill. My father worked nights, so there was no one home to watch me until time for school. The nursing supervisor told her to bring me along and they'd let me sleep in the nurse's lounge until my father got home and could pick me up."

She remained calm, but he saw her eyes lose focus as she

remembered. "I fell asleep. It was just getting light when I woke up. I knew I'd find my mother at the nurse's station, because my father and I used to pick her up after work. She told me I could sit with her for a little while, because it would soon be time for morning medicines and breakfasts." The expression in her eyes grew more distant as the picture she saw became clearer.

"The building started to shake," she want on. "Things started to fall. She pushed me under the desk. The sound was awful."

She closed her eyes and raised one hand to her ear, then lowered it to the table as she seemed to realize the sound was in her memory. Jack covered her hand again. She seemed on the brink of telling him more. She looked torn for a moment, as though sharing it would relieve the weight of it. Then she apparently chose against it, coming to herself once again with a forced smile. "Anyway—I came out of it alive. Obviously I'm grateful for that. But my mother died, and I spent two and and a half days trapped under a desk in absolute blackness, unable to move, grieving and terrified." She sighed, as though relieved to have the story over. She sipped her wine and said with a trace of irony, "And that's why I screamed at you in the elevator."

"I'd say you were entitled," he observed quietly. "Your father must have been so thankful when they found you."

She hesitated a fraction of a second—enough to tell him some hook in the problem rested there. She stared at his hand, still on top of hers, and ran a finger lightly across his fingernails. He felt as though he'd placed them in a socket, but he didn't move.

"One of the rescuers placed me in my father's arms. His fingers were raw and bleeding from helping them dig. His fingernails were broken. He was sobbing." She looked into his eyes, pulling her hand out from under his and crossing her arms. "They'd found my mother first, and I remember he kept saying to me, 'She's dead, Genny. She's dead.' Not 'Thank God you're alive, Genny,' but 'She's dead.' We tried to pick up our lives again, but I'd developed this quirky behavior and he didn't know what to do with me. I went to live with his sister..." She smiled. "A wonderful woman. Emily reminds me of her. She took me to a psychologist who helped me adjust enough that I could go back to school and function somewhat normally. My father visited occasionally, but my mother's death destroyed him. He died shortly after I got married."

Stacked up against hers, Jack thought, his personal problems paled significantly. The waiter arrived with salads, then removed the flatbread and replaced it with a hot, fragrant loaf of wheat bread on a cutting board. Something about the homey aroma helped to lighten the atmosphere.

"The biggest upheaval in my life," Jack said, wielding the knife tucked into the board, "was my marriage. Had it been a professional step, it could have destroyed my career. I went for looks and class, but I failed to notice that neither penetrated the epidermis."

Genny nodded, holding her bread plate up as he speared a slice of the loaf with the tip of the knife. "My husband had more substance than that, but I was seventeen and he was eighteen, and I married him because I needed someone of my own. Not someone I could give to, but a man who could give *me* the strength and security that left with my father."

Jack passed her the small pot of whipped butter. "Didn't work out?"

She shook her head, feeling herself begin to relax. "We had one of the shortest marriages on record. Two weeks."

He blinked. "Seriously?"

She nodded, dipping her fork into a bite of Bibb lettuce and spinach. "Quite."

Jack tilted his head consideringly. "Mine lasted ten years, but I suppose if you added up the time we held any real feeling for each other, it wasn't much longer than two weeks."

Genny frowned. "Why did you stay ten years?"

He chewed and swallowed, thinking about it. "Her father was in business with my father, and they were both so pleased. Then Dani was on the way and I was in too deep to escape."

"A lot of men wouldn't have felt that way."

He shrugged. "I was promoted, spent a lot of time away from home, and it was fairly bearable."

"What finally made you leave?" Genny asked.

"I didn't. She did." If he felt any pain over her defection, it wasn't visible. "She ran away with a man on my staff." His voice quieted. "They were both killed in a fast car on an Italian mountainside."

"I'm sorry."

"It's over." He topped off her wineglass. "Live and learn."

Genny guessed he didn't even hear the trace of bitterness in his voice. He'd adjusted to the defection and death of an unfaithful wife, but not without cost.

"Incidentally—" he replaced the bottle and frowned "—can you fly in a plane?"

She nodded. "If I don't drink anything."

"Makes you sick?"

She shook her head with a slightly embarrassed grin. "I can handle the plane, but not the tiny bathrooms." She changed the subject. "Aren't Dani and Lisette trying to find you a wife? Francie had me list my qualifications for a husband so she could help me shop."

He grinned broadly. "No. I'm out of business as far as the marriage market is concerned."

Jack was surprised when she frowned scoldingly. "Why? Just remember to be sure the looks and style are more than skin-deep next time. Have her X-rayed or something."

He laughed softly, imagining his proposal. "Will you marry me, darling? And will you submit to a CAT scan?" He frowned at Genny as she giggled. "Why are you coming down on me? Unless you've had a second husband, you've been single longer than I have."

That was true. And for a good reason, but not one you could bring up over dinner with a virtual stranger. "You have more to offer than I have."

"Such as?"

"*Two* beautiful daughters, a wonderful home, a comfortable life-style, yearly visits to New Hampshire." She smiled a little shyly. "And you're a very nice dinner companion."

He nodded his gratitude. "Then maybe I should have *you* X-rayed," he teased.

She smiled, but there was a blunt edge of pain in it. "You could have me scanned, but the claustrophobia wouldn't be revealed. And you'd find yourself in the same position again— wondering how to get out of something in which you'd gotten in too deep."

He frowned. "How could that affect you as a marriage bet? Unless your husband wanted to live in a telephone booth or something?"

Curious emotions crossed her eyes. They moved quickly, and

he had difficulty isolating them, but he was sure one of them had been shame. She gave him a smile she had to force past whatever she was really feeling.

"It had ramifications you can't even imagine," she said. "Trust me. You'd be better off turning your X-rays in another direction."

She was teasing, just as he'd been. This had been a little verbal sparring over dinner. But he remembered what she'd said before. "You'd find yourself in the same position again—wondering how to get out of something in which you'd gotten too deep."

He studied her smoky blue eyes, her ever-ready smile, and wondered if it wasn't already too late.

Chapter Four

"When are the cousins from hell arriving?" Dani asked from the backseat of the rented van Jack guided from the airport through the green New Hampshire countryside.

Lisette and Emily giggled. Jack aimed a scolding look in the rearview mirror. "Next week. And that is not a good attitude with which to start a reunion." His frown sharpened on Emily's reflection, though he had difficulty keeping a smile out of it. "Really, Em."

"Face it, dear," she said frankly from the middle seat she occupied with Genny. Luggage was stacked in the small space beside them, under everyone's feet, and in the storage area behind the back seat. Genny sat near the open window, the rushing air holding any sense of confinement at bay. "Except for your father, your family really is a collection of posterial pains."

"Posterial pains?" Lisette repeated in confusion.

Dani looked up from a fashion magazine to translate. "Pains in the butt."

Lisette and Francie laughed. Genny turned to her daughter to frown her disapproval. Francie quickly sobered, but Lisette still found it funny.

"You won't like them either, Genny," Lisette predicted. "Wait till you meet them. Trey's a zombie, Robbie's a baby, and Aunt Sheila acts like—"

"That will do," Jack said firmly into the mirror. "People give you exactly what they think you expect from them. Let Genny decide for herself."

"Uncle Drew's okay," Dani said, opening a perfume sample

in the magazine that suddenly filled the car with a strong floral scent. "Though you'd never guess he and Dad are brothers."

"Half brothers," Lisette corrected. "Yeesh! That smells like those rotten flowers you put in your closet."

Dani sighed over her ignorant sibling. "They're not rotten, they're dried. Your closet smells like a locker-room hamper."

"It does not!"

"It does too! Grandma puts a bandana over her face to walk into it."

"She puts it over her *eyes* to go near your room. Tom Cruise posters everywhere you look!"

"At least he's not a baby like Neil Patrick Harris!"

Lisette looked horrified. "Doogie Hauser is a doctor!"

"A sixteen-year-old doctor?" Dani snorted. "Give me a break."

Genny saw Jack exchange a wry look with Cavendish, who sat beside him. Jack looked tired, she thought. In the four days she'd spent with the Flemings helping Emily and the girls prepare to leave, her employer had worked long hours of overtime. She guessed he must be exhausted by now.

She also got the distinct impression he'd rather not be making this trip. She had no idea why, but she'd noticed that mention of the visit always dimmed his usually cheerful demeanor. She wondered if it had to do with the administrative changes he'd mentioned.

She turned to Emily, expecting she might intervene in the girls' dispute. Instead Emily stared at the passing countryside, her gaze unfocused.

Genny turned in her seat and asked gently for quiet.

"Well, don't you think Tom Cruise is sexier than Neil Patrick Harris?" Dani asked. "I mean, you're older..." She shrugged, her wide eyes innocent of any slander. "Don't you like a man with a little maturity?"

The three girls waited for an answer.

Genny had to smile. At about her age, Tom Cruise, though gorgeous, was not her idea of a mature man.

"I can't give you a fair answer," she said. "I'm in love with Sean Connery myself."

"He's old, Mom!" Francie complained. "Even you're not *that* old."

An amused gaze snagged Genny's from the rearview mirror.

"Is it the father figure that appeals?" Jack asked, "Or the flamboyant James Bond past?"

"Neither," she admitted. "Despite his age, his image is hardly paternal. I guess style and genuine sex appeal just don't age."

Jack turned to Cavendish with a grin. "Watch yourself," he warned. "The lady likes older men."

Cavendish cleared his throat then gave Genny the barest smile over his shoulder. "You have only to say the word, Genevieve. However..." He turned back to Jack and said gravely, "When I volunteered to leave your father's household when you set yours up all those years ago, you might have warned me this could happen."

"Well, *you're* not exactly a teenager, Daddy," Dani said with brutal honesty. "Maybe Genny could go for you."

"Thank you, Danielle," Jack replied with a wince.

"Could you?" Dani asked Genny.

"Your father and Cavendish are both safe from me," Genny said lightly, though the conversation was making her a little uncomfortable. She deliberately kept her eyes from the rearview mirror. "This is a great time in the history of the world for a woman to remain single. I plan to take advantage of that."

"Won't it get lonesome?" Lisette asked.

Genny kept her smile in place. Loneliness was a fact of life for her; she'd learned to cope. Before she could reply, Francie said, "She's just kidding. We have a plan to find a dad."

Lisette, instantly alert, wanted to know. "What is it?"

"He has to—" Francie spread the fingers of one small hand, ready to tick off requirements.

Genny interrupted quickly. "It's our secret," she said, fixing her daughter with a look that told her she'd appreciate her keeping it that way.

"Maybe we could help you look," Lisette offered, her dark eyes eager. "If we knew what you wanted."

"That's probably something Genny should do herself," Jack smiled at his daughter in the mirror. "After all, you'd probably match her up with Doogie what's-his-name."

"No, I wouldn't," Lisette denied gravely. "He's mine."

ANDREW FLEMING'S HOME was a large, rambling two-story structure situated in the middle of a leafy birch woods. Genny stared at it as the girls ran toward a white-haired man walking down the few porch steps. It had no architectural classification that she could recognize, but seemed to simply spill into its surroundings, as though each successive generation had added on what appealed to it, a greenhouse here, a deck there, so that the house had a modern but comfortable, portly-dowager look.

She found it wonderful. Windows and French doors winked in the afternoon sun, and tables and chairs spread all over a flagstone patio gave the impression that, in the summer months at least, much of the living was done outside. She expelled a small sigh of relief. A claustrophobic could relax here.

Genny watched as Andrew Fleming caught his granddaughters in a hearty embrace. Then Dani drew a suddenly shy Francie forward.

"This is Francie," Lisette said. He smiled at the child, then drew Emily forward and gave her a hug.

Genny saw the unconsciously defensive gesture that made Emily bring her arms up between them to avoid body-to-body contact. Andrew appeared momentarily surprised, then his features composed as though he understood what had made her draw back.

"Emily, you look wonderful," he said, bright dark eyes smiling into her momentary confusion. "Don't you know you won't get any mileage out of this invalid business if you insist on looking healthy and beautiful?"

Emily patted his cheek, smiling in spite of herself. "Andrew, you are still so full of it. This is Genny, my nurse." Emily reached behind her to draw Genny forward.

Genny offered her hand and had it swallowed in Andrew's large, firm handshake. Those bright dark eyes looked her over with care.

She could see Jack in him, she thought. He had the same angular shape to his face, similar dark features, the same tall, broad frame. But that wasn't what defined their relationship for her. It was in the directness of his glance, the strong, vaguely defiant angle of his chin, the straight set of his shoulders that looked as though they'd borne many burdens and shrugged nothing off. She sensed solidity, dependability, purpose.

Andrew raised an eyebrow, his glance softening. "Where were you when I was in the hospital this spring? My nurse looked like Walter Cronkite—complete with mustache."

Behind Jenny, Jack laughed. "She was in Oregon. You got sick in the wrong place, Dad."

"Apparently. Welcome to Birchwood, Genny."

Andrew reached beyond her to clasp his son in a quick, strong embrace. Then he held him at arm's length and studied him like a watchful parent.

"Well," he said finally, "you don't look like a man who must have worked day and night and kept his finger on every detail to pull in the kind of figures you did this year."

Jack dismissed the suggestion of praise with a grin and a twist of his right hand. "It's all in the wrist. And Cavendish's cooking."

"Cavendish, how are you?" Andrew shook the butler's hand and grinned broadly.

"I'm well, sir," Cavendish replied. "And I've been working on my backhand."

"Splendid." Andrew rubbed his hands together. "And your poker tactics, I hope."

Cavendish nodded. "Ready to devastate you at either, Mr. Fleming."

"Big talk."

Cavendish nodded again. "Big talent. I'll put the car away, and bring the bags in."

"You'll need help," Jack said, hanging back as Andrew began to shepherd the girls and women toward the house.

"Sir..." Cavendish began to protest frustratedly.

Jack turned him toward the van. "I know, I know. You're perfectly capable, and it's your job and all that, but there are sixteen bags in the car, man."

Cavendish rolled his eyes. "You have so much to learn about propriety."

Jack shook his head. "This isn't Hyde Park, Cavendish, it's the wilds of New Hampshire. Loosen up."

Cavendish pushed the van's sliding door open and hesitated a moment, fixing his employer with a steady look. "You should too, sir."

Jack pulled two bags out, put them on the drive, then looked up at him in surprise. "Do I look tense to you?"

"No," Cavendish admitted. "But I know you are."

Jack looked back at him, trying to work a bluff, but he should have known better. Cavendish didn't blink. Jack reached in for two more bags.

"It's just hard for me to be the odd man out," he admitted quietly.

Cavendish removed a tapestry bag and stacked it with the others. "You're not," he said.

"Yes, I am," Jack insisted.

"You're the only one who thinks so, sir."

"I'm the one who counts."

They reached for the same bag, but Cavendish pulled it out of Jack's reach. "You're the one who's mistaken."

Jack faced his employee, both hands on his hips. "You know, Cavendish, many employers wouldn't take kindly to being constantly corrected."

Cavendish smiled. "I know. But many employers wouldn't help me with the bags, either. It all balances out. Would you get the door, sir?"

A bag under each arm, and one hanging from each hand, the large Englishman headed for the house. Jack watched him go, thinking that whatever could be said about the unusual shape and circumstances of his life, it was certainly populated with interesting people.

"Wow!" FRANCIE GAPED at the size and elegance of the upstairs room to which Andrew showed her and Genny. She stayed close to Genny's side as though disoriented by the elegance. Genny put an arm around her, a little startled herself.

The room was larger than their living room and filled with gray oak furniture—two double beds, two dressers, an armoire, a desk and small sofa. The bedspreads and draperies were polished cotton in a floral pattern of old rose and mossy green. Folded on a trunk at the foot of one of the beds was an old quilt.

Genny went to it immediately, running the tips of her fingers reverently over the old fabrics and the surgically precise stitches.

It was done in a friendship-knot pattern, one that required skill and patience because of its curved seams and many small pieces.

"This is beautiful," she said, sitting on the edge of the trunk for a closer look. "Is it a family heirloom?"

Andrew came to lean against the bedpost and smile down at her. "My mother made it while my father served in France in World War I." His expression became thoughtful, his smile filled with memories. "It took her all the time he was gone, and there are probably as many tears in it as stitches."

Genny removed her hand from it, feeling suddenly as though it held emotions she had no right to touch.

"You know about quilts?" Andrew asked.

Unable to stop herself, she put the tip of a finger to a perfectly curved seam. "Just enough to know how much time and skill were required to complete these." She drew her hand away again and smiled at him. "I have a small project going at home, but it was too bulky to put in my suitcase. I'll have to spend my free time admiring your mother's work."

"You're welcome to, of course. Jack told me on the phone how much you've done for Emily, emotionally as well as physically. I want to thank you. Every member of my family is very important to me."

Genny thought it interesting that he considered Emily part of his family when she was his son's mother-in-law. She shrugged off his praise. "That's a good nurse's job."

He nodded. "But I know you've gone above and beyond." He glanced at his watch. "Dinner's in two hours. Emily's right across the hall if you'd like to check on her. Otherwise you're welcome to rest, or to wander anywhere, inside or out." He smiled at Francie, who sat at the foot of the second bed. "I understand you're quite a dancer. For you there's a large, glassed-in sun porch covered in linoleum."

Francie blushed and put both hands over her face.

He laughed. "No need to feel embarrassed. Someone with a talent should be working on it all the time. My housekeeper, Mrs. Pratt, ran to town for a few things for dinner, but she should be back any moment. If you'd like anything and you can't find me, ask her."

Genny followed him to the door. "Thank you, Mr. Fleming. I'm sure we have everything we need."

He stopped on the threshold. "Call me Andrew, please. I'm going to call you Genny whether you like it or not."

"Please do. Thank you."

Genny closed the door behind him and turned to her wide-eyed daughter.

"Mom!" Francie exclaimed in a loud whisper. "I've never seen anything so beautiful! Have you?"

Genny had to admit that she hadn't. "Never. But try not to get too used to it," she cautioned, still reeling from the swift and radical change in their circumstances. She tried to ground herself in reality. "In a month, we have to go back home."

Francie leapt off the bed and onto Genny's. "Well, what about him, Mom?"

Genny tucked a wayward strand of blond hair behind Francie's ear. "Who?"

"Him." She pointed to the door. "Mr. Fleming. Andrew. You could marry him. You said in the van you like older men."

"Francie..."

"He'd be perfect!" Francie went on with enthusiasm as Genny went to the window to examine the view. The flagstone patio apparently surrounded the house. She looked down on a large pool, an elegant barbecue grill and more tables and chairs. Beyond, the birch woods seemed to stretch into infinity.

Francie moved to stand between Genny and the window. "Mom, are you listening?" she asked with the good-natured patience for which Genny had often been grateful.

Genny leaned down to wrap her in a hug, her heart filled with affection for her child's sweetness, and with a mother love that ran so deep she often felt as though it were the well from which she drew her own life.

"Of course I'm listening," she said.

Francie, wide-eyed, carried on her case for Andrew. "He's got this great house so he must be rich! He seems very nice and I think he liked us."

Genny laughed at the notion that the complicated game of finding a mate could ever be considered so easy. And she'd caught a look in Andrew's eye when he'd put his arms around Emily that made her wonder if he wasn't already in the game—with another player. "Francie, you can't just pick out a man who looks like he has everything you need and decide I'm going to marry him.''

''Oh, I know that,'' the child said with a superior roll of her eyes. ''You have to go out on dates and do some kissing and stuff.'' Then she asked gravely, ''Do you think an older man would be able to carry you up the stairs, though?''

Genny was saved from having to consider that question by a knock on the bedroom door. Francie ran to open it.

''Hi, Dishy!'' she exclaimed, already as comfortable with Jack Fleming's butler as Dani and Lisette were. She opened the door all the way to admit him.

Cavendish looked very proper, despite his burden of four suitcases and a stuffed Garfield Francie had left in the car. After a forward approach through the door met with the clatter of a wide bag against the frame and a giggle from Francie, he turned sideways and crab-walked into the room.

''I swear!'' he said, setting everything down in the middle of the rose-colored carpeting. ''I'm sure the Queen of England moves with less luggage.''

Genny laughed and pulled Garfield out from under his arm. ''It only looks that way, Roger, because she has such a large staff and you, unfortunately, work alone. Are you considering leaving the Flemings for the royal family?''

He straightened his impeccable jacket. ''Now, what would all of you do without me?''

''I can't imagine.''

Francie came around him to look up into his face, her own bright features fixed with an expression of speculation that made Genny open her mouth to utter a warning—but not quickly enough.

''You said in the van you would think about marriage, Dishy,'' Francie said candidly, arms folded in concentration.

Cavendish didn't even blink. ''I've not only thought about it, I've done it. In the past, that is.''

Genny straightened, distracted enough to stop her daughter from prying further. That was something she hadn't known.

''Where is she?'' Francie asked. ''Did you get a divorce?''

Cavendish hesitated only a moment, nothing changing in his demeanor but the texture of his voice. ''She died, Miss.''

Genny put a hand on his arm, feeling guilty that she hadn't

stopped Francie's question. "I'm sorry, Roger. I'm afraid Francie's campaigning for a father and interviewing all likely candidates. Feel free to run for you life."

He squared his shoulders, the glimpse of grief in his eyes lightened by a flash of humor. "The Cavendishes are not cowards. However—" he headed for the door "—I have yet to bring up Mrs. McGovern's bags, and I should lend a hand with dinner." He pinched Francie's chin. "Perhaps we could discuss marriage another time?"

Genny followed him, then reached around him to open the door. "Thanks for bringing our things up."

He bowed. "It was my pleasure. Please remember that I'm still at your disposal, even though we're not at home."

"Thank you, Roger."

Genny closed the door behind her and turned to find Francie sitting cross-legged in the middle of her bed, Garfield in her arms. Her sunny mood had been eclipsed. "I made him feel bad, didn't I?" she asked.

Genny went to sit beside her, wondering how to explain the complicated concept that personal feelings and secrets sometimes had to be shared and other times had to be protected, and that one of the skills of friendship was to be able to determine which was which.

"You brought up something it probably hurts him to think about," she said gently. "But I'm sure he knows you asked because you were just interested."

Francie sighed and hugged Garfield a little harder. "He always seems to happy. Well, not ha-ha happy like Lisette or Dani, but happy for him—you know." She straightened her shoulders and mimicked the royal tilt of his head. "Like a king would be if he was happy."

Genny nodded, pulling her close. "I know. Lots of people have many sad things in their lives, but they keep going cheerfully because they're very brave, and because it's usually the best thing to do." She pulled away and smiled. "But I'd be careful about asking personal questions, okay? Everyone is very nice to us, but we're not a part of their family even though they treat us that way. We're here because I have to take care of Emily. That's my job. And we mustn't take advantage of their kindness. Okay?"

Francie nodded, her brow clearing. Genny drew a deep breath, congratulating herself on having handled that well.

"You mean," Francie said, leaping off the bed to drag her suitcase onto it. "I have to find you an older man *outside* of the house."

"MOM? MOM!" A loud knock on the bathroom door followed Francie's desperate cries.

Genny slid up out of a foot of fragrant bath bubbles, her heart pounding. "What?" she asked anxiously.

"Can I go down to the family room with Lisette until dinner?"

As Genny's pulse dribbled back to normal, she wondered why nine years as a mother hadn't conditioned her to remember that the desperation in a child's voice didn't necessarily mean dismemberment or impending death.

"Okay, but remember to mind your manners," she called.

"Mom, I know that," came Francie's reply in a tone of mild indignation.

"I know you know it," Genny replied. "Please just *remember* that you know it."

"Okay. Dani says Emily is still asleep, so you don't have to hurry."

"Thanks, Francie. See you at dinner."

Genny sank back into the bubbles with a contented sigh. To think that her fellow nurses were hurrying from home to home in traffic to care for grumpy patients in dire circumstances, and she was lounging in a bubble bath. A niggling guilt tried to form, but she wouldn't allow it. In a month she'd be back to that routine, so there could be little harm in enjoying her good fortune while she could.

With forty-five minutes left until dinner, she washed her hair, rinsed off, wrapped herself in a bath sheet and stepped onto the plush blue bath mat that matched the blue-and-silver wallpaper.

She toweled her hair, leaning over the counter to examine her face critically in the wide mirror surrounded by dressing room lights. No serious wrinkles yet, but she was definitely no longer an ingenue. Thank God for makeup, she thought, and walked out of the bathroom into the bedroom.

She stopped in stunned surprise halfway to the bed when she

noticed the bear asleep on it, his head comfortably pillowed on her lacy pile of underthings.

Her heartbeat quickening, her mouth going dry, she tried to make sense of the situation. There was a bear asleep on her bed. No, not a bear, she decided after a second look. Bears did not have white spots. But it was definitely the size of a bear. Turned away from her, its head tucked down, its reddish-brown body from muscular shoulders to rump took up most of the bed.

She stepped sideways, intent on reaching the bedroom door Francie had apparently left open and calling for help. She rounded the foot of the bed and, incredibly, encountered a second one asleep in front of the trunk.

This one woke instantly at her strangled gasp of surprise, baring long teeth and shouting a sound that chilled her to the bone as it rose to stand on four powerful legs. The one on the bed awoke also, surreal yellow eyes pinning Genny to the spot with ursine severity.

Genny heard herself laugh nervously. They weren't bears, they were dogs. She laughed again, then sobered instantly when the one on the bed leapt down and approached her as the other closed in from the side. Just dogs, she told herself bracingly. Very big dogs.

Backed into the corner of the room, she looked into their collective glare and said firmly, "Now look. I have to be at dinner in fifteen minutes and I still have to dry my hair."

They did not seem impressed.

She took a side step toward the door and the one closest cut her off. Then he told her off in a very big voice.

"Don't shout at me," she said. "I'm a guest here. You're making me nervous and your friend—" she pointed to the other dog "—was sprawled out all over my clothes!"

The dog who'd been on the bed took exception to being singled out and leapt at her pointing finger. Genny drew back, screaming.

"Bull! Bear!"

At the shout of a male voice, both dogs abandoned their prey and ran to Jack, tails wagging, yipping excitedly, as he walked into the room.

Genny closed her eyes and leaned back against the wall. She

put a hand to her pounding heart—and realized that nothing covered it but the selvage end of a towel.

"Are you all right?" Jack asked. She felt his warm hand close over her bare arm and pull her out of the corner.

She opened her eyes to see his filled with concern mingled with amusement. "I'm sorry," he said, his eyes going over her bare shoulders and limbs as though looking for injury. "I usually take this room. They're Dad's dogs, but they're used to bunking with me."

Still trapped between mortification over being caught in a bath towel, and annoyance because she'd been made to look silly when she'd just lectured Francie on the need to remember their place, she had difficulty forming an answer.

"I know they're big," he said, his tone reassuring, "but they never bite."

"No." She drew a breath and gave the now-docile dogs a dry glance. "I don't imagine they have to. They could swallow a large man whole. What are they, anyway?"

"Saint Bernard and Newfoundland mix," he replied, still studying her doubtfully. "Do you want to sit down?"

She wasn't sure there was enough towel to allow that without embarrassment. She shook her head, her sense of humor returning as she remembered thinking her room had been invaded by a bear.

"I walked out of the bathroom, and one of them was stretched out there." She pointed to the bed, laughing softly. "His head was turned away from me and I thought he was a bear. You called one of them 'Bear,' didn't you?"

He reached down to stroke the ears of one of the two dogs sitting obediently near him. "The one with the white tip on his tail." He patted the other. "This one's Bull. The names are corny, but what else can you expect of a man whose fortunes are related to the stock market?"

As he looked up, he noticed the bed where one of the dogs' imprint remained, and the small pile of pink lace right beside the depression. He studied it a moment then turned back to her, a suspicious tug at his bottom lip. She wondered if he was thinking how much smaller "Brunhilde's armor" was than the one she'd modeled for Emily the day she'd met him.

"Is everything undamaged?" he asked.

"I'm sure they're fine," she replied, trying to sound firm and final. She failed miserably when his deep green eyes met hers. She added quickly, "I'd...better get dressed."

Jack couldn't think of a good excuse to stay. He wanted to. Her hair was a short, half-dry golden tangle, her shoulders were ivory smooth and delicate, her legs slender and shapely. He couldn't help but fantasize over what was under the towel. God. He was losing it.

He glanced briskly at his watch then turned to the door. "You're right. I'll get these guys out of your hair." The dogs followed at the snap of his fingers, running ahead of him into the hall and waiting. "Take your time," he said, pausing in the doorway. "We'll wait for you."

"Thank you," she replied politely but coolly.

He pulled the door closed, smiling to himself as he led the dogs downstairs to be fed. There was a certain satisfaction in knowing what she'd be wearing under her clothes.

Chapter Five

The living room was quiet. Contemporary overstuffed furniture in sand and white stood emptily on the broad expanse of sand-colored carpet. Beyond the wide windows, the birch forest shone like an orchard of gold coins in the setting sun. In a crisp cotton dress of small black-on-white polka dots, Genny stopped for a moment to admire it.

Then the distant sound of conversation drifted to her ear and she followed it. She walked through a long gold-and-white dining room where a Louis XV table was set with sparkling china and crystal. She stopped again, staring. It was beauty of quite another kind, but almost as breathtaking as the view from the living room window.

The sound of laughter rose, and she followed it to a door at the end of the dining room. She placed her hand on it, prepared to push into what she presumed was the kitchen, when she heard Cavendish's voice, loud with frustration.

"Damn it, Louise," he said, "I will not eat my meals at the table with the other guests, I'll take them with you. I'm hired help, just like you are."

A quiet, cultured voice returned, "We are hardly the same, Cavendish. And you may call me Mrs. Pratt."

There was a groan of exasperation. "No, we are not the same. That's the very point I've been trying to make during our last three visits. We are man and woman. There's a correlation here your stubborn colonial pride refuses to acknowledge."

"Pass the garlic."

Genny withdrew her hand and left through the living room,

retracing her steps. So Cavendish wasn't a candidate for Francie's daddy deal after all. He was trying to put together a deal of his own.

The sound of loud giggles came from beyond the stairs. Genny went in that direction, hoping she would find Emily there. For a woman who'd been asleep when Genny had been in the bathtub, she must have moved quickly, because her room was empty when Genny, finally free of the dogs and dressed, tried to collect her for dinner. Emily was the reason she was here, after all.

Genny rounded a corner under the stairs into a large room filled with books, large throw pillows, a sophisticated television, VCR, stereo system—and people. Andrew and Jack, casually but smartly dressed for dinner, stood smiling down at Dani, Lisette and Francie sitting on pillows in the middle of the floor. Emily, in a blue silk dress with a cross-wrapped top chosen to camouflage the results of her surgery stood between the men, watching closely what was happening on the floor.

Genny stepped into the room to find her daughter holding center-stage as she showed off the unique skill of affixing the bowl of a spoon to her nose through some breath/friction application. Francie made an *O* of her mouth, blew loudly on the spoon, rubbed the inside of the bowl with her thumb, then applied the bowl to her nose, the handle of the spoon hanging down. It stuck. The applause was hearty and unanimous.

Francie held her arms out dramatically, bowed, and let the spoon drop to the floor.

"What talent!" Andrew praised, laughing

Emily, turning to share a laugh with Jack, noticed Genny in the doorway and went to draw her into the room.

"This child really is going to support you in your old age," she said. "I know showmanship when I see it, and Francie's got it."

Genny blew a kiss at Francie as the child waved to her from the floor. She smiled wryly at Emily. "I think she needs an act with more universal appeal, don't you?"

Emily dismissed that as a problem with a wave of her hand. "If she's this entertaining at nine years old, the rest will come."

"When the time comes to launch her career," Jack said, shepherding them out the door and toward the dining room, Andrew following with the girls, "I'd like to hire on as her agent and make my fortune. Mm. Dinner smells wonderful."

Everyone sat down as Cavendish served Mrs. Pratt's elegant chicken Kiev, pilaf, and asparagus with all the flourish it deserved.

"Why is Louise hiding in the kitchen?" Andrew asked Cavendish as he serve the cherries jubilee after dinner.

"I'm not sure, sir," Cavendish replied, igniting the brandy with a graceful swipe of a fireplace match. "But I'm certain it's related to Yankee stubbornness. Shall I tell her you've asked for her at the table?"

Andrew nodded. "Please."

As Andrew, Emily and Genny raved over the meal and the girls stared wide-eyed at the flambéed cherries, Cavendish leaned over Jack's shoulder and said under his breath, "One doesn't have to resist dealing with women, sir. One simply has to know how to do it."

Jack raised an eyebrow at him. "And you're doing so well. You're out here, she's in there and, unless I'm mistaken, all she's done since we've arrived is give you the cold shoulder."

Cavendish straightened, obviously offended by his lack of faith. "Well, I've just begun, sir." He snuffed out the flames by adding more kirsch.

"Really?" Jack looked surprised. "I could have sworn your campaign's going into its third year."

"Women require patient handling, sir. Excuse me."

Louise Pratt was a short, plump woman with graying dark hair in a neat bun, soft dark eyes and a gracious though shy manner.

As Andrew introduced her to Francie and Genny, she smiled warmly at the little girl and looked at Genny with polite but sharpened interest.

"Genny's been my nurse since I came out of the hospital," Emily explained, "and I decided I couldn't do without her for an entire month."

Mrs. Pratt nodded, formally polite. "I hope you enjoy your stay. If you'll all excuse me..." She disappeared into the kitchen with a threatening glance aimed at Cavendish.

"Hates to be fussed over," Andrew explained. "Cavendish if you'll serve the jubilee..."

The butler seemed to have to force his attention away from the kitchen door to the task at hand.

"Genny, do you play tennis?" Jack asked.

"Ah—no," she replied.

"Grandpa has two tennis courts," Lisette informed her from the end of the table. "And a swimming pool, and an old cabin that his great-grandma lived in a hundred years ago."

"It's an old log cabin that's been abandoned since my grandfather built this place," Jack explained. He grinned at his daughter. "Lisette thinks of it as part of the entertainment around here."

"And it has a tunnel!" Lisette went on, her eyes growing huge. "Because our great-great-grandfather's uncle stole stuff and hid it in there."

Genny turned to Andrew in surprise, wondering if Lisette was exaggerating or had somehow misunderstood.

"It's true," he said. "Did some time in the local jail, according to my mother."

"Wow!" Francie caught Lisette's excitement. "A tunnel!"

"The tunnel's off-limits to you girls," Jack said. When Lisette nodded as though the caution was very familiar, he fixed Francie with a steady look. "You can play in the cabin as long as you don't touch the trapdoor that goes into the tunnel."

"We'll go there tomorrow," Lisette promised excitedly. "We'll bring stuff for a tea party."

"Tomorrow, I'm working on my suntan," Dani said, then smiled winningly at her father. "But will you take me to town this week to see if they still have that aerobics class at the park?"

"Sure." Jack turned to Genny. "The Parks Department has dance classes for younger girls, too. Lisette really enjoyed it last year. Maybe Francie would like to come, too."

"Can I, Mom?" Francie asked eagerly.

Genny hesitated. The suggestion was kind, but it further blurred the professional line she was trying so hard to draw between his family and hers. Maybe it wasn't practical to expect that to extend to the children. "Yes, if you'd like to," she finally replied.

The girls asked to be excused and ran off, chattering excitedly. Andrew watched them go with a smile. "It's good to have life in this place again. Now that I chair the board from here, I don't see the daily changes take place in the kids. I can't believe how much they've grown and changed since last year.'' He laughed and smiled at Emily. ''We old folks are changing too, I suppose, though we hate to admit it.''

The remark was innocent, but Genny saw Emily stiffen. Andrew noticed her downcast eyes, then closed his own for an instant, obviously realizing how she'd interpreted what he'd said.

''Emily...'' he began.

''Well, I'm off to bed,'' Emily said, standing and smiling stiffly at her companions. ''Got to get my beauty sleep, and God knows it takes longer now than it used to. No, Genny—'' she put a hand out to stop her as she rose to follow ''—I can manage by myself.''

''I'll help you,'' Genny insisted, pushing her chair in.

''Stay and finish your coffee.''

Genny hooked an arm in hers. ''I'm finished.''

''I want you to enjoy yourself,'' Emily said stubbornly.

''I'm here to look after you,'' Genny said. ''And I'll enjoy myself if you'll let me do that. Are you ready?''

As Emily glared at Genny mutinously, Andrew raised an eyebrow at Jack. ''Well. Someone who knows how to handle her.''

Jack sipped his coffee. ''I asked for a nurse who was SWAT team-trained,'' he said.

Chin high, Emily disengaged Genny's arm and left the room. Genny cast a look back at the men, torn between an urge to laugh and an urge to scold them for their teasing. Deciding against either course, she said good-night and followed Emily to her room.

Andrew went to the sideboard, picked up a bottle of brandy by its neck, snagged two glasses in his other hand and carried them to the table. ''Still touchy,'' he observed, pouring.

''Very,'' Jack said.

''I didn't mean she—''

''Of course you didn't,'' Jack interrupted before Andrew could finish an unnecessary apology. ''She's just sensitive about everything. She feels ugly and unfeminine, but Genny's helped her a lot. She'll come around.''

Andrew nodded, offering Jack a glass of the aromatic brandy. Then he toasted him with his.

"What are you doing for yourself these days?" he asked, after taking a smooth swallow.

Jack leaned an elbow on the back of his chair and frowned, swirling the brandy in his glass. "For myself?"

"For yourself," Andrew repeated. "The girls look wonderful, you're seeing that Emily's taken care of, your district of First Westward Bank is so healthy it's almost scary. But how are you?"

Jack swallowed another mouthful, avoiding Andrew's eyes. "I'm fine. I'm always fine."

Andrew considered him a moment and shook his head. "You're on automatic. Your brain's doing everything. Are you ever going to put your heart to work again?"

Jack gave him a dry glance. "Try living with three women without employing your heart."

"I mean in your own interest," Andrew clarified. "Not theirs. Are you ever going to get over Sarajane?"

"I was over her a month after I married her."

"I don't mean over the love. I mean over the hurt and the betrayal. It'll eat you alive if you don't. I know about that, Jack. I at least had your mother."

It was on the tip of Jack's tongue to remind him that his mother hadn't had him. But that would have been cruel, and though Jack had suffered for that in more ways than even Andrew would understand, he knew that it had really been no one's fault. It had been one of those things for which there were no excuses and no explanations.

"How's Drew?" Jack asked, wanting to change the subject. He realized too late he'd only succeeded in complicating it.

Andrew shook his head ruefully and took another drink. "How would you be if you were married to Sheila? There must be a faulty gene in the men in this family—gold digger X—that makes us gravitate toward the wrong women."

"How is he otherwise? His Bend district looks as good as mine."

Andrew nodded. "You're both brilliant—in different ways. I talked to him on the phone yesterday and he sounded well, but as though he needed a rest. Pushes himself beyond the limit, just like you do."

Jack stared into his brandy. "Another faulty gene."

Andrew met his eyes as Jack raised his head. "Soon as Drew arrives, we have to talk about my successor."

Jack downed the rest of his brandy and put the glass aside. "Yes," he said. But he wasn't ready to talk about it. God, he wasn't ready.

"ANDREW WASN'T REFERRING to your surgery, you know," Genny said, helping Emily on with the top of a pair of silky pajamas.

Emily sighed. "I know."

"Then why did you make him feel as though he'd said something to hurt you."

"Because he did," Emily replied defensively.

"Emily..."

"I know! I know! It was petty and small of me, but damn it! Dani's going sunbathing, the little ones are going to take dance lessons, you're probably going to find a man this summer, and I'm...I'm old and deformed!"

"You know what you need?" Genny asked as she went to the bed to prop up the pillows.

Emily looked at her suspiciously. "Yes, but you'll be fired if you suggest it."

Genny grinned, throwing the blankets back. "You need contact with other women in the same situation. I'm sure there's a support group—"

"No." Emily's voice was adamant. She snatched a book out of a tote bag she had yet to unpack at the foot of the bed and straightened, frowning. "I will do no such thing. It's bad enough that I feel sorry for myself. The last think I need is to feel sorry for them, too."

Genny folded her arms. "I'll look in to it anyway."

"I won't go."

"We'll see."

"No, we won't." Emily came to stand within inches of Genny and shake her book at her. "It's my life, Genny, and you've been hired to make it more comfortable, not to take it over." Emily angled her chin and lowered her voice. "Now," she said, "if we can't come to terms on your duties, maybe...maybe we'll have to find another nurse."

Genny tried valiantly not to smile. She'd been a nurse long enough to know that a patient's threats and ill temper were often the result of medication, pain or simple depression. And she had a feeling Emily's depression was complicated by unresolved feelings for Andrew Fleming.

Genny helped her into bed and pulled the blankets up. "Do you really think you'll be able to find another nurse who'll put up with you?"

Emily's eyes filled with regret, then pooled with tears. She rested her head back against the pillows and put a hand over her eyes. "It's a wonder anyone puts up with me. I'm sorry." She let her hand fall to the blankets and smiled thinly. "You know I didn't mean that."

"Yes," Genny replied gently, then teased her with a threatening look. "Even if you did, your son-in-law hired me and he's on my side."

Emily shook her head and snatched her reading glasses from the bedside table. "Who isn't? Go on to bed. I'll be fine."

"Want a last cup of tea or anything?"

"No, thanks. Good night."

Genny wandered downstairs in search of Francie and passed a room she'd noticed earlier that appeared to be a library, or possibly Andrew's office. From beyond a gray oak door left slightly ajar she heard the sound of male voices and laughter. Whatever reason had made Jack reluctant to return to Birchwood, it had nothing to do with his father. Both men seemed delighted to see each other.

Possibly, she speculated, it had to do with the brother who would be arriving in a week. Judging by Emily and the girls' reactions, they didn't enjoy that part of the Fleming family.

Genny found Francie downstairs in the playroom. She and Dani and Lisette had already changed into pajamas. The two sisters lay on the floor in sleeping bags while Francie lay on folded blankets. Their eyes were glued to the television where a scaly green monster rose out of a lake to the strains of tension-building music.

Mrs. Pratt appeared with two large bowls, one filled with popcorn, the other with corn chips. She smiled politely at Genny then sailed past her into the room. She placed one bowl between

Francie and Lisette and the other in front of Dani. They thanked her absently, their attention still focused on the screen.

At home Genny adhered to a strict nine-o'clock bedtime for Francie, but she hated to pull her away from the cozy group.

"They're fine, Mrs. Scott," Mrs. Pratt said, apparently reading her mind. "Mr. Fleming lets them watch television as late as they want and sleep in their sleeping bags. They love it and they don't bother anyone."

Francie overheard the discussion and crawled out of her blanket cocoon to throw her arms around Genny. "They get to sleep here all night! Can I stay with them, Mom? Pleeease? Mr. Fleming said it's okay as long as we stop giggling after midnight."

Genny hugged her, knowing the companionship meant as much as the privilege to stay up late. "Okay," she replied. "But remember to be quiet, okay? This is kind of a working vacation for Mr. Fleming and his father, and Cavendish and Mrs. Pratt need their sleep."

"Okay, I promise." Francie hugged her fiercely then crawled back into her blankets to lose herself in the movie.

Genny turned to thank Mrs. Pratt and found herself standing alone in the doorway. A little wave of loneliness lapped against her. The Fleming men had each other, Francie had Lisette and Dani, Mrs. Pratt and Cavendish at least had sparring partners, and Emily didn't want anyone at the moment. Genny felt unnecessary.

She hurried upstairs to her elegant room, scolding herself. How anyone dared whine in these beautiful surroundings, she couldn't imagine.

She threw open her French doors and stepped out to a small balcony. The aroma of a summer night, rich, floral, musky, wafted around her on a light breeze. She breathed deeply and smiled into the gathering darkness. Treetops were silhouetted against a dark purple sky. Subtle movement in the woods carried to her ears in the quiet.

The scent and sounds of nature eased the strange feeling of loneliness. Loneliness had been a large part of her childhood after the earthquake that killed her mother and ruined her young life. But once Francie had come along, her life had gained purpose. Her daughter's company and her work with Nursecare had filled her days so that she'd felt fulfilled. She'd long ago accepted that a man was a luxury she couldn't have, and she'd been happy in her own little world.

Was it the Flemings that made her want more, she wondered. She frowned into the dark, thinking that didn't make sense. They weren't a whole family, either. But they were secure, emotionally and financially. Unlike herself who lived from paycheck to paycheck and fell apart at the closing of an elevator door.

She folded her arms and sighed. So Jack Fleming was more competent than she was—he could afford to be. He'd been given everything. She, on the other hand, had lost a lot and sometimes felt the world close around her like a tight, dark vise.

Not that she disliked him. For all his wealth and privilege, he was one of the kindest men she'd ever met. She was just jealous, she decided, because he treated her and Francie as though they were all on a par, and that just wasn't so. At the moment they shared these beautiful surroundings, but he belonged to it, and she just worked here.

She turned to go back into her room when a door opened downstairs, casting a wedge of light across a corner of the flagstone patio. It was thrown into shadows again when the door closed.

A male figure walked slowly toward the woods, hands in his pockets, tread silent. The figure was leaner than Cavendish, and his hair was not the beacon in the dark Andrew's would have been. So it had to be Jack. Genny moved quickly out of the light pouring from her room and into a dark corner of the balcony.

She wasn't sure what prompted her to watch him rather than retreat to her room and allow him the privacy he obviously sought. She didn't seem able to help herself. Something in the slight slump to his shoulder, visible even in the shadows, made her stare after him with frowning concern.

At the moment, he didn't look like a man who had it all together. He looked troubled. He stopped to lean against the trunk of a birch that was ghostly gray in the darkness. He stared into the woods for a moment, then turned toward the house with a sigh she heard on the balcony. He rested a shoulder against the tree, then she saw his face tilt up. "Oh, Juliet?"

She hesitated, embarrassed. Then she stepped into the light, placing her hands on the railing and smiling down at him. "Sorry. I was just enjoying the night."

She saw his smile. "Do you have everything you need?"

Silence rang between them for a moment as each realized the question suggested things he hadn't meant.

"I'm very comfortable," she replied, taking the question the way she was sure it had been intended. "And so are Francie and your girls, hip-deep in popcorn, corn chips and something large and reptilian bent on destruction."

He laughed softly, the sound rippling up to her, making her feel suddenly better about everything.

"The Swamp Thing," he said. "I just looked in on them. How's Emily?"

"Grumpy, but fine." Genny hesitated, feeling guilty about intruding upon his solitude. "I apologize for..."

He straightened away from the tree, stopping her with a quick, "Nonsense." He stared up at her, his manner suddenly sober. "You're a welcome sight tonight, Genny." He stared another moment, apparently reluctant to end their conversation. Then he added quietly, "Good night."

"Good night," she replied.

She went inside, feeling vaguely uneasy. Despite her many reminders to herself of her professional capacity, in the past several hours her daughter had almost proposed marriage on her behalf to her employer's butler, she'd been caught wrapped in a towel, and been discovered spying from a shadowy corner of her balcony.

She groaned quietly as she changed into a functional pair of cotton pajamas. She didn't know what was wrong. She was a good nurse and no patient had ever had reason to complain of her behavior. Tomorrow, she resolved, pushing her empty suitcase under the bed, she would be more circumspect. She would do her job as mother and nurse and maintain a professional distance between herself and Jack Fleming. She slipped into bed, trying to forget the romantic image of Juliet.

JACK LEANED BACK on a chaise, staring at the starry sky and listening to the water lap lightly in the pool. The thought crossed his mind that in the darkness, Genny's hair was like moonlight. Then he reminded himself that he was a banker approaching forty, too sedate and too old for such callow similes. And he had other problems he should be working on instead of letting his mind indulge itself with images of the pretty nurse.

This particular reunion was important. His future depended upon what happened when Drew arrived—indeed even his past would be validated by what his father chose to do.

Not that he had a planned strategy. His father would make a wise and logical decision. But he should be deciding what to do afterward, how to cope with the decision, whatever it was.

Instead he had a woman on his mind. A very different kind of woman than the one that had attracted him fifteen years ago, driven him to delirious heights then deep, dark despair.

He wasn't sure why he was upset by his reaction to Genny. He hardly knew her, and she seemed aware of him only as an employer. This relationship would probably proceed no farther than his mind.

He smiled when he thought about how carefully she tried to maintain her clinical decorum. A sigh followed the smile when he remembered her wrapped in a towel, thoroughly intimidated by Bull and Bear. He'd noticed silky, delicate shoulders, slender arms, graceful thighs and ankles.

He stood, disgusted with himself, and headed for the back door. He had enough women in his life. Daughters and mothers-in-law, he could manage. Wives were beyond his understanding. His own had been cruel, unfaithful and treacherous. His father's had been frighteningly similar, and his brother's was less malicious but a royal pain all the same.

No. Life was too filled with complications at the moment to allow another one.

Chapter Six

"I have a friend coming to visit today," Emily said, passing Genny a small crystal bowl of strawberry jam. She looked up from her breakfast of fruit and toast to give her nurse a teasingly superior tilt of her eyebrow. A tennis visor protected her eyes from the sun on the patio, and she had to readjust it when her expression made it slip. "So, you'll have to put someone else through their paces. I don't have time to take my walk, do my exercises or listen to your daily lecture on the pros of a prosthesis."

"There's always this evening," Genny said with a bland smile, "and I intend to have my lecture recorded and placed in your Vaughan Monroe cassette box."

Emily looked at her in amazement. "You are relentless."

Genny shrugged. "Your good health is my responsibility as a nurse. Balancing your bosom is my responsibility as another woman."

"Bosoms?" Jack appeared from the direction of the garages. He was dressed in khaki shorts and a mossy-green knit shirt that lightened his eyes. His grin was wicked as he took the chair between Emily and Genny. "Sounds like this conversation has potential. Can anyone join in?"

Emily challenged him with a look. "Only if you qualify. Do you own a bra?"

His grin broadened. "Several."

Emily blinked.

"I do have several in my possession," he explained reasonably. "You didn't say I had to wear them."

Emily swatted his arm. "Those left behind after a tryst don't count. Why aren't you in the study with your father?"

"He's on a conference call with Drew and a couple of board members. He'll be busy most of the morning. I'm free to discuss bosoms until noon."

Emily sighed. "I don't want to hear another word about bosoms. Margie Peck is coming to visit me this morning, and she's staying to have lunch. I'd prefer she didn't arrive and find me with the two of you talking about chests." She glanced at Genny imploringly. "It would do a lot for the state of my health if you'd entertain Jack while Margie's here."

"Ah..." Genny groped for a believable excuse. She suspected time spent with Jack Fleming would confuse an already-complicated relationship. She'd awakened this morning determined to be professional. "I have to make sure Francie..."

"Francie and my girls have been invited to our neighbors to spend the morning and have a barbecue lunch," Jack said, apparently pleased to be able to decimate her excuse. "You were helping Emily with her bath when the invitation came, and Francie didn't want to disturb you, so I gave her my permission."

Genny was quiet a moment, uncertain whether or not to be annoyed.

"I explained it was conditional on your approval," he said. "Of course, I could go bring her back, but it wouldn't make you very popular."

Genny saw his good-natured amusement and was tempted to relent. But she also saw broad shoulders under the knit shirt, strong hands folded over his flat stomach, and long, tanned legs stretched out beside the table.

A small frown pleated his brow under her study. Added to her confusion was the uncomfortable feeling he knew she found him appealing.

"There must be something I can do for Mrs. Pratt," she insisted.

Jack shook his head. "Cavendish is already underfoot in the kitchen." He stood and offered her his hand. "Your job today is to accompany me to town."

"I don't want to go to town," Genny said calmly.

Jack put both hands loosely on his hips. "Yes, you do. Francie told me just this morning that you're a quilter in your spare time and you've been eyeing my grandmother's quilt. She said you told her you were hoping you'd have an opportunity to go to town to buy fabric.''

Defeated, but not entirely displeased, Genny turned to Emily. ''If you're sure you won't need me.''

Emily's smile had a speculative quality. ''No, thank you. Just relax and have a good time.'' She smiled up at Jack. ''Try to wear her out, would you? She's been walking me into the ground for four days now.''

''That's her job.'' Jack leaned down to plant a kiss on Emily's cheek. ''Sure you don't want anything. A cassette tape of music from this century, perhaps?''

Emily pointed. ''Go.''

Jack offered Genny a hand up, then frowned at her white blouse, skirt and stockings. ''You don't have to wear a uniform around here, you know?''

Emily had told her that several times, but Genny thought it reminded her what she was doing in this beautiful place.

''Change into something comfortable,'' he said. ''I'll wait.''

Ten minutes later Genny returned to the patio in jeans and a yellow cotton sweater.

With a parting wave for Emily, Jack took Genny's hand and pulled her after him across the patio and onto the path that led into the birch woods.

Genny doubted the wisdom of her decision almost immediately. The woods were green and sun-dappled and intimate. Birds called, insects buzzed, and the soft, loamy earth made her feel as though she were on someone's plush carpet. And Jack still had a hold of her hand.

A bright blue sky domed their path, and the tall, spindly, white-trunked trees reminded her of an illustration in one of Francie's books. This path led to a castle guarded by a knight and a fiercely loyal dragon. So much for a professional mind-set. She tried to shake off the fanciful mood, but the surroundings were too perfect to allow it.

The path narrowed, and Jack dropped her hand to take the lead, explaining over his shoulder. ''This leads to the highway, then it's just a half mile to town.'' He stopped to point through the trees to his right. ''The old cabin is on the far edge of the woods.''

Genny peered in the direction he pointed. He placed warm, strong hands on her shoulders to turn her several degrees. His long arm came over her shoulder and pointed again. She felt his chest against her back, his breath at her temple. Through the trees she glimpsed the small cabin but her brain didn't register it. It was busy dealing with Jack's closeness.

He frowned down at her. "Something worrying you on a beautiful morning like this?" he asked. He rubbed gently where his hand rested on her shoulder. "You're stiff. Would you rather I hadn't let Francie go?"

"No, of course not," she denied quickly. "I'm glad you told her she could go. She doesn't have many friends outside of school, and she adores your daughters."

"Then, what is it?"

"Nothing."

He shifted his weight and folded his arms, apparently determined to have an answer. "When there's nothing wrong, your eyes are clear and your smile sparkles. When something's bothering you, you eyes go gray and you have a frown that would discourage a Russian tank. You're wearing it now."

She lowered her eyes, wishing she were less transparent. "I'm sorry."

"Now don't play the shy, amenable nurse," Jack said on a laugh. "I've seen you do the shimmy in a bra, I've seen you wrapped in a towel, I've seen you gazing at the moon from a balcony..."

"That's just it," Genny blurted. "I'm usually very circumspect professionally, but ever since I—" She almost said "ever since I met you," but hastily changed her tack. "Since that day on your patio, I've been caught in one stupid episode after another and I—"

"You're worried about your image, is that it?"

"I'm worried about..." She didn't know how to explain it. Putting it into words would suggest the very familiarity she was trying so hard to deny.

Jack listened patiently, apparently prepared to let her talk herself out.

She sighed and finished lamely, "I don't know. Please forget the whole thing."

He smiled down at her, his expression amused and disturbingly indulgent. "Your actions as a nurse have been above reproach. As far as the interesting episodes..." The indulgence in his eyes took a wicked turn. "I've enjoyed them. Most of the women I come in contact with look and behave as though they've been programmed for glamour and dullness. Relax on the professionalism, okay? You're allowed to be a friend to Emily as well as her nurse, and since we're all interested in Emily, you're stuck with us, too. On the other hand—" he became serious "—if you're uncomfortable because you'd rather not come with me, you don't have to."

He was giving her an opportunity to back out—and she suspected from the challenge in his eyes that he didn't mean simply from the walk to town. She should take it, she told herself.

Instead she admitted quietly, "I'd like to come." And then she smiled, because the honesty felt good.

His eyes acknowledged her admission and what it meant. Nothing big. Nothing certain. But something.

He smiled and took her hand again. "All right, let's go."

In a moment, they walked out of the woods onto a paved, four-lane highway. Their emergence into civilization seemed to bring with it a sanity Genny had begun to think she'd lost among the birches.

Her hand in Jack's, they walked along at a comfortable pace, talking about Emily and the girls, and the unexpected relationship between Cavendish and Mrs. Pratt.

We're just good company for each other, Genny told herself. We already know neither of us has plans that include a serious relationship. He's been hurt and I'm an emotional pygmy. Friendship should be safe enough.

The sign that welcomed them to Bridgebury boasted that the town had been established in 1781. Genny stopped to stare at it in amazement.

"Lewis and Clark arrived in Astoria in 1805, and we think of ourselves as so steeped in history. This town was settled thirty-five years before they ever set foot in Oregon."

Jack smiled, drawing her along. "This is New England, remember. This is where it all started. Wait until you see some of the buildings downtown."

Genny started to follow the pavement over a small gurgling stream, but Jack pulled her off the road and through a grove of leafy oaks. "I think you'll like this entrance to town better," he said.

Genny stopped again and drew in her breath. A covered bridge hidden by the grove stood in charming dilapidation, spanning the stream.

"I wish I'd thought to bring a camera," she lamented as he pulled her along.

"We'll come back again," he promised. "Will it upset you to go into it?"

"No," she said. "It's open at both ends. Come on." Her voice was eager, excited.

They entered the shadowy interior, their footsteps causing musical creaks though the bridge felt sturdy. Sunlight through the gaps in the carpentry made exotic patterns on the walls and the floor of the structure.

Jack turned to Genny to point out a heart carved on the wall just as she looked up at the ceiling. A bar of sunlight landed right across her eyes, lighting them to silver. He saw warmth and pleasure in them, and felt his heart bump when she swung her gaze to him.

"I wonder how many wanderers and children have hidden here," she asked, pulling on his hand as she kept walking slowly, looking around with smiling interest. She noticed the heart and pointed to it. "How many lovers have made promises here and stolen kisses?"

"Many, I'm sure," he replied, pleased to discover he sounded normal. "But those are their secrets and that's as it should be. Come on. I'll show you the chandlery."

It was a simple board-and-batten structure with the original windows wavily catching the light. It'd been repainted a dark gray-blue with white trim and now housed a museum and gift shop. The old sign that said Cushman's Chandlery, est. 1791 still swung over the front door.

Genny sighed and closed her eyes. "Can't you just see men in stockings and three-cornered hats and ladies in dust bonnets?"

"Is that all they're wearing?" There was a smile in Jack's voice, and Genny opened her eyes to respond to it.

"You're in a lighthearted mood today," she noticed as he led her down the cobbled street. "No banking stuff to worry about today? No profits and losses and all that?"

"No. I'm a tourist today."

"But this is your home," she said.

The faintest cloud passed across his face, then was gone. "Yes, sort of," he said. "What would you like to do? We've got antique shops, boutiques, gifts and souvenirs, a leather shop..."

As he toured her quickly up and down the street, pointing out the shops so that she could decide where to start, she wondered what she'd said to upset him. He'd put it aside quickly enough, but she knew he'd done that out of courtesy. She'd hurt his feelings, or brought up something unpleasant. 'But, this is your home.' She remembered the words. To her own mind they seemed harmless enough, but something had rocked his fun mood.

Feeling guilty and responsible, she tried to bring that gleam back to his eyes. "Depends," she said, studying him, arms folded. "How sturdy a shopper are you?"

He frowned warily. "Don't tell me. You're one of those 'shop till you drop' types."

She shrugged. "I can be in the right company. But I wouldn't involve a neophyte like yourself in such an expedition. Point me to the fabric shop and I promise not to dawdle."

"No," he said squaring his shoulders dramatically. "I can handle it, if I know there's compensation down the road."

She raised an eyebrow, suspicious. "Compensation?"

"Fish and chips and a Watney's at Malone's across the square."

"What's a Watney's?"

"An English ale. But you can have a Pepsi or an iced tea."

"Sounds great. And I'm game for a Watney's."

Jack put an arm around her shoulders and led her toward a gift shop with Bridgebury T-shirts in the window. "You're okay, Genevieve. Let's start here. The girls will whine if we don't bring something back for them."

"I'LL HAVE TO COME for fabric another time," Genny said, taking a cautious sip of the dark ale. It was strong but pleasant.

"Why?" Jack asked, passing the malt vinegar across the table.

A platter of fragrant, lightly battered fish and chips steamed between them.

She indicated the pile of packages on the floor beside them
containing T-shirts for the girls, a package of English shortbread
for Emily, chocolates for Mrs. Pratt, a *London Times* for Cavendish and a small cactus for the window garden in Andrew's
office.

"Have you forgotten we're on foot?"

He grinned over his tankard. "No, but I thought you had.
We'll take a cab home, so get whatever you want. Where do you
want to go for the fabric?"

"A thrift shop sometimes has fabric scraps."

He nodded. "The Presbyterian Church has one."

When they'd finished eating, Jack smiled at her as he reached
for his wallet, then stopped, his attention suddenly arrested by
her mouth. Her heart skipped a beat. He picked up his napkin
and, reaching across the table, dabbed it at her upper lip.

"Foam mustache," he explained. "Cute, but if you're concerned about professionalism..."

She rolled her eyes, embarrassed. "I think I give up on it. It
seems impossible to maintain under the present circumstances."

The thrift shop had three twenty-gallon leaf bags filled with
fabric scraps. Genny opened one and then the other, unable to
believe her good fortune.

"There are wool swatches in this one." On her knees on the
hardwood floor, she leaned into the second bag. "This looks like
cotton, and this—" she peered into the third, then smiled up at
Jack "—is all solids. Do you believe it?"

He flattened the top of a paper bag on the bundles he carried
so that he could see her. "Which are you getting?"

She waved for the clerk, a tall, slender matron with elegantly
styled gray hair. "I have to have them all. At five dollars a bag,
they're a steal." When his eyes widened, she looked at him in
concern. "You're not going to get hysterical, are you?" she
asked, grinning. "I mean, I know this is where men usually lose
it. They're tired, they're carrying everything, and the thought of
one more package sends them over the edge. And I still need a
few rolls of batting."

"Batting," he repeated without comprehension.

"Stuffing. Three rolls. They'll be pretty big." She got to her feet and put her hands on his arms in teasingly dramatic concern. "You're sure you can handle it?"

He was aware of every one of her fingertips in contact with his skin. He made himself relax. "We're going to be a tight squeeze in your standard four-passenger cab. Are *you* going to be able to handle it?"

"As long as we can open a window."

Genny settled Jack, their packages and the three giant green bags on and around a wrought iron bench in front of the shop.

"You wait right here," she said. "I'll run across the street for the batting, ask the clerk to call us a cab, and I'll be back in a few minutes." She had difficulty keeping a straight face at the picture he made. "You look a little like a yuppy Santa Claus," she said, indicating his preppy shorts and shirt and their booty.

His smile took on a threatening quality. "You're pushing it, Miss Nightingale."

"Right. I'll hurry."

Jack watched her step off the curb, look left then right, then run across the street, her small leather shoulder bag slapping against her hip. She looked leggy and graceful in the slim jeans, and he stared at the tantalizing sway of her bottom until she disappeared into the Bridgebury Emporium.

It occurred to him that he hadn't had such a good time since...since the early days with Sarajane when he'd thought her charm and laughter were genuine.

True to her word, Genny was out of the emporium in five minutes, the upper half of her invisible behind three large rolls of something white squished in her arms. He laughed softly when she had to turn sideways to check to cross the street.

He waved her on, and she came blindly toward him, laughing. "Got it!" she exclaimed as he took them from her and added them to their other purchases. "The cab said five minutes."

"Did you ask him to attach a trailer?"

"Ha ha."

Genny reflected as they stuffed everything into the vehicle that there might have been more sense to Jack's suggestion than she thought. The back seat was stuffed, and Jack still held one giant leaf bag.

The cabby ducked down to look out at them from behind the

wheel. He wore a battered straw hat and a toothless smile. "Want me to come back for ya?" he teased.

Decisively Jack put the bag in the middle seat, climbed in beside it, then reached for Genny, pulling her onto his lap. He pulled the door closed.

Genny's throat closed immediately, and she felt her heart begin to thump. She made a small sound of distress.

Jack rolled the window down, gently rubbing a circle at the small of her back. "Better?" he asked.

She drew in a deep draft of air and felt an almost instant relief of the pressure inside her. But she noted in mild alarm that not all her symptoms disappeared. Her throat still felt tight. Her heartbeat was no longer wild, but it was very strong.

As the driver pulled away, calling his dispatcher with Birchwood's address, Jack splayed his hand against her back to hold her steady. His other forearm rested across her knees. She felt bracketed, but not quite closed in. She wondered about that.

His knees under her were muscular but somehow comfortable, the shoulders around which she was forced to place her arm, solid and warm. Her chin bumped against his cheek when the cabby made a turn. She felt his eyes on her but refused to meet them.

"Don't you need a quilting frame?" he asked suddenly, startling her out of her concentration.

She shook her head, hoping she had a voice. She felt almost too breathless to speak. "I've never had the luxury of one," she replied, concentrating on the simple question in order to relax. "There isn't room in our apartment. I just use an embroidery hoop and work in small pieces, then put it all together on my sewing machine."

"I think there's an old frame in the attic," Jack said.

She leaned away from him, bumping her head on the roof of the cab as she did so.

"Ouch!" Jack sympathized, reaching a hand up to give the crown of her hair a rub. "You okay?"

She winced and nodded, also reaching up to rub and inadvertently covering his hand with hers. She drew it away instantly.

"A quilt frame?" she asked, her tone exaggeratedly interested. "Really?"

"Really. If it's not worm-eaten, I'll bring it down for you."

They were home in a matter of minutes, which seemed to take an eternity. The moment Jack pushed the door open, Genny leapt out—to come face-to-face with Cavendish.

"Hi, Roger," she said brightly, ignoring his raised eyebrow. "Look what we bought!"

Jack climbed out, pulling the bag after him. Cavendish looked at it a moment and smiled thinly. "Garbage. How nice, Genevieve."

Genny elbowed him. "It's not garbage, it's fabric scraps. I'm going to make a quilt."

"Is your room short of blankets, Miss?"

"Not for warmth, Dish," Jack explained. "For entertainment. Art. Help me with the stuff in the back, will you?"

As Emily walked onto the patio and Genny ran up the steps to report their purchases, Cavendish leaned toward his employer.

"I don't suppose, sir," he asked, his expression neutral, "that it would have worked as well to put Miss Genevieve in the middle seat and the bag on your lap?"

Jack handed Cavendish another bag. "As well, but not as delightfully."

Cavendish studied Jack's face a moment, then concluded with a grin, "Then, you've had a good day, sir?"

"Very good, Dish. Very good." He led the way toward the house, batting under one arm, the other dragging a bag of scraps.

Cavendish followed, smiling.

"I LIKE THIS STUFF." Francie sat in the middle of Genny's bed in pajamas, half the contents of one bag of swatches spilled around her. Bull lay on his back on her other side, four tree-trunk-size legs folded gracefully over as he snored rhythmically.

She held up about half a yard of something lavender covered with a delicate pink design.

Genny, on her knees on the floor, elbow-deep in another bag, looked up. "Put it aside and we'll use it in one for you."

"How come you're doing this?" Francie asked, pulling another swatch out, studying it, then putting it aside.

"Because I finally have time to," Genny replied. "I made your baby blanket, and once I made myself a vest. But I haven't had much time lately to just do fun things."

Francie pushed the bag aside and stretched out between it and Bull, her chin supported on a hand. "If you had a husband you'd have more time because he'd do half the work, so you wouldn't have to work so hard, right?"

Genny smiled, wondering how many women dreamed of just such an ideal. "Something like that."

"Dani said that you came home from town sitting in her dad's lap."

Genny looked up with a start to meet Francie's bright-eyed stare. "If he likes the opera, we wouldn't have to keep looking for a dad, would we?"

"The cab was crowded with all our stuff..."

"Cavendish said to Emily that Mr. Fleming could have put you in the back and held one of the bags on his lap." Francie let that sink in. "But he didn't."

Genny frowned, caught between embarrassment and horror. "How did everyone come to be talking about this?"

Francie shrugged. "'Cause everyone saw you."

Genny opened her mouth to speak, then unable to think of just what to say, got to her feet and paced across the room.

"It's okay," Francie assured her. "Everybody thinks it's neat." She turned onto her back, holding a swatch of fabric up to the ceiling and studying it. "Have you thought about Mr. Fleming as a dad? I mean, I know he isn't old, and you wanted someone—"

"I don't want someone old!" Genny exclaimed, pacing toward Francie. "I don't want anyone at all. At least not right now. I was sitting in his lap because the cab was crowded, and Mr. Fleming is already a dad, and I'm sure his life is complicated enough."

Francie sat up, frowning at her. "Get a grip, Mom. I was just telling you what everybody said."

Genny sighed, walking back to the bag, gathering the opening in one hand and dragging it behind a chair. She smiled weakly at her daughter. "I'm sorry. I didn't mean to shout at you. Let's just forget this daddy thing for a while, okay? It was just sort of a joke and it's kind of getting out of hand."

"It's nature taking its course," Francie said importantly.

Genny straightened in the act of stuffing in the swatches Francie had pulled out of the bag on the bed. She didn't like the sound of that. "What do you mean?"

Francie shrugged. "I don't know. It's what Dani's Grandpa said."

Genny sat on the edge of the bed with a groan. So Andrew also knew she came home from town in Jack's lap, and had apparently been part of the discussion. She could move to the Klondike, she thought. There'd been a resurgence in gold mining. When Nursecare fired her for consorting with patients in the fullest sense of the word, she might support herself and Francie with a pickax and a pan.

There was a rap on the door and Genny rose to her feet with another groan. Emily had promised to let her know when she was ready for bed. She wasn't sure she could face her under the circumstances.

It was Jack, still wearing the gray slacks and black shirt he'd worn at dinner. The color made his eyes the shade of an evergreen. Under his arm was a roll of batting. He handed it over.

"Somehow this got left behind in a corner of the kitchen," he explained. "Bear thought you'd brought it home for him to use as a pillow."

She took it from him, forgetting the speculation their trip to town had caused. She was aware only of how good she felt in his presence. How alive.

He looked beyond her, spotted Francie and waved, then rolled his eyes when he noted the dog asleep on the bed.

"Bull!" he called, walking into the room to coax the dog off the bed.

Bull looked at him upside down, snuffled and closed his eyes, silently explaining that he was comfortable where he was. Francie laughed.

Jack tugged at Bull's two-inch-wide collar until the dog allowed himself to slip off the bed and land on his feet with a loud thud. He stretched, shook himself and followed his master's pointing finger into the hall, giving Genny one sad-eyed look over his shoulder.

Genny groaned. "Now I feel like a traitor. Please explain to him that he's leaving at your insistence and not mine."

Jack smiled at Francie. "Why don't you take him down to the

playroom. Lees said to tell you it's time for *The Creature from the Black Lagoon.*''

"Oh!" Francie scrambled off the bed, paused to hug Genny, then raced out, calling Bull to follow.

Jack turned to Genny, pleased to have her alone at last. He'd seen her at dinner and over a glass of wine on the patio, but everyone else had been there, too.

He couldn't quite believe he was behaving this way after all he'd promised himself when Sarajane left. Yet here he was in her doorway, afraid to step in, unwilling to walk away.

He indicated the bag she'd been packing up on the bed. "When does the project begin?" he asked.

"It's begun," she said, pointing to color piles on the desk. "I was looking through to see what I've got." She felt shy suddenly, and a little confined. She leaned a shoulder on the opposite side of the door frame from where he stood. "You should be proud of yourself. You survived a 'shop till you drop' experience with your sanity intact."

His gaze moved over her face, a little frown appearing between his eyebrows. "Not entirely," he said.

The statement was nebulous, but his expression left little doubt about what he meant. Genny looked up at him, lips parted in confusion and indecision.

Jack wondered what it would be like to kiss her. He saw the wary look in her eyes, the pulse ticking in her throat, and suspected she was thinking the same thing. This would be a risky move, one that could change everything. And he already faced an enormous change in his career this summer—one way or another. Accepting an emotional jolt might be tempting fate. Then why are you here? he asked himself.

"Well." He straightened. "I'll be busy in the morning, but tomorrow afternoon we'll see if we can find the quilt frame. Good night."

She wanted to tell him how much fun she'd had, how she'd be looking forward to seeing him tomorrow afternoon, but the words refused to form. It wouldn't be fair. He'd insisted there be no formality between them, but he didn't understand there could be no intimacy, either.

She seemed unable to buck the tide of what was slowly but

surely developing here, but she could prevent herself from contributing to it.

She said a polite good-night and closed the door. She leaned against it, for the first time since her aunt had put her in therapy, railing at the Fates that had set up the circumstances that placed her in the rubble of a hospital, and made a disaster of her life where men were concerned.

Through the door came the strains of Vaughn Monroe's rich, lazy voice singing "Racing With the Moon." Seemed she wasn't the only one feeling sorry for herself.

Pulling herself together, she started across the hall, determined to cheer Emily up. The woman in her was at a loss, but the nurse had work to do.

Chapter Seven

"Used to climb this tree when I was a boy." Andrew slapped the trunk of a burned-out white pine. It stood on a high hill at the edge of the birch forest, charred and naked, its limbs amputated. Andrew stepped back and stared up at it, his eyes and his smile wistful. "It was strong and green in those days and so was I." He glanced at Jack and smiled, stuffing his hands in the pockets of a leather-buttoned cream-colored cardigan.

"We must have a shared destiny, the tree and I, because I'm beginning to feel like it looks." At Jack's frown of concern, Andrew amended, "Well, maybe not that bad. But definitely as though my days as a force to be reckoned with are over."

With a little groan he sat under the tree, folded his knees up, rested his arms on them and looked down at the red roof of Birchwood visible through the trees. "I want to talk about you and Drew, Jack," he said, swinging his gaze to his son. It was filled with love and respect. "Will you let me?"

Jack sat beside him, leaning back on an elbow. Drew was the last subject he wanted to talk about, but he knew it was the reason he'd been invited on this walk. "Go ahead," he said.

Andrew said quietly, carefully, "He's your brother, Jack. When I'm gone, I hate to think you'll never see each other except to haggle over the will."

"You know I wouldn't do that," Jack sat up, brushed off the elbow of his sweatshirt and leaned his forearms on his drawn-up knees. "Besides, I'm not entitled."

Andrew's dark eyes showed traces of temper. "I've never treated you differently than Drew."

Jack nodded. "But the fact remains—you weren't married to my mother. You can't turn the bank over to your bastard son. It isn't done."

"You're saying you don't want to be president of First Westward Bank?"

Jack shook his head. "It's what I've wanted all my adult life. I've always felt it would validate my existence, but Mom told me over and over that however much I might deserve to take over for you one day, I couldn't expect to. That even though I'd inherited your fiscal savvy, I'd have to find success elsewhere."

"But I brought you into the bank right after college. You've been an important force in it since then."

"Because my mother had died and you felt obligated," Jack said.

He regretted the quick reply instantly. His father's pained expression doubled his guilt.

"I felt obligated," Andrew enunciated, a catch of emotion in his voice, "because I have two sons and neither is more *real* to me than the other. In fact, if I were to admit to feeling closer to either of you, it would be to you because I loved your mother so much, and Drew's mother did nothing but cause me grief."

Jack had never met Helene Fleming, but among his father's staff the stories of selfishness and blatant emotional cruelty were legendary. Her death had been mourned by no one.

"But Drew's lived his whole life trying not to be like her. He's a good man and a good banker."

Jack looked his father in the eye. "Then why quibble over a decision? He's more than capable of taking over for you. Give him the job."

"What I want to do," Andrew said, uncharacteristically cautious. Jack knew what was coming before the words were spoken. "Is put you jointly in charge."

Jack didn't hesitate a moment. "That's out of the question. I'm sure if you proposed that to Drew, he'd tell you the same thing."

Andrew sighed, apparently unable to deny that. "And if I appoint Drew," he said, "you'll quit, won't you?"

"Not out of spite."

"But you will."

"Yes."

"So whatever I do, I alienate one of you."

"No." Jack put an arm around Andrew's shoulders. "You wouldn't alienate me, I just couldn't work under him. We hate each other, Dad."

"No, you don't," Andrew insisted quietly. "It's just that neither of you understands that it's all right to love each other."

Jack ignored that. "I'd quit the bank, Dad, but not you. We'd still come every summer and every Christmas."

Andrew ignored him. "Drew never understood about your mother."

"You can't expect him to. Just like you can't expect us to love each other. To him I'll always be your secretary's bastard trying to lure you away from him, and to me he'll always be the privileged pretty boy who had everything I wanted and couldn't have."

Andrew put both hands over his eyes. "Your mother's love saved me, Jack," he said, his voice muffled and heavy. "Her death a month after Helene's—when we finally had time—was the ultimate injustice. I can't tell you how much I still miss her."

"I know." Jack's throat constricted. Laurie O'Connell had been a woman of strength and kindness and a love that was without limit for the man she was committed to for life, and the son she bore him.

Jack had been about eight when he'd realized he and his mother were his father's second family and not his legitimate one. He'd wept at the realization that all the times he and his mother were lonely for him, he was living with another woman and another son. He'd insisted angrily that it wasn't fair.

"It's something I've chosen to do," his mother explained patiently, lovingly. "No father who lived with us could love you more—even when he isn't with you."

It hadn't made sense to Jack for many years, and he often now admitted to himself that it still didn't. It took the wasteland of his own marriage to make him realize love didn't have to make sense or conform to rules to be real. It sure as hell was simpler when it did, but there were some people for whom simplicity wasn't possible.

He accepted his family situation and loved both his parents with a devotion no simpler arrangement could have fostered. But his brother was another story.

"Don't torture yourself, Dad," Jack said, getting to his feet, helping Andrew to his. "Do what you have to do. I've never expected it would be any other way."

Andrew frowned at him. "Is it easier to sit back than to fight for what you think you deserve?"

Jack frowned back. "I'd have to hurt you to do that."

Andrew shook his head. "No. I love you both, and accept you both for all you are to me. You'd have to hurt *you* to do it. You'd have to bargain with Drew."

"Exactly," Jack said. "And I won't."

Andrew shook his head and started down the hill. "Now I really feel like that damned tree," he shouted over his shoulder.

GENNY SPREAD OUT a handful of fabric squares on the small table in the corner of the kitchen and moved them around while she drank a midmorning cup of coffee. Cavendish had driven the girls to town for their dance class, she'd seen Andrew and Emily head off in his car right after she and Emily had returned from their walk, and she had no idea where Jack was.

Mrs. Pratt pushed aside a pasta salad she worked on at the counter and came to the table to refill Genny's cup. She paused a moment to study the array of disconnected patches on the table.

"I'm trying to establish my pattern," Genny said, moving the colors around like pieces in a shell game. "It's just going to be a patchwork quilt, but something still isn't right." She moved a claret-colored square in place of a dark green one next to a pais-ley square that carried both colors. "I like that, but that puts the green one down here next to orange and I suddenly have contrast rather than harmony."

Mrs. Pratt studied the squares a moment, put the pot down on a corner of the table and moved the green square to the other side of the paisley, taking the deep gold square it replaced and putting it beside the orange.

"There," she said, picking up the pot. "Harmony."

Genny studied the lineup of squares in amazement, wondering why she hadn't seen that. It was perfect. She smiled up at the housekeeper. "Thank you. Are you a quilter?"

Mrs. Pratt went back to the counter, shaking her head. "No, but I used to sew for my girls and my husband—before he left, that is.'' Then suddenly she said, ''You aren't much like her, are you?''

''Who?''

''Sarajane Fleming.''

''Ah—no,'' Genny replied. ''At least, I don't think so. And anyway, it doesn't matter. I mean, I'm not—''

''I appreciate the box of chocolates you brought back from town yesterday,'' Mrs. Pratt interrupted. ''*She'd* have never thought of that.''

''I'm glad you liked them,'' Genny said. ''But Mr. Fleming bought them.''

The housekeeper nodded. ''But he said they were your idea.''

Genny shrugged. ''We were in a shopping frenzy. Look, Mrs. Pratt, I...''

Mrs. Pratt began to peel an onion and said without looking up, ''I have a portable sewing machine you're welcome to use when it's time to put your squares together.''

Genny gave up trying to correct the impression Mrs. Pratt obviously didn't want corrected. ''Thank you,'' she said. ''I suppose a quilting purist wouldn't agree, but I'd like the girls to help me with this, and it would save a lot of time to put the squares together by machine.''

''You're welcome.'' The housekeeper bustled about the kitchen, adding over her shoulder with a philosophical grin, ''Never trust a purist. Nothing alive every stays that way honestly.'' Genny gathered up her squares and took them and her cup of coffee outside, suddenly in need of sunshine and fresh air.

A splash in the pool brought her head up as she prepared to sit on a chaise near the garden. She approached the pool behind the shelter of a privet hedge and saw a long, sleek figure move the length of the pool with startling speed, turn without a movement lost and swim toward the other end to repeat the procedure again and again. It was Jack.

Anger emanated from him. It was in every powerful pull of his arms, every precise turn, every tilt of his head to draw in air. The line of his body was so taut she was surprised by the grace with which he moved.

She hadn't known him that long, but she'd never seen him angry, or even ruffled about anything. Occasionally she caught him with a distant, thoughtful look but it usually contained more grim acceptance than anger. She remembered Andrew's hasty departure this morning, his manner unusually abrupt and quiet, and wondered if father and son had quarreled.

She put her things down and went toward the pool, knowing Jack might not appreciate an intruder at this point, but drawn by a need to offer help if she could. She had no idea how, but that didn't seem to matter. She suddenly found herself pulling off her sandals and sitting on the edge of the pool, dangling her feet in the warm water.

He spotted her from the middle of the pool and turned onto his back, coasting to the end, apparently taking a moment to compose himself.

She held up her cup and saucer. "Shall I get you one of these?" she asked. "Nothing like a shot of caffeine after healthy exercise."

He drifted lazily toward her, emerging from the pool by her knees, water dripping from his head and shoulders as he slapped one hand on the tiled rim and slicked his hair out of his eyes with the other. "Only if you put a shot of bourbon in it," he said, hoisting himself up beside her.

His eyes were dark and turbulent, at sharp odds with the faint twist of a smile on his lips. She saw hurt and confusion there. She handed him his towel.

"I'll get you a cup," she said, trying to scramble to her feet.

He stopped her, catching her arm and pulling her down beside him. "No. Just sit there."

He dried his face, buffed at his hair, then let it stand in short disarray as he looped the towel around his neck and gave her a sidelong glance.

He opened his mouth as though to speak, then shook his head, dabbing at an errant drop of water at his temple with an edge of the towel.

"I'm a good listener," she prodded gently.

He pulled the towel off and dropped it beside him. "What makes you think I need to talk?"

"You made a Jacuzzi out of the swimming pool," she replied, "without benefit of motor or electricity."

He gave her a faint smile. "I was working off steam."

She nodded. "I hope it worked. You wilted the woods."

His smile broadened and he nudged her with his shoulder. "You're very clever this morning. Why aren't you picking on Emily?"

"She escaped with your father."

That was it. Something about his father. Genny sensed the tension in him instantly. She went on teasingly, "The girls are in town with Cavendish. Mrs. Pratt is preparing lunch and I wouldn't want to do anything to stop that. There's no one else to pick on. That leaves you."

"Where does it leave me?"

"How about in the attic looking for the quilt frame?"

He considered her a moment, then tucked his knees up gracefully and unfolded to his feet. He reached a hand down to her. "Give me five minutes to change and I'll meet you at the door at the far end of the upstairs hall."

IN SHORTS and a white T-shirt, Jack led the way up the steep, dimly lighted stairway. He stopped at the top to help Genny up the rest of the way. He pointed to the steeply pitched roof and the clutter.

"Can you handle this?" he asked gently. "There is a way out, but a headlong rush at these stairs could do serious damage to your anatomy." His eyes ran over her quickly and he grinned. "God, I'd hate to see that."

His gaze drew her in, held her, confined her. She dropped her eyes. "Then don't make me feel closed in," she advised quietly.

She walked around him into the jumble of stored memories. Sheets covered what must be large pieces of furniture. There were old lamps, skis propped against the wall, paintings stacked in a corner, several neatly stacked boxes marked Christmas, and a dress form. Genny went to it, putting her hands at the nipped-in waist. It smelled of mustiness and something herbal. She wondered if it was still the wearer's fragrance after all these years.

"Look at this!" she exclaimed. "This must be twenty inches. Maybe only eighteen."

Jack was wading through the remnants of his father's past toward the back wall of the attic where many tall things were propped. "That would be after the owner's corset was cinched, wouldn't it?" he called over his shoulder.

Genny continued to stare at the form mournfully. "Even in a corset I wouldn't be that small. Even with love handles surgically removed..."

He stopped behind something shrouded in white and waggled both eyebrows wickedly. "You have love handles? Really?"

She nodded grimly. "It's where the chocolate-covered Oreo cookies settle."

"Let me see."

"You're supposed to be looking for a quilt frame."

Frowning, he turned back to the motley collection of things. He pushed aside skis, poles, curtain rods, an oar, a fishing pole, a piece of unfinished molding.

"Ah!" With a sound of satisfaction, he turned to her, two tall turned posts in his hands. "Here it is." He fingered a little bag stapled to the top of one of the posts. "Complete with fittings. My father is so organized."

"I guess you can't deal with other people's money and not be."

"True."

Genny had hoped the mention of his father would spur him to talk about what had upset him this morning, but he simply wound his way back to her, the contraption balanced on his shoulder. He yanked the sheet off a medallion-backed love seat and sat down, putting the pieces of the frame at his feet. He tore off the small bag and examined its contents.

Genny sat beside him. "Is everything there?"

He spread out the screws and nuts in the palm of his hand, then leaned over the pieces, checking the posts for the holes by which to connect them. "I think so," he said, concentrating. "As I recall, it's a simple affair that's fastened halfway down, like a rack that opens out for folding laundry." He turned to look at her. "Right?"

Their faces were inches apart—close enough that their noses would bump if either moved. Genny saw into his eyes, beyond their simple green color to the brown and silver that darkened them—to the pain held over from earlier.

Jack looked into her eyes and saw sympathy—or maybe, empathy. He'd never seen that for himself in a woman's eyes—at least not in a woman who wasn't his mother or his mother-in-law. Sarajane had been out for herself, and the few women with whom he now kept company seemed always to have a look of avarice or lust.

He was as pleased as the next man to inspire lust in a woman, but he'd just as soon know he'd done something physical rather than financial to earn it.

He felt the temper that had simmered in him since that morning cool and quiet. A different kind of warmth began to take him over.

Genny lowered her eyes to the frame. He recognized the movement as a diversionary tactic. Surely a grown woman with a child wasn't afraid of being kissed.

She straightened, her glance apologetic, asking for understanding.

She was beginning to feel confined, he guessed. He could feel the thickening atmosphere himself and it had nothing to do with the dimensions of the room.

"Shall we take it downstairs and see if it goes together?" she asked, her voice breathy and small.

He smiled gently, leaning into his corner of the love seat, trying to relax her as well as himself. "I won't come any closer," he promised. "Let's stay up here for a while." He looked around at the tangible memories with a sigh. "Sometimes the past is more comfortable for me than the present."

Genny leaned into her corner. The distance kept her clearheaded. "Why?" she asked with a frown. "You have two beautiful daughters and you're such a success. Your family and your employees adore you."

He put an arm on the elegant turned wood that trimmed the back of the love seat. His finger traced a curlicue. "Well, some of them do."

"You think your father doesn't?" she asked, prepared to argue with him.

He raised an eyebrow in surprise. "No. Why?"

Confused now, she stammered. "Well...he...you argued this morning, I thought. I saw him leave, obviously upset. Then you were surpassing Olympic records in the pool. I thought..."

"We'd been arguing about my brother," he explained. "Dad wants to retire in January, and he wants to name one of us to take over as president of the bank."

She nodded, thinking she saw the problem. "And you're competitive, and your father's afraid one will resent whoever's chosen?''

"Not exactly." He sighed, wondering why, after so many years, he still found his family history so difficult to explain. "Drew and I hate each other. We always have. Dad knows if he appoints one of us, the other will leave the company."

Genny digested that. No matter how open-minded she tried to be, as someone who'd practically grown up an orphan without anyone in the world but a kind old aunt, she thought that attitude disgraceful. "Forgive me," she said carefully, "but isn't that small of both of you?"

He thought a moment, then nodded. "I suppose," he admitted. "But the reason behind it isn't. Drew is my father's legitimate heir. I'm the result of his long liaison with his secretary. I hate Drew for belonging, and he hates me for being part of a family in which I've no real right."

Genny stared at him, speechless. "I'm sorry," she whispered at last. "I'd no idea. You and your father seem so close."

"We are, until the subject of Drew comes up."

"Is your father planning to appoint him?"

Jack shook his head. "He hasn't made up his mind. Each of us has his strengths, and Dad isn't sure what to do."

She frowned. "Then why are you angry before you know who he intends to appoint?"

Jack stood, as though the thrust of what he felt propelled him to move. He took a few steps, folded his arms, then turned back to her. "I guess because, deep down, I'm always angry about my situation. There are no villains really, so there's nowhere to direct this anger. My father fell in love with my mother because his wife was a coldhearted witch. Out of cruelty, she wouldn't give him a divorce. She was a major stockholder in the bank and often threatened to decimate the company if my father tried to leave her. He felt a responsibility to his partners, his employees, his investors and every customer who trusted the bank with his money.

"My mother kept him sane." He shook his head, his eyes reflecting his anguish. "She was the dearest, kindest, most openhearted woman, and she gladly lived a kind of half-life as my father's mistress because he was everything to her."

He paced away again to stop and toy with the beads on an old lamp shade. "As soon as I understood the kind of life we were living, I thought the only thing in the world I wanted was for my father to come for us. I had his name, but I never felt like I had him. The day I graduated from Harvard he invited me to join the bank and gave me a large number of shares." He gave the rows of beads a desultory slap, so that their faint jangle seemed to fill the quiet attic. "Now I know it was the worst thing he could have done for me. It admitted me into his life, but only so far. I'm accepted, but I'm still not legitimate. Had I been allowed to go my own way I might have done as well and not spent a major part of my life bumping up against closed doors." He turned back to her and leaned a hip on the table where the lamp stood. "No matter what I accomplish, the fact of my birth will always make me second-class."

Genny went to stand beside him, her heart filled with sympathy and a curious understanding. Her childhood had been so different from his, yet there was an emotional parallel there.

She put a hand on his shoulder and rubbed gently. "I know what it's like to feel second-class. I grew up feeling guilty for having survived the earthquake. I remember looking into my father's eyes when the rescuer handed me to him and knowing, even at six years old, that it didn't really matter to him that I was alive. He'd have preferred that my mother had lived. But I was helpless to control that, just as you're not responsible for the circumstances of your birth." She smiled at him and made a helpless little gesture with her shoulder. "I think you should think of yourself as born out of love, instead of out of wedlock."

Another thing Jack had never experienced was sympathy for his circumstances. His father thought acknowledging him solved everything, his mother had simply expected him to understand, Sarajane had used it to hurt him, and around the office, the subject of his birth was fair game for gossip. He was treated with respect because he did his job well, but he knew people talked about him behind his back.

But Genny's eyes were brimming with compassion. The fact that her empathy came out of her own misfortune touched him deeply. It was hard to reach out of your own misery to comfort someone else.

Her eyes on a level with his as he leaned on the table and she stood, Genny saw the subtle change take place in them. The darkness there was no longer simply pain. Something began to glow in the turbulence. She came to full alertness, the hand she held to Jack's shoulder experiencing a subtle vibration, as though a current ran between them. Like a real electrical charge, it made it impossible for her to move her hand.

Jack felt the hand on his shoulder stiffen, and waited for her to run. Her smoky-blue eyes were wide with what appeared at first to be confusion, then changed unmistakably to longing. Her fingers tightened on his shoulder.

His impulse was to close both arms around her and pull her close, but he remembered in time that that would frighten rather than excite her. He tilted his head slightly to the side and leaned forward to close the few inches between them. Her hand remained on him as though she couldn't move it.

Her lips were warm and dry, supple but artlessly trusting as she met his careful advance.

Genny felt both panic and excitement at the touch of his mouth. Jack's kiss was tender, his lips mobile but nondemanding as they moved gently on hers. She was very much aware that he hadn't touched her with his hands. She wondered vaguely why she felt frightened.

As she felt her own response rise from a long-restrained sexuality, she realized for the first time in her life that being held tightly didn't always require physical confinement. In a less intense but no less desperate way she felt the same revving of her heart, the same breathlessness, the same need to get away that she experienced in one of her claustrophobic episodes.

But right beside the urgency to escape was a need to stay, a desperation to remain in contact with his mouth, to feel the strength and solidity that had been so lacking in her life. She wanted to put her free arm around him, to let him embrace her, to try to brave the panic—but she simply hadn't the courage. The hesitant feelings alive in her for the first time in more than a decade brought home to her with startling clarity how much she was missing.

She dropped her arm and took a step back.

Jack accepted her withdrawal philosophically. He'd even expected it to come earlier. What he wasn't prepared for was that he'd made her cry.

She turned to the stairs, but not before he saw the quiver in her chin. He forgot himself and grabbed for her hand, stopping her. She turned to him, panic bright and real in her eyes. With a powerful yank that should have required more muscle than she had, she tore away from him and ran to the stairs.

He found her leaning a shoulder against the window trimmed in leaded glass at the end of the hall, staring down onto the patio where the girls, just back from dance class, were comparing steps.

Sunlight through the window made gold floss out of the tips of her short curls and her eyelashes. It highlighted the creamy lipstick on her trembling mouth. Guilt filled him.

"I'm sorry," he said quietly. "I didn't mean to upset you. And I didn't mean to grab you. I just...forgot."

She turned away from the window with a faint smile, burying her hands in the pockets of her shorts. "You needn't apologize. You didn't upset me, you...pleased me. You just reminded me of what I can never have." Her eyes brimmed again for an instant, but she tossed her head and refused to let them fall. "I can identify with the feeling of bumping up against closed doors."

Jack started to move closer then stopped, frustrated. He understood, probably for the first time, the enormity of the problem she faced. The very closeness that even friendship required was almost impossible for her. He could liken her physical dilemma to the emotional isolation he'd always felt. And for that very reason, he couldn't simply leave her to it. .

"If kissing me pleased you," he said, "I don't think this is something we should give up on prematurely."

She shook her head, her tone firm though her eyes were sad. "It's something we shouldn't even consider. Believe me."

"I've learned to trust my own instincts in most things," he insisted gently.

"Surely even the vice president of a bank knows enough to back away from a hopeless situation."

"A man doesn't get to be vice president of a bank by assuming anything is hopeless without giving it his best shot."

She began frustratedly, "I'm telling you—"

"And I'm telling you," he interrupted implacably, "that we're going to find a way to hold each other without frightening you."

She made a helpless gesture with her hands. "Jack, it's so much more than that. You don't realize—"

"And then," he interrupted again, "we'll take it one step at a time until we can get close enough to at least assess what we have here."

She folded her arms and fixed him with a firm look. "I know what it is," she said. "It's trouble."

He grinned. "Did you know my full name is John T. Fleming?"

Genny rolled her eyes, unable to withhold a smile, willing to be wrong. "You're telling me 'Trouble' is your middle name?"

He shrugged a shoulder. "No, it's Terrence, after my maternal grandfather, but it was a hell of a lot of trouble when I was a kid. That and my unorthodox parentage have made me stubborn in the face of trouble. Are you going to help me carry the frame downstairs, or not?"

Genny sighed, privately pleased she'd lost. It would end as she'd predicted; she knew it would. But for a time, at least, she could get as close to Jack as fate and her neuroses would allow her. One day soon she would be grateful for the memories.

"Sure." She followed him to the foot of the attic stairs where he'd propped the frame.

He handed her the bag of fittings and balanced the frame over his shoulder, hooking an arm over the forward end of it as though it were a pair of skis.

She followed him to the main staircase, dodging the back of the frame as he made the turn in the hallway.

"You're dangerous with that thing," she teased. "I don't know whether to get in front of you or stay behind."

Now that they were leaving the narrow corridor, he hooked his free arm around her shoulders and pulled her into it. "The safest place," he said, his smiling glance significant, "is right by my side."

Genny returned his smile and curled an arm around his waist, content, at least for the moment, to let herself believe that.

Chapter Eight

"Do you wonder that we all dislike her?" Emily whispered to Genny as the family gathered on the patio to welcome Drew and his family. "She has a Garfield personality stuffed into a body a size too small for it. And she sounds like something out of Tennessee Williams."

Sheila was a sight to behold, Genny decided. In a tight pink skirt and a tighter sweater, she gave Cavendish instructions on handling their luggage.

"*Do* be careful with that," she said in a regal tone as the man pulled a suit bag out of the trunk of the pale blue Mercedes. "It has my Giorgio things in it and most of Drew's Mizrahi wardrobe."

"Yes, Miss," Cavendish replied without looking up.

"And when you take this in—" she tapped a fingernail the same shade of pink as her outfit against the top of a makeup bag "—guard it with your life. My collagen cream is almost as much as our mortgage. And you can imagine what that's like in Orion Estates." She took a second look at him and shook her head. "Well, maybe you can't, but I tell you, it's a fortune."

Two boys in designer sweatpants and T-shirts emerged from the back of the car at Sheila's prodding. The oldest, about twelve, looked bored and indifferent. His younger brother, probably ten, was rubbing his stomach. "I think I'm going to be sick," he said. It sounded to Genny like more of a threat than an expression of distress. "The pollen count must be high here. I have a splitting headache and I can't breathe."

"When it gets more serious," Dani whispered on Genny's other side, "maybe he won't be able to talk, either."

Emily giggled, then sobered instantly at Genny's scolding look.

Sheila pushed her boys toward Andrew, who descended the steps of the deck toward the car. "Say hello to your grandfather, boys. Hello, Daddy!" She called in a yoo-hoo voice. "Drew, here's Daddy!"

Genny wasn't sure what she'd expected Jack's half brother to look like—a villain, possibly, with an aquiline nose and beady eyes, the image of the hateful mother everyone had disliked.

She hadn't expected him to look so much like Jack. He was an inch or two shorter, a little thicker in the chest and shoulders, but as he approached his father she saw the same resemblance in them she'd noticed with Jack. And the same affection. The men embraced, and Jack turned away to help Cavendish with the luggage. As the butler leaned into the trunk to remove Sheila's makeup case, Jack pulled out a green nylon ditty bag, speaking quietly to Cavendish who barked a heartfelt laugh.

Emily and Sheila greeted each other with polite indifference, and the children squared off. Dani introduced Francie to the boys. Trey, the oldest, gave her a desultory "Hi." Robert said, "Just what we need around here, another *girl.*"

Francie opened her mouth to reply, but caught Genny's warning eye and closed it again.

"You poor, poor darling!" Sheila was saying as she embraced Emily with exaggerated care, taking pains to avoid close contact with the front of her, though she didn't mind staring down. "Is it just awful? Do you feel as though the joy has gone out of being a woman?"

Emily went pale, her expression a mask of barely held control. Genny went quickly to her side and offered her hand to Sheila.

"Hello, Mrs. Fleming. I'm Genny Scott."

Distracted from her torture of Emily, Sheila smiled speculatively, her eyes going over Genny's nondesigner shirt and shorts with obvious distaste. "Who are you?" she asked.

Genny answered politely, though with difficulty, "Emily's nurse."

"Oooooh." Sheila drew the word out as though that explained something that hadn't been clear. "You're *employed* here."

"She's a guest here," Jack corrected, walking by with a bag in each hand and one over his right shoulder. His tone was icily formal, but Genny could see the temper in his eyes. "How are you, Sheila?" The question was an obvious concession to good manners.

Sheila didn't like Jack—or she was afraid of him; Genny couldn't decide which. But the woman squared her shoulders and drew a breath before answering. "I'm fine, Jack. How are you?"

"Good," he replied. He tapped her makeup bag. "I'll put this on your bed. Wouldn't want any damage done to that collagen." The implication was that she needed it.

Genny saw that occur to Sheila after Jack had disappeared into the house.

Her nerves already strained by this family's hostile undercurrents, Genny considered ducking back into the house when Andrew approached her with Drew.

"Drew this is Genevieve Scott," Andrew said warmly, "a nurse and friend Emily brought with her from Portland. Genny, my son, Drew."

Smiling, Drew offered his hand. Genny saw nothing artificial in him. His eyes were brown rather than Jack's dark green.

"I'm happy to meet you," she said. "Your father's been boasting about you for days."

"Has he?" Sheila asked anxiously.

Drew gave his wife a quelling look. "He forgets between visits that I slaughter him at tennis," he said to Genny, "and that he's still into me for fifty-three dollars from the poker game at Christmas."

Andrew laughed. "That was only because I'd had too much wassail."

Drew raised an eyebrow. "There was no wassail on the tennis courts last summer."

Andrew cleared his throat. "There were juleps, though."

Drew put an arm around Andrew's shoulders. "Well, this year," he suggested, "you might want to stick to iced tea. Prime rate just went up again. You're now into me for a considerable sum."

Andrew pretended shock. "You're charging your own father interest?"

"Heartless capitalist," Jack said in a light tone as he stepped onto the patio, the bags disposed of. His tone was jocular but his smile forced. He offered his hand.

Drew looked at it a moment, then up into his brother's eyes before taking it. Genny had heard the edge to his teasing remark. Drew released his father and shook hands with Jack. The exchange looked a little more like a sizing-up to Genny than a greeting. She got the distinct impression blood would be shed over the appointment during this family get-together. What alarmed her most was Jack and Drew looked evenly matched.

"Read your report," Drew said. "You're looking good."

Jack nodded. "You, too. Good work bringing in Hubert Freight. They like to make money and borrow it."

"I'd forgotten how small this pool was." A whining voice was pitched loudly enough to interrupt their conversation. Everyone turned to Robert, who stood near the pool, frowning.

"You can play tennis with us," Andrew offered.

"At home," Robert returned, "everyone has roller blades."

"Here," Drew said quietly, "we have a pool and tennis courts. Try to make do." The irony in his voice was unmistakable. He shook his head at Andrew. "I suppose every generation feels this way about the succeeding one, but I'm beginning to wonder if the world will make any strides when they take over if they can't watch it happen on a big-screen television or listen to it on a CD."

"When you boys were growing up," Andrew said, his choice of words making both brothers stiffen, "I thought this generation would be limited to whatever could happen on a basketball court. But look at you now. Just goes to show you. Come on inside. I'll bet you could use a beer, Drew."

Andrew went into the house, and Drew and Jack turned to follow, exchanging a look that united them in its irony, but divided them in the memories Andrew's casual comment had provoked. Jack swept a hand toward the door, encouraging Drew to go in ahead of him, and Drew accepted the courtesy with a nod.

Genny watched them walk away with a pang in her heart. For all Jack's talk, she saw something in his eyes when he looked at his brother. It was cryptic and elusive, but it wasn't hate.

Sheila shepherded the boys toward the house. "Come along. We'll have a cold drink, then you can change into your trunks and go swimming."

"I don't want to go swimming," Trey said, slouching along after her.

"Dad should have bought me roller blades," Robert said, frowning. "This is going to be so dull."

"We talked about it, remember, and your father isn't convinced they're safe."

"*Everybody's* got them. They're safe."

Trey made the great effort to turn his head toward his brother. "Gordy Fletcher broke his head," he said wearily.

"Fletcher's a dweeb."

"Dan Flabetich got seventeen stitches in his—"

"Shut up."

The trio disappeared into the house. Dani, Lisette and Francie came to join Genny and Emily.

"Let's run away," Dani suggested. "Let's go to New York and go shopping."

"I wish we could just go home," Lisette pouted.

Francie put both arms around Genny's waist and leaned against her. "I like it here, but those guys really are creepy."

"They're very spoiled," Emily said with more compassion than she'd shown so far to Drew's brood. "Their father's very busy, Sheila thinks everything important in life revolves around money and position, so Trey and Robert have grown up thinking they have to have designer everything, that they have to be entertained every minute, and that you can't be happy otherwise." She smiled at the girls. "Maybe your jobs this summer could be to show them how wrong that is. Be their friends because they're part of your family, not because their shoelaces cost a hundred dollars."

Francie straightened, her eyes wide. "They do?"

Emily laughed. "I was teasing." She leaned over Francie and gave her a hug. "I know they're not your cousins, so you don't have to do this, but you're such a sweetie. You'll help, won't you?"

Francie, bowled over by the compliment and being included with Dani and Lisette, agreed immediately. "Sure!"

Dani and Francie headed for the house, hand in hand. Lisette trailed behind, saying over her shoulders, "I'll try. But the first time Robert calls me a dweeb he gets it. Pow!" She made an appropriate gesture with her fist.

Emily smiled at Genny. "That kid's got a lot of me in her."

Genny put her arm around Emily and laughed. "I'm proud of you, Em. That was very understanding and very Christian of you. Sheila really is something."

"I will never understand what attracted a man like Drew to a woman like her." She shook her head, sighing. "But then I never grasped what Jack saw in my daughter, either."

"I guess sometimes it's hard to see beyond what you want to see."

"I suppose," she said thoughtfully, wandering toward the house. "At the time they met, Jack was moving up in the bank. Sarajane was lovely to look at..." She stopped, her brow pleating, pain tightening her features. She shook her head and her eyes focused somewhere in the past. "She'd been such a pretty baby. Her father and I were so proud of her. She was very smart, always top in her class, aggressive and clever. Then...when she became a teenager, it was as though something snapped or broke inside of her and all that beauty and cleverness took a wrong turn. I guess she discovered she could use it to get things. Then she met Jack and decided she wanted him."

Genny squeezed her shoulder. "I'm sorry, Emily," she said.

Emily came out of the past with a toss of her head. She drew a deep breath, leveling her emotions. "I don't want anything else to hurt Jack. My daughter took everything he had to offer in love, emotional support and material things, then ran around on him, taunted him about his parentage, then left him with the two girls without a warning. He's been through enough."

They were still halfway between the pool and the house and she lowered her voice. "Despite the way it all came about, this is a good family. But Jack, understandably, I guess, has his grudges. I think he lives on the fringe of the family because that's where he thinks he belongs. I want to see him part of it—loved, happy, secure—and with a brother he'll be able to count on when Andrew's gone."

Genny felt her throat constrict. She wished that for him, too. "I think the potential's there," she said softly.

"You saw it, too?"

"They want to be friends. You can see it in their eyes."

Emily put an arm around Genny's shoulders. "How can they

hope to become friends when they can't accept that they're brothers?''

THE HOUSE WAS CHAOTIC for several days while routines were established and the children jockeyed for position in the hierarchy. The playroom and the pool area were often the scenes of hot arguments.

"Who wants to watch that dork? I want to see *Jake and the Fatman.*"

Genny, walking by the playroom on her way to the kitchen, heard Robert's complaint and saw Lisette come unglued. "Dork? Dork? You're a dork! Doogie Hauser is the best doctor in..."

Francie, apparently taking Emily's mission to heart, suggested, "Why don't we watch *Doogie Hauser* and record *Jake and the Fatman,* then Robby can watch it in the living room while we're watching *Horror Hour.*"

Both combatants stopped to consider. Though logical compromise seemed to have less appeal than argument, they reluctantly agreed.

Francie noticed Genny in the doorway and waved. Genny blew her a kiss and went on to join the others for coffee. She couldn't suppress a little swell of pride. It had been a small victory, but her daughter had been responsible for it.

In the living room the men sat in a cluster of chairs near the window facing a dusky sky, ragged treetops silhouetted against it. Andrew, Jack, Drew and Cavendish were engaged in a lively discussion about who would take the American League pennant, and Emily and Sheila sat on a sofa at a right angle to a marble fireplace, its hearth filled for summer with a basket of dried flowers. Sheila was carrying on about a party she'd attended that had included Princess Diana.

Genny seriously considered joining the men, but as Sheila leaned to the low table where Mrs. Pratt had left a coffee service, Emily beckoned Genny with desperate vigor.

"That ring Charles gave her is just exquisite," Sheila was saying. "And her clothes! I tell you, they're just elegant. I told her she should ignore all the fuss in the press about Harry being spoiled. Children need a lot of latitude. I mean, he's going to be king one day. Who wants a leader who accepts the word, 'no'?''

"Even a king," Emily said, her voice unusually quiet as though she were taking great pains to keep it that way, "should learn that he isn't alone in the world, that other people's needs and opinions also count."

Sheila shrugged the shoulder of a very expensive, very tight white silk blouse. "Oh, I don't know. I'm very free with our boys and look at how well they're turning out?"

Emily opened her mouth to reply. Not trusting what might come out of it, Genny sent her a cautioning glance. Fortunately Sheila chose that moment to notice that the coffeepot was empty.

"Well," she said. "Mrs. Pratt isn't her usual efficient self this evening. We're out of coffee."

Emily sipped at her own full cup. "It's her evening off. That was your third cup, Sheila. You'll have insomnia."

"Cavendish!" Sheila called across the room. "Cavendish, would you refill the coffeepot, please?"

It should have been obvious to anyone that the butler was off duty, that he'd been invited into the men's discussion as a friend. Sheila, however, didn't seem to notice such things.

Cavendish pushed away from the table, but Jack, sitting beside him, stopped him with a hand on his arm. "Coffee's in the kitchen, Sheila," he said.

Drew cast him a critical glance, but said nothing.

Sheila was obviously hurt at the notion of getting it herself. Genny couldn't help but wonder if she was driven by pure selfishness, or if she was the product of the same kind of upbringing she was inflicting on her boys and simply knew nothing else.

"I'll get it." Genny carried the pot toward the kitchen, thinking it was the least she could do to restore peace. The Flemings had enough problems without building a tempest over a coffee pot. She ignored the rebuke in Jack's eyes as she passed their chairs. She hefted the pot on the sideboard near where they sat and found that it, too, was nearly empty. "Be right back," she promised, smiling into the uncertain, vaguely confused male faces.

She was not surprised when Jack joined her in the kitchen. Coffee dripped and gurgled from the coffee maker as she filled the empty pots with hot water to keep them warm.

"I was trying to make a point," he said, coming to lean on the counter beside her.

"I know." She smiled and reached around him for a tea towel to wipe off the sides of the pots. "I'm just trying to make coffee."

"You're not a servant here."

Her smile broadened as she glanced at him again. "I know that, too. Even the servants here aren't really servants."

"Genny…"

"Jack, it's such a small thing." His name came off her lips so easily it startled both of them. She blinked and he grinned. "I'm not sure Sheila can help it," she went on, trying to divert his attention back to the matter at hand. "She just lives in another world."

"As long as she's here," he said quietly, "she should live in this one."

"Maybe she doesn't know how."

"How can she—" Their quiet disagreement was interrupted by the sudden arrival of Lisette and Francie at a dead run. Lisette ran to the pantry while Francie went to the refrigerator. There was a quickly muttered "Hi," from the appropriate quarter then they left, again at a run, one carrying a bag of potato chips, the other a two-liter bottle of Pepsi. Lisette paused in the doorway to explain, "Commercial. Doogie's about to operate. Bye."

As running footsteps receded down the hall, Jack shook his head as though to clear it of a hallucination. "Where were we?" he asked Genny.

She poured fragrant, steaming coffee into the pots. "I think you were about to praise me for my resourcefulness and offer me a raise in salary."

He took the hot pot from her and put it aside, then turned her toward him. "Nice try," he said. "Now listen to me."

Surprised by his intensity, she complied.

"Let me tell you something about Sheila." He spoke quietly, probably in deference to everyone sitting just beyond the kitchen door. But she'd come to notice in the past few days that he spoke quietly when he was upset or irritated, as though it helped him contain his temper. "She'll push you just as far as you'll let her, particularly if you let her get the impression you're part of the staff here."

"Jack," she said reasonably, "I am part of the staff."

He wanted to shout at her for her stubbornness, but that was the second time she'd used his name, and he suddenly found it difficult to be angry.

"If she starts using you that way," he warned gently, "I'm going to climb all over her. If you don't want that to happen, next time let her get her own damned coffee. All right?"

"All right," she relented. "I just thought it would be nice if you all had a peaceful evening."

"You're not responsible for keeping the peace."

"We're all responsible," she insisted. "I don't have a family, so the issue doesn't come up from Francie, but do you want your girls to remember when they're grown that the only thing that happened at their family reunions was that their aunt pushed people around, their cousins whined and everybody argued?"

Jack ran a hand down his face and extended both arms in a gesture of surrender. "I give up!" he groaned.

She smiled and walked past him with both pots of coffee. "Thank you," she said.

"I AM NOT GOING to a meeting of bionic women who are putting their lives back together by means of artificial body parts. I won't do it!" Emily walked around Mrs. Pratt's portable sewing machine set up in a corner of the sun porch, shaking her finger at Genny. "You had no right to call without asking me."

Genny lined up two bright fabric squares and sewed them together. She matched up another pair. "I told you three days ago I was going to look into a support group."

"But you didn't *ask* me."

"You didn't tell me not to."

"Yes, I did, but as usual you never listen to me. You do what you think is right for me, not what I think is right."

Calmly Genny sewed up the second pair. "That's because," she said, sewing the two sets together on the width, "my job as your nurse is to see that you get better. If I did what you thought was right, I'd let you waste away in front of a television with a box of bonbons, your Vaughan Monroe tape and a subscription to *Variety*."

Emily walked around the machine, leaned over it and glared into Genny's face. "I'm retired! And if I choose to be a settee potato, I'm entitled. And how do you think you can make me go to this thing when the time comes?''

Genny maintained a neutral expression. ''I'll see that no one's left at home to keep you company but Sheila.''

She could not have hoped for a stronger reaction had she threatened to have her carried to the car. Emily gasped indignantly and stormed from the room.

Genny sighed and slumped in her chair. She looked at her reflection in the window next to which she sat. ''And you call yourself a peacemaker,'' she said.

She had half her squares assembled when Cavendish returned from town with the girls. They were giggly and loud, feeling a little ''loose,'' Genny guessed, because Drew and Sheila had taken the boys sight-seeing. Dani had bought a New Kids on the Block tape, and they used the other end of the sunroom to practice a dance routine they'd learned in class.

Genny stopped to watch them, marveling at how much fun they were having. She'd always considered herself fortunate that Francie was a cheerful child, anxious to take part in whatever was happening, able to make her own fun if she had to occupy herself. But she positively glowed in the company of the Fleming girls.

She revered Dani, who gave her as much sisterly affection and abuse as she gave Lisette. She and Lisette had become inseparable. They often quarreled, but tiffs were soon over because a partner in the next endeavor always seemed to them more important than the disagreement.

Genny watched them execute a simple but perfectly coordinated side step with skillful precision, and felt a little pinch of pain. This was what she'd dreamed of during her own lonely childhood—a small brood of children playing and laughing together. Children who would have one another to lean on instead of the quiet, solitary existence she'd known after her mother died.

They broke formation, collapsing in giggles when Lisette stopped and Francie collided with her.

''Okay, let's try it again,'' Dani said, coaxing them back into line. ''Only this time give the temptation walk a little hip like Janet Jackson does.'' She put an arm to the back of her head and moved right with a playfully sultry little bump and grind.

Francie and Lisette huddled together, giggling uproariously.

"Okay, let's do it." Dani reset the tape, took her position, shooed the younger girls in place and waited for the music.

The first effort was a disaster, and they all ended up on the floor in hysterics. Genny laughed out loud, but she thought she spotted the problem.

She abandoned her quilt and took a place at the end of the line. The girls scrambled back into formation, delighted by her participation. She leaned around the giggling pair to look at Dani. "I think your longer step is overreaching theirs. Try taking a small one, or leaving a little more space between you." She grinned. "They don't have quite as much hip to swing yet."

Lisette thought that was funny, but Dani accepted it as a compliment and gave her sister a superior glance as she started the tape again.

Genny led the line as they shuffled right, then mimicked Dani's sexy walk, the move very close to a standard routine in her Jazzercise class.

They were close, but not quite coordinated. "Okay," she directed, counting out a few beats then pointing in the other direction. "Shuffle left!"

That was considerably better. By the time they moved right again, they were coordinated, aligned, and feeling the music. Dani squealed and counted the beats with a clap as Genny got into it, snapping her fingers and ba-ba-ba-ing with the music as she swung her hip to the right, moving blindly in the rapport of the moment.

The girls' giggles provided no clue to her audience, because they'd been giggling steadily for a week and a half. She hipped full tilt into Jack, her shoulder smacking into his solar plexus with a jolt that brought her out of her dancer's euphoria with a little scream of surprise.

Startled and speechless, she looked into his eyes for one eternal moment of silence. Against her shoulder and the length of her upper arm, she felt the ridged muscles of his chest and stomach and his body's vibrant heat.

She looked quickly into his eyes, hoping to encourage thought rather than emotion, but was sabotaged. She saw laughter in their green depths, and something else that defied definition in the instant allowed her. It occurred to her in a part of her brain still functioning that she didn't have to be able to identify it to know that it was trouble.

In a quick move Jack took her hand, wrapped an arm around her waist, and dipped her to the floor like the last move in some dangerous tango. She hung there, her head an inch from the floor, physically trusting him implicitly, emotionally terrified.

"Sorry," he said, pulling her smoothly up. "I know that isn't what your routine called for, but that's all I remember from my four sessions at Miss Melody Brown's School of Dance when I was ten."

Genny was vaguely aware of the girls' giggles, of Andrew's grinning figure leaning in the doorway, of the tape playing on, although the performance had come to an abrupt halt.

Jack congratulated himself on the well-executed dip. His other choice had been to push her away to break the contact with his body. He'd felt every inch of her that touched him from his sternum to... God. Was this really going to happen to him after so many years of comfortable bachelorhood?

"Daddy, you went to dance class?" Lisette asked, her voice high with disbelief.

He nodded. Genny took the opportunity to move safely out of reach. He forced his mind to focus on an answer. "Only a couple of times. The first time a girl put her arms around me, I refused to go back."

Lisette came to wrap her arms around his middle. "Didn't you like girls? How come you had us?"

"Well, I was younger, then," he replied, grinning. "I thought girls were weird and ugly. I didn't know they grew up to look like Genny. And I had you," he said with a warmth in his voice that made Genny willing to forgive him everything, "because I was smart. Now, Grandpa and I wanted to know if you ladies were in favor of tacos for lunch at Gringo's."

The affirmative was unanimous. Andrew plastered himself to the molding as the girls raced past him to wash their hands.

He laughed lightly at his son. "I didn't know you took dance lessons." Then his glance swung consideringly between Jack and Genny. "But, then, there's probably a lot I don't know, isn't there?"

Chapter Nine

"I told you I wasn't going." Emily remained stubbornly at the breakfast table, pretending total absorption in the contents of her coffee cup.

Genny, and Jack who had volunteered to drive her and Emily to the Cancer Support Group meeting in Bridgebury, waited by the door, ready to go.

"Then why are you wearing makeup?" Genny asked.

Emily looked up, startled. "Is that illegal in New England?"

Genny folded her arms, trying to show that she was prepared to wait. Jack leaned back against the door frame.

"I think you want to go," she said. "I think you know you need to go, you just don't want to face pitying or patronizing behavior. But these are all women dealing with the same things you're faced with. I'm sure that won't be a problem."

Emily stared at the empty place across the table from her. "I'm doing all right."

"You could be doing better."

"I'm not going to sit around and moan with a bunch of misshapen women."

Andrew walked into the kitchen at that moment and stopped with a grin, his hand on the refrigerator door. "Moaning and misshapen ladies? Where are you two going?"

"The cancer support group in Bridgebury," Genny replied without a smile for his levity. "Emily doesn't want to go."

"Oh." He sobered instantly and went to the table, sitting beside Emily who turned in her chair to face away from him. "Lost your nerve?" he asked gently.

"No, my breast," she replied, her back stiff. "And I'm not going to pour out my soul to a bunch of well-meaning but sanctimonious biddies. How I live with it is my business."

"But you're not living with it, are you?" He reached out to tug at her arm and turn her back toward him. "You're living in the past, torturing yourself with old glories."

"I was beautiful then," she said, her voice low and husky, her eyes glimmering with unshed tears. She angled her chin. "And I was good. I was the best."

"Then how could the removal of one breast have changed all that?" he asked reasonably, then answered his own question. "It hasn't, Emily. So, a part of you is missing—a part of you that signified for you your feminine self. I know you can't be shallow enough to think that means the woman in you is dead."

She listened silently, her composure barely held in check. Genny felt her own throat close, and Jack shifted his weight, as though Emily's pain hurt him.

Andrew put an arm on the back of her chair. "I lived with one very cruel woman, and I've loved a very good one. I know about them. What makes up what they are is nothing physical. It's love and spirit and generosity. It's a strength I could never hope to have because I'm just a man." His hand closed over her shoulder and he rubbed gently. "Come on, Emily. Go to the meeting and make something spectacular of the next thirty years."

Emily closed her eyes and her tears fell. Andrew took a napkin from a silver holder in the middle of the table and dabbed at her eyes.

"We'll wait for you in the car," Jack said. He took Genny's arm and pulled her out with him into the sunshine.

Perhaps it wasn't so hard after all, he thought, to see what had kept his mother's love steady all those years.

THE WOMAN AT WHOSE HOME the meeting was held was small and pale, a blonde with a buzz cut that Genny guessed indicated chemotherapy. Her smile was warm and genuine as she drew them into a comfortable sunlit living room and introduced them.

One of the members was a grandmotherly woman who sat in a corner rocker, holding the bottom six inches of a child's sweater on round needles. She worked the difficult pattern flaw-lessly, seemingly without looking at it as she spoke with the other ladies.

Another was a young mother who'd brought a pair of three-year-old twins whom she constantly chased and admonished with good-humored exasperation. The thought of her facing a life-threatening illness while raising toddlers almost brought Genny to tears, but she was so cheerful, and apparently enjoying the moment so much, that Genny relaxed.

The last, and the one with whom Emily seemed to identify, was a woman about her age with the looks of a fashion model. She explained that she'd been a graphics designer in New York City until her husband retired the previous year to New Hamp-shire.

"I still free-lance," she said, "thanks to a fax machine."

"Joanie also models at Pierre Bonham's in Manchester," said the young mother, wrestling one of her twins for a fireplace poker, "and for a couple of catalogues."

Emily seemed fascinated, despite herself.

Noting Emily staring at her, Joanie smiled. "My prosthesis is so good, I'd wear a bikini." Then she sighed and groaned. "Un-fortunately I haven't had my thighs replaced."

Emily relaxed and leaned back in her chair.

"THIS IS STUPID," Robert said. "Guys don't quilt."

Trey ignored him, concentrating on stitching through the bat-ting without catching the backing. "My track coach," he said absently, "does needlepoint. Says it...focuses your concentra-tion."

"We could be watching *Monster Truck Challenge*," Robert sulked.

"But Dani and Emily are watching *Days of Our Lives*," Trey reminded.

"There's another television in the living room," Genny said.

Robert gave her a disgusted glance. "Mom's watching *Don-ahue*."

"You could play tennis."

"Dad and Grandpa are playing Uncle Jack and Cavendish."

Genny liked the sound of that. She patted Robert's shoulder.

"Well, I'm happy to have your company." After just a few days she was discovering Trey was less bored than simply introspective, and Robert was amusing, even if he had inherited his mother's tendency to complain.

"Why are you doing this anyway?" Robert wanted to know. "I mean, Grandpa could *buy* you another blanket."

"Quilting is my hobby," Genny explained. "Only at home I'm usually too busy to do it. Here, every time I sit down at the frame, someone sits with me and asks me how it's going and ends up helping me. In the old days they called this a friendship quilt because everyone helped."

Robert sighed and leaned back, holding his needle at a distance as though it might turn on him. "Well, it makes me crabby, not friendly."

Genny took it from him and tucked it into the square he'd been working on. "Just think that years from now, when someone is wrapped in this quilt, it'll have your stitches in it."

"They'll probably fall out."

Genny leaned closer to inspect his work. He'd taken only a few stitches and they were large but carefully made. "No, they won't. You're doing a fine job."

"Can I have another cookie?"

Genny passed him the plate of oatmeal cookies Mrs. Pratt had brought in.

"Well." Jack walked into the room in white shorts and a sweater, a light patina of perspiration on his brow. "I'm pleased to see such diligence."

Robert sighed. "There's nothin' else to do around here. All the TVs are taken."

Jack offered him his racket. "Want to take my place? I've got a date."

Robert was out the door in an instant.

Trey angled Jack a grin. Whatever quarrel the brothers had, it had no part in Jack's relationship with his nephews, Genny noticed, nor in Drew's with Dani and Lisette.

"Date?" Trey asked in disbelief. "At your age, Uncle Jack?"

Jack rapped Trey's bent head lightly as he took Robert's vacated chair. "Actually, my date's with Genny."

Genny looked up in surprise. "Oh?"

"We've been invited to high tea at the cabin." Jack glanced at his watch. "In five minutes."

Genny smiled. "By whom?" For Francie and Lisette, the cabin had become a haven from the boys when they needed privacy for their little-girl rituals.

Jack frowned in puzzlement as he helped himself to a cookie. "A very pretty little lady in a long pink dress and a white hat with a veil. Didn't recognize her."

"Long skirt, no chest?" Trey asked.

"You've seen her, too?"

Trey shook his head as though the workings of the female mind were beyond his comprehension. "It's Francie, but you have to call her Abigail." Trey rolled his eyes. "Lees is—" he snorted "—get this, Marjoleine."

Jack whistled. "I don't suppose we can get away with calling her Marjie, either."

"I wouldn't try it."

Jack turned to Genny. "We are asked to be prompt."

Genny tipped her needle into the fabric and looked at Trey in concern. "Will you be okay?"

Concentrating on his stitches, he replied without looking up. "Just leave the cookies."

"Abigail" answered Jack's knock on the cabin door. In a woman's décolleté dress that opened to her waist, displaying fragile ribs and a still-undeveloped torso, Francie bowed formally. Down the dress, Genny caught a glimpse of striped shorts.

"Good afternoon," Francie said in a sultry voice that complemented the chin-length veil on her white hat. "I'm so happy you came." She turned into the cabin and called, "Marjoleine, our guests are here." Under the veil were dark eyebrows that extended to her hairline, deep blue eyelids and cherry-red lips.

Genny wanted to laugh and cry at once. The girls were playing, but there was something prophetic in the imitation—something that was hard for any mother to look in the face without remembering the infant she'd held in her arms.

Lisette came to the door in a black dress suspended by spaghetti straps that hung to her waist. She'd wrapped a gauzy red scarf around her neck to match the cherries on the black velvet picture hat placed at a jaunty angle. She'd apparently been made up by the same hand as her cohostess.

"We're the Fleming sisters," she said with a little curtsy. "I'm Marjoleine, and this is Abigail." She extended her hand in a theatrical gesture toward the cabin's interior. "Do come in."

The one room's furnishings were spare but clean. Genny knew Mrs. Pratt kept it tidy because the girls loved to play in it.

A curtain sectioned off a corner of the room. "What's in there?" Genny whispered to Jack as the girls busied themselves at the table.

"The bed," Jack returned under his breath. "Want to see?"

She caught his devilish grin and shook her head. "I believe you."

The table was set with things commandeered from the kitchen, and a jam jar filled with dandelions was placed in the middle. Beside it was a fat brown teapot and a plate of misshapen butter cookies.

Francie pulled out two chairs on the far side of the table. "How *are* things in London?" she asked.

"Dreadfully sticky," Jack replied in an Etonian accent and without hesitation. He put an arm around Genny's shoulders. "The memsahib and I were planning to summer in the south of France, then we received your invitation and changed our plans."

Lisette smiled as she took the chair opposite Genny. "I'm sure the queen will miss you."

It was easy to fall into their fantasy. "Not at all," Genny replied. "She's fishing in Scotland, I hear."

"Our grandfather fishes," Lisette said, glancing at Francie. "Shall I pour, Sister?"

"Please, dear," Francie replied.

"He's a banker, you know," Lisette went on, pouring carefully.

"Our father, too," Francie said, passing Jack the cup.

Jack nodded. "Thank you. Yes, we've done business. Good man. Fine family."

"Our mother's a nurse," Francie provided, passing a full cup to Genny. She added gravely, "She saves lives every day."

Jack looked impressed. "Is that a fact?"

Genny saw the same pinch of emotion in his eyes she felt. This was fantasy, but it wasn't. The girls had built a world the way they'd like it to be and were living in it this afternoon. Genny was almost afraid of being drawn into it too deeply.

"Are there just the two of you?" Jack asked, apparently not sharing her fear.

"Our older sister is a movie star married to Tom Cruise," Francie replied, adding wide-eyed, "we get free tickets to the movies all the time."

Jack kept a straight face with difficulty.

Genny sipped her tea. It was tepid and very, very strong. "Wonderful tea," she said. "May I have your recipe?"

Lisette shook her head with a sweet smile. "Then you wouldn't come back to see us, would you? And Sister and I do enjoy having you visit."

JACK AND GENNY WALKED back to the house arm in arm.

"The south of France could not have been more fun," Jack said. "Guaranteed."

Genny grinned up at him. "You've got Tom Cruise for a son-in-law. You can go anytime you want."

He looked up at the sky with an absent smile. "Their little tea party was an interesting blend of fantasy and reality."

Genny nodded. "That's childhood, I guess. Accept the part of life you like, and dress up the rest. How'd the tennis match go earlier?"

"The way things always go when the three of us do anything together. My father takes such pains to give us equal attention, to ask both our opinions—as though we were a pair of jealous eight-year-olds." He didn't like to analyze too closely whose fault that was. "And Drew has a better backhand than I do. I was glad when Abigail arrived with the invitation."

"Isn't it all right for Drew to be better than you at something?" Genny asked.

He shook his head as they wound their way through the birches. "I have to be better."

"Why?"

His eyes became troubled. "If I'm not, then my father's second family wasn't worth the risks he took to keep us, or the pain it caused everyone. He never really got to have my mother, and he has the perfect heir in Drew, so I'm basically unnecessary."

Genny couldn't decide whether to punch him or hold him. "Jack!" she cried. "An individual isn't worth his existence because of what he provides others. He's worth it because he *is*. He earns his place in society that way, but his right to be is guaranteed by his birth. Love conceived you, Jack. Drew can't even say that. I wonder how many times in his life he's envied you?''

Jack shook his head, unable to believe that had ever been true.

''I understand Emily enjoyed the support group meeting,'' he said.

Genny accepted the evasion. She was getting used to him changing the subject when it became too personal. She couldn't fault him; she did the same thing herself.

''Very much,'' she said. ''Once she discovered they spend their time helping one another deal with life rather than bemoaning what it's taken from them, she relaxed. I think she even benefited.''

He squeezed her shoulder. ''Good work.''

''I think the credit goes to your father.''

''Part of it,'' he conceded. ''But you're the one who looked up the group and arranged to go.''

Genny laughed softly. ''I am pretty wonderful. After all, I am Abigail's mother and I save lives every day.''

Jack kissed her temple. ''You even knew the queen was fishing in Scotland. Impressed the heck out of me.''

CAVENDISH WAS SERVING raspberry charlotte when Andrew rapped his spoon against a water goblet. Conversation stopped.

''I have an announcement,'' he said, folding his arms on the edge of the table and leaning forward.

Sheila stiffened, her wide eyes turning to Drew. Drew took a sip of coffee and waited.

Genny felt her own fingers clench, and turned to Jack. He appeared calm, but she could guess what he was feeling.

Jack folded the napkin in his lap, placed it on the table, then leaned back in his chair, pretending mild interest. Inside, he hoped he was braced for whatever was about to happen.

''Most of you know George Spears,'' he said, smiling. Genny saw Sheila frown, as though unable to understand what that name had to do with anything. Jack smiled and relaxed. He saw Drew do the same.

"He's managed our Salem branch for thirty years," Andrew went on, for the benefit of those at the table who didn't know who he was. "He trained Drew and Jack. He's a single man and the bank has been his life. He's devoted all his energy to it— and to us." He smiled at each of his sons. "He's retiring at the end of the week and I couldn't let the occasion pass with just a small branch party. So I'm bringing him here to spend a few days with us just to let him know how much I appreciate his loyalty and hard work."

"You'll never get him to come," Drew predicted. "He hates fuss."

Andrew nodded, looking pleased with himself. "That's why I'm having him kidnapped."

Cavendish, topping off everyone's coffee, interposed formally, "That's illegal, sir. Perhaps we should begin collecting your bail after dinner."

"I've already arranged it with several of his colleagues," Andrew went on with a wry grin at the butler. "He's scheduled to fly out of Portland airport on Friday to spend some time with his sister in Florida. I called her and asked if it would be all right if he were a few days late. Jacobs, the assistant manager of his branch is driving him to the airport, but instead of putting him on a plane to Florida, he's going to get him on the New Hampshire flight, traveling as far as Denver with him to make sure he doesn't run away from us. All we have to do is pick him up in Manchester."

"That's where you three come in." Andrew turned earnestly toward Dani, Lisette and Francie, sitting together at one end of the table. "I've watched you dance, and I'd like you to provide the entertainment for the party we're having for him."

Sheila slouched, visibly disappointed. That hadn't been the announcement she'd hoped for.

Dani shrieked, and Lisette and Francie huddled together, giggling. Trey and Robert looked disgusted.

Andrew turned to Robert. "I'm counting on you to be master of ceremonies."

Robert winced. "What's that?"

"You'll announce the girls."

After a moment's consideration, Robert's expression changed to one of sinister glee. "Can I say whatever I want?"

The adults laughed, but Dani leaned toward him threateningly. "Not unless you want to die an ugly death," she replied.

"Trey will write you a script," Andrew said, smiling at his older grandson. "And maybe a poem for the girls to recite about George's accomplishments."

"Grandpa..." Trey began to protest.

"I'll give you a list of highlights to work from."

Sheila looked somewhat mollified, Genny thought. She must have felt if it wasn't time for her husband to be put in the spotlight, her children would be a comfortable second. "We'll go to Bridgebury for some new clothes tomorrow," she said to the boys, clapping her hands together at the prospect.

Drew turned to her, his expression complex. Genny saw annoyance, pity, a very pale flicker of affection, and a glimpse of sadness. She felt as though she'd looked into the soul of the man Jack thought had everything and seen a lonely man.

Sheila caught his glance, patted his knee and said, "We'll get you something new, too, dear."

Drew dropped his napkin on the table and pushed his chair back. "If you'll all excuse me, I've a few phone calls to make. Mind if I use your office, Dad?"

"Of course not," Andrew replied. "Cavendish will bring you a brandy."

"Make it a double," he said.

"Would you all excuse us, too, please?" Jack stood, walked around the table and pulled out Genny's chair. "It's a beautiful evening for a walk."

Genny turned to Emily, prepared to protest, but Emily made a shooing motion toward the patio. "Go on," she said. "I won't need you for anything, and it is a beautiful night."

"Watch your step in the dark," Andrew cautioned.

Jack grinned. "I always do."

Jack put an arm around Genny's shoulders and led her across the patio toward the trees. He looked in the direction of the cabin, invisible in the darkness. "I wonder if the Fleming sisters are in this evening."

"Oh, they must be enjoying an evening out," Genny replied, leaning in to him. "I imagine they're in great demand."

"But not for their tea."

Genny laughed. "No."

As they wandered toward the trees in the cool, fragrant night, Genny's mind wandered back to Drew leaving the table. She said without planning to, "I feel sorry for Drew."

"So do I," Jack agreed. "The boys are all right, but Sheila's pretty much of a loss."

Genny stopped at the rim of the woods. The path into it looked dark and narrow, the low branches crowding over it to make it appear small and confining. She turned her back on it and leaned a shoulder against the ghostly trunk of a birch. "I think he still loves her."

Jack shrugged a shoulder. "Maybe. There's no accounting for taste. Tired already?"

"No," she said, her voice suggesting self-recrimination. "The dark is very confining to me. Walking into the woods would feel like walking into a cave. You go ahead, I'll wait for you."

Jack looked at the trail on which she'd turned her back. It looked like an invitation into velvety blackness to him, a remote and comfortably quiet place that would renew and restore him. How sad, he thought, that it held only fear for her.

"I'm sorry," he said.

She shook her head. "Don't be. It's just that...in the darkness, I lose my way out."

He hooked his arm in hers and pulled her back toward the lights of the house.

"Isn't it amazing," he said, a smile in his voice, "that it hasn't occurred to my father that someone might *not* enjoy watching his grandchildren perform?"

Genny laughed softly. She had thought about that. "Isn't that charming? Of course, you haven't seen the girls perform," she said. "Don't sell them short."

He laughed throatily. "I've seen you, though, and I was mightily impressed."

"Thank you," she replied regally. "Your dip would have made Miss Melody Brown proud, I'm sure. I think your father so enjoys his family, he just presumes everyone else will find them totally entertaining. And George might."

"How's the quilt coming?"

Genny took the hint. Another evasive tactic before the subject got around to Drew again.

"Very well. Emily and the girls have been helping me. Even

the boys put in a few stitches yesterday. The frame works beautifully, incidentally. Thank you.''

"Thanks go to my grandfather. He made it, I believe.''

"Did you know him?'' Genny asked.

"No.'' Jack took her hand to help her over the low brick wall. "He and my grandmother were very upset about Dad's relationship with my mother. I never met them.''

Genny laced her fingers in his, hearing the small sound of loss in his tone. How sad it must be, she thought, to have grandparents who disapproved of you and didn't want to know you.

"I'm named after him, though,'' Jack said. He sank onto a chair on the patio and pulled her into his lap.

She looked worriedly toward the house, pushing at his shoulders. "Jack...''

He wrapped both arms around her waist and held, his grip loose enough to let her feel she could escape, but tight enough to prevent it. "Relax,'' he said. "Everyone knows we're attracted to each other. It won't horrify anyone to find you in my life.''

When she leaned her weight against him, relaxing, he thought he might be making progress. "Sheila doesn't approve,'' Genny said quietly.

"Like we care?''

She leaned an elbow on his shoulder. "What do you know about her?''

"Why?''

"To help me understand her.''

"Why do you want to?''

"Because this whole family is connected. You're all individualists, but I think you act and react to one another as though you're inextricably connected, despite all your denials.''

"Oh, you do?''

"Uh-huh.'' Genny expelled a soft sigh as his hand stroked gently, absently, up and down her spine. The darkness was distant, the bright floodlight over the patio was far enough away to cast only a soft glow where they sat. Her head grew heavy. She had to think about what she'd been saying. It helped to slump against Jack and concentrate on the fingers on her back. "At first I thought they were just another couple who'd acquired everything after so many years of marriage, but lost each other. Now I'm not so sure.''

Jack shifted slightly to make her comfortable, stroking the arm that was uppermost to keep her warm. He had trouble focusing on the conversation.

"You want to know why?" she asked.

"By all means," he said.

"Tonight at the table when she talked about taking the boys shopping," she explained lazily, "I saw in his eyes how disappointed he was. I gather from their designer-everything life-style that's about all she thinks about. I just wonder if that would bother him if he hadn't once had a lot more from her."

"She was a spoiled rich girl when he married her," Jack said. "I know because I'd just married one myself two months previously."

"But wasn't he a spoiled rich boy?"

"Yes." Jack was silent a moment, then he added grudgingly, "But he's always worked hard."

"And you admire that about him."

"Don't put words in my mouth."

"They're in your eyes," she said gently. "You'd probably feel a lot better if you'd let them get to your tongue."

The French doors onto the patio opened, followed instantly by the sound of shouting. Genny tried to sit up but Jack held her to him, admonishing in a whisper, "Ssh. They won't even notice us if you sit still."

"You're a spendthrift!" Drew's voice was loud and angry. Genny had thought at dinner that he looked like a man about to burst. "Do you ever have another thought in your head that doesn't involve money? You're enough to break Donald Trump!"

"And you're a cheapskate!" Sheila's voice shrieked. "One lousy new shirt for the party and you act as though I asked for a new Mercedes."

"That's because it always comes down to that with you! Who the hell cares about a new shirt! I've enough now to clothe the top half of the free world."

"Appearance is important." Sheila's voice quieted, the tone cajoled. "Honey, you have to get serious about why we're here."

Drew's voice sounded weary, despondent. "A new shirt will not do that, Sheila."

"You've got to be his choice, Drew."

"My father has two sons. Much as I hate to admit it, Jack's as good at what we do as I am."

"But he's—"

"Be quiet, Sheila." There was the sound of footsteps on the flagstone that led to the garages. "Go inside."

"Where are you going?"

"For a drive. Don't wait up."

"Drew!"

His answer was the lifting of the garage door, followed by the purr of a sophisticated engine as the Mercedes drove away. The door hummed closed.

A whispered epithet filled the ensuing silence. The French doors opened then closed with a loud reverberation of glass.

Neither Genny nor Jack moved or spoke for a long moment. Then Genny sat up slowly, looking over Jack's shoulder to the deck. Seeing no one there, she put a hand to her forehead and emitted a little groan.

Jack patted her hip. "Sounded like love to me," he said dryly.

Chapter Ten

"Mom!"

"Genny!"

Genny looked up from tightening the quilt frame in time to find herself tactically flanked by Francie and Lisette. Each child took one of her hands and tugged until Genny was out of her chair.

"Come on, Mom," Francie said excitedly, tucking Genny's purse under her arm. "We're going to the airport."

"To get Uncle George," Lisette explained. "He's not really our uncle, but you'll like him. He's never been here before, but he comes to our house in Portland a lot. Daddy wants you to come with us."

"But why?" Genny asked as they tried to pull her toward the door. "I..."

"Do you think," Jack asked from the doorway, "that I'm driving for an hour and half alone in a car with these two?"

Genny grinned, thinking how wonderful he looked in khaki pants and a white cotton shirt with a single, broad khaki stripe.

"So, I'm to be your bodyguard against two nine-year-old girls?" she asked, shaking her head over his temerity.

Jack needed a moment to answer. Backlit by the sun porch's glow, she looked like she did in his dreams—gossamer, ethereal—like something he might reach for but never catch.

He finally nodded. "I can deal with either of them alone," he said. "Together they're like a nuclear weapon with a giggle payload." He glanced at his watch. "Can we move along? We're just going to make it."

Lisette tugged on Genny while Francie, used to having the question tossed at her, asked gravely, "Do you have to go to the bathroom first?"

"DAD, CAN WE ADOPT Francie?" Lisette asked from the backseat of Andrew's Cadillac, borrowed for the trip. Seat-belted in the back, she and Francie played Old Maid on the seat between them.

Jack glanced away from the road to meet Genny's smile. "You can't adopt children who have parents, Lees," he said. "You know that."

"What about kids who only have one?" she asked seriously.

Jack had to think a minute. That had apparently not been the silly, off-the-top-of-her-head question he'd thought it was.

"They belong to the mom or dad they have," he replied reasonably. "You wouldn't want to take Francie away from Genny, would you?"

"No," she said, obviously indignant that he'd thought so. "We'd adopt her, too."

"Honey, you can't adopt an adult," Genny said, smiling over her shoulder at the girls.

"Why not?" Francie asked.

"Because they no longer need parents," Jack answered.

Lisette frowned. "You mean you don't need Grandpa?"

"Of course I do. But as a friend. He doesn't have to take care of me...anymore." Jack hesitated, thinking as he heard himself speak that wasn't precisely true.

"But you have lots of friends."

"Yes, but none whom I love in the same way I love Grandpa. Or who love me the way he does."

"That's because you're his son."

"Yes."

"Then you need him because nobody else can do for you what he does. So why can't adults be adopted? Doesn't everybody need that?"

She had *him* convinced. He glanced at Genny with a grin. "How about it? Want to be a Fleming?"

"Adults get married instead of adopted," Francie put in knowledgeably. "That solves everybody's problem. The kids get a mother or a father, and..." She paused in her explanation.

"Like, if it was us, Lees, Mom would get a husband, your dad would get a wife, and Mom would get a in-law father."

"A father-in-law," Genny corrected.

Lisette was silent a moment. "That would work," she decreed finally. "Why don't we do it?"

Genny didn't dare glance in Jack's direction. "Because a man and a woman have to be in love to get married."

As the words came out of her mouth, she knew she'd set herself up for correction.

"Sometimes they just live in the same house and don't get married," Francie informed her. "Is that because they're not in love?"

Genny let her head fall back against the headrest. "I was having a nice, quiet morning with my quilt," she complained softly to Jack, "then you play upon my sympathies and I find myself in a social studies workshop!"

He laughed. "Does that mean you don't want to be adopted?" When she didn't answer, he suggested helpfully, "We still have the marriage option."

"People live together," Genny said, raising her voice to carry to the back seat, "for all kinds of reasons. Sometimes it's because marriage can be scary because you have to promise to stay together forever."

"But everybody gets divorced."

"That's why many people don't get married. Because they're afraid that will happen to them."

Francie sighed noisily. "They don't get married when they love somebody because they don't want to get divorced from them. So they *don't* promise to love that person forever even though they really do, just so they won't break the promise?"

Genny had to play that over in her mind once more. The inherent logic in it was startling. "That's about right," she said.

"But if they want to live with that person, don't they love them even though they didn't make the promise? And won't it still hurt when they leave whether they made the promise or not?"

"Probably."

"I don't get it," Lisette said.

"I do," Francie told her. "It's chicken."

HAND IN HAND, Jack and Genny ran into the airport terminal fifteen minutes late. Lisette and Francie were alongside searching for George.

"Poor guy," Jack said as they ran. "Kidnapped, then left to cool his heels in a strange airport. I never miss that turn into Manchester."

Genny laughed. "You can be excused for being distracted. That was quite a discussion."

"Maybe we could send the girls to a rabbinical college," he suggested. "They love the restless, searching mind. Do you see him?"

"I don't even know what he looks like."

"Short, round, glasses, looks like a banker."

In the middle of the terminal, Jack turned in a circle as knots of travelers bustled around them. Strollers, baggage carts and an occasional wheelchair rolled past. The air was warm and smelled alternately of expensive perfume and warm bodies.

"Daddy!"

Jack homed in on Lisette's voice and saw her and Francie heading for the double glass doors.

"He's getting a taxi!" she shouted as she ran.

Jack followed her pointing finger and spotted a short, rotund man walking toward a taxi waiting by the curb. His first thought was that Lisette was mistaken. The man wore wildly colored Bermuda shorts, lime-green knee socks and a cotton hat with fishing flies attached to the band. Also, George knew they were coming for him. Why was he getting a cab?

Calling out George's name, Lisette and Francie ran out of two different doors, bracketing their prey.

Pulling Genny with him, Jack hurried for the sidewalk, remembering George's weak heart. Lisette on one's trail could be an alarming experience. In tandem with Francie, she was downright terrifying.

He found George backed against a vending machine, effectively treed. He clutched a suitcase and a briefcase in his arms for dear life. Lisette chattered at him, introducing Francie.

"We're going to have a biiig party for you," she was saying, her arms stretched out to show how big. "And Dani and Francie and I are going to dance for you."

"That's your idea of banker's attire?" Genny asked under her breath as they approached.

Jack shrugged, at a loss to explain. "The freedom of retirement must have gone to the part of the brain that controls clothes sense."

George Spears had knobby knees, Genny noted, was as wide as he was tall, and looked like someone's doting uncle—someone's frightened doting uncle, at the moment.

"Hey, George." Jack extended his hand. "Sorry we're late. I took a wrong turn."

Still clutching his bags, George looked as though he didn't recognize Jack—or as though Jack were the last person he'd expected to see.

Jack gently pushed the girls aside and pulled George away from the vending machine. He wrestled the suitcase from him and set it on the ground.

He gave the short, broad man a small shake. "George, are you okay?"

An embarrassed smile suddenly bloomed on George's face, then grew into a laugh.

"Would you be okay if you were on your way to celebrate your retirement in Florida before vacationing in Mexico, and were kidnapped at LAX and dragged onto a plane headed for Denver?"

That did explain the clothes, Jack thought.

George's laugh grew louder. "The way Jacobs dragged me away, I'm sure everyone watching though I was a convicted felon. He even went with me to Denver and put me on the plane to Manchester to make sure I didn't deplane somewhere else. Then I get here, there's no one to meet me, and I head innocently for a cab and am chased down by two pretty little bulldogs."

George put a hand over the briefcase he still clutched to his heart and paused for breath. He frowned at Francie. "And one of them I don't even recognize."

Jack introduced Genny and Francie, then waved the confused cabdriver on. He put an arm around George, picked up his bag and led him toward the parking lot. "Come on," he said, laughing. "We'll get you home and get some good New England home cooking into you and you'll feel better."

George resisted. "Come on, Jack," he wheedled. "Tell Andy

you couldn't find me. I don't want a party and a lot of fuss, I just—''

"Too late," Jack said. He indicated Lisette and Francie. "The girls are part of your entertainment, and they're already into heavy rehearsal."

Lisette looped her arm in George's and smiled winningly. "Come on, Uncle George. You're gonna love it."

Francie tugged on his briefcase. "I'll carry that for you," she offered.

He hesitated a moment then handed it over, looking helplessly at Jack as the girls led him off to the car.

Jack and Genny followed several paces behind. "Those two are quite a team," Jack observed, drawing Genny into his arm.

She hooked a thumb in a belt loop of Jack's slacks, smiling at the sight the slim little girls made leading the large, quiescent man. "The only thing Francie's ever wanted as much as a father is a sister. And a sister who's as into dance as she is, is like a gift from heaven. It'll be hard to break them up at the end of the summer."

"You mean you will let me adopt her?" Jack teased.

She gave him a light jab in the ribs. "No, but maybe we can be the first unmarried people to share custody of each other's children."

He shook his head. "A unique solution, but I'm sure with a little thought we can do better than that."

ANDREW MET THEM at the bottom of the patio steps and wrapped his friend in a bear hug.

George laughed and slapped Andrew's back. "Fine way to treat someone who's given faithful service. Half the people at Sea-tac think I'm an extradited felon."

George shook his head, obviously embarrassed. "Anyway, we said our goodbyes before you left on vacation. We've been together a long time, Andy. You know how hard these things are for me."

Andrew put an arm around his shoulders and drew him up the steps toward the family. "I know. I know. But we can't let your years of loyalty go without recognition. We're having a dinner in your honor day after tomorrow. Just the family—to let you know how much you mean to us. Until then, you have the best room in the house.

For a moment George Spears looked as though what Andrew proposed could be the worst experience of his life. Then Jack and Drew pulled him onto the patio, settled him in a chair, put a drink in his hand and began to regale him with memories of how he'd helped them through their early mistakes.

Genny watched them sit on either side of George, apparently united in their father's wish that the man be feted. Their hostilities were set aside as they bolstered each other's stories and even laughed together over reminders of their fiscal innocence.

Genny looked up to find Emily watching from across the patio. She caught Genny's eye and winked. Genny felt buoyant, lighthearted. Things were looking up all around.

"YOU SAID YOU LIKE THEM over easy."

"Those are over hard."

"You said you hate a runny yolk."

"Those yolks couldn't run if you set their tails on fire."

Genny stood in the kitchen doorway as Cavendish and Mrs. Pratt waged their softly spoken argument. Cavendish in a white apron and wielding a spatula, finally slapped the tool on the counter, yanked off the apron and confronted the much smaller woman calmly whipping batter with a whisk in a blue pottery bowl.

"I was trying to do you a favor, Louise, by preparing your breakfast," Cavendish said, his very correct voice betraying a sharp edge this morning. "But all you have done is criticize and complain. As you did when I took you to town to the film, when I helped you stir the fudge and when I went to town for the nutmeg you'd forgotten, which you'd also forgotten to tell me you wanted whole and not ground!" He said all that in one breath and paused to draw another. "You're a mean-spirited woman, Louise. God knows why I ever found you attractive."

He sighed, squared his large shoulders and went on pleasantly. "Well, you'll be relieved to know the attraction has passed. I appreciate a strong woman as much as the next man, but there is a point at which a woman ceases to be self-sufficient and becomes self-indulgent. If you must do everything for yourself to continue to prove to yourself that you never needed the wastrel who left you, and that every man who crosses your path is the same, then by all means wallow in your self-deception. I'm on my way.''

Cavendish turned on his heel and marched to the door. Genny barred it with her arm, concerned. "On your way where, Roger?" she asked, afraid he meant to go back to Portland.

"Figuratively on my way, Genevieve," he replied with a stiff bow. "Out of the life of this harridan. I'll be leaving with the family as originally planned week after next. Good morning."

Genny went to the coffeepot as though she'd heard nothing. "Want a cup?" she asked the housekeeper.

Mrs. Pratt gave her a shrewd glance. "Men are just more trouble than a woman needs," she said, making the whisk flash.

Genny leaned against the counter and sipped her coffee. "I know many men who validate that statement. I also know many who prove it wrong."

Mrs. Pratt put the bowl aside, wiped her hands on her apron and reached into a bottom cupboard for an iron griddle.

"Nothing makes pancakes like iron," she said. "Nice even heat. That's what it takes." She placed it on the burner and turned the heat on low. Then she stared at it as though she'd forgotten what she'd intended to do with it.

"Roger Cavendish is a very good man, Mrs. Pratt," Genny said.

"He lives in Oregon," she replied, still staring. "I live here."

"Is that an impossible hurdle?"

"I left good employment once to follow a man. It stranded me in a small town in Nevada without a penny to my name. It took me eighteen months to get back home."

"Cavendish wouldn't—"

"It's better this way, Genny."

Genny opened her mouth to argue that, when the kitchen door burst open and Sheila walked in wearing an elegant pink sweat suit. Genny identified it as the kind one posed in but didn't run in. She looked pale and out of sorts. She sank down at the table.

"Coffee?" Genny asked, hoping Jack wasn't listening. She'd have to hear his lecture all over again.

"Make it a double," Sheila said, leaning her head on her hand.

Genny carried the cup to the table and sat opposite her. "Are you all right?" she asked.

Sheila considered that a moment, then shrugged a shoulder. "I used to think so. Now I'm not so sure."

It became obvious to Genny that they weren't on the same wavelength. She tried again. "Are you feeling ill?"

"I'm sick of a lot of things." Sheila looked around at the pristine kitchen and the sun pouring in through the windows over the counter. "Mostly I'm sick of coming here."

When she dropped her head on her arm and burst into noisy tears, it took Genny a moment to react. Mrs. Pratt, at the griddle, glanced over her shoulder without sympathy.

Genny put a hand to Sheila's arm. "I'll get you some water."

"I don't want water," Sheila wept. "I want to go home!"

Her cry was so plaintive and childlike, Genny didn't know how to respond.

Mrs. Pratt turned away from the stove, waving her spatula in the air as though she intended to use it. "For the love of God, go then!" she cried. "Go! All you do when you come here is whine and complain—you that's got everything a body could humanly wish for! The linen's too coarse, the food is too rich, the laundry isn't done right, the house is too warm, the house is too cold. There is nothing here that will satisfy you, so go! Go!"

"Mrs. Pratt!" Genny grabbed the housekeeper's arm as she stood over a now-silent, horrified Sheila.

JACK PUSHED OPEN the kitchen door, intent on bacon and eggs and hotcakes—and saw his father's housekeeper about to bash his brother's wife with a pancake turner. He took a moment to look again. Yes. That was what was happening.

His doubts were confirmed when Genny caught Mrs. Pratt's hand and relieved her of her weapon. The housekeeper raced past him in a torrent of tears.

He stood still, waiting for Sheila to demand that he file suit immediately. Instead her face crumpled and she began to sob, running for the back door.

He looked at Genny, who appeared as mystified as he felt, pancake turner still in hand. He pointed behind her where the pancake was beginning to burn. She ran to it and turned it.

"What in the hell..." he began to ask.

She shook her head. "I don't know. Mercury must be retrograde or something."

He frowned, pushing the bowl of batter toward her as she reached for it. "What does that mean?"

She shrugged a shoulder. "I don't know. I have this friend Margo Power who's into astrology, and whenever things go wrong for me she looks it up and sure enough, Mercury's retrograde. Can you cook?"

"Only marginally," he replied, sounding offended that she'd asked. "That's why we have Cavendish."

"No good. He left in a temper ten minutes ago."

"Roger Cavendish?"

"The same. The kids'll be down any minute, and we're going to be eaten alive if breakfast isn't ready. Will you get me the bacon out of the fridge, please?"

"Right."

At that moment the kitchen door flew open, a very surly-looking Drew took a quick look around and, apparently not finding what he'd come in search of, turned to leave. Belatedly he turned back to Genny and Jack and with great effort said politely, "Good morning," then disappeared.

Jack smiled blandly at Genny. "We're leaving right after breakfast. I have a feeling Devil's Island could be more fun than this place promises to be today."

The next moment the outside door opened and George Spears jogged through wearing his colorful shorts, a hot-pink sweatshirt and a towel around his neck. His face was flushed, his eyes a little feverish.

"Morning," he said breathlessly as he pushed his way through the swinging door to the living room.

Genny turned to Jack, feeling as though they'd somehow crossed onto an unfamiliar plane.

Jack stared at the swinging door. "Maybe we won't wait till after breakfast," he said.

Chapter Eleven

Genny stood in a natural corridor of granite and felt deeply, almost spiritually, the mastery of nature as craftsman. The brochure tucked away in her pocket described The Flume as a gorge created by glacial activity, but the beauty and power of what she saw had to be felt rather than explained.

The granite rock, which made up so much of New England and had been the bane of early farmers, rose high overhead, extending to a height of ninety feet on both sides of a crystal clear pool lined with colorful stones. A quaking aspen grew in the middle, catching the bright midmorning sunlight.

Genny had always been sensitive to beauty, but today she felt it like a physical touch. Her feelings for Jack, she realized, had given beauty a new dimension.

"Think you can handle the narrow trail?" Jack asked. "Or would you rather go back and check out the gift shop?"

The high walls of granite narrowed the path considerably up ahead, but she felt fearless today. And there was no obstruction overhead. She took Jack's hand and led the way.

Jack wasn't sure what to make of her attitude this morning. He'd expected an argument about their going off together.

Instead she'd happily come with him. The pretension that they could dismiss or deny what was developing between them was over. He had to plan his next move carefully.

The narrow trail went on for some time but she moved ahead steadily, the rocky path made slippery by moisture and undergrowth. It finally emerged onto a small green plateau that disappeared into a forest.

She walked to the very edge, overlooking other visitors winding their way up the narrow path, to get a different view of the quaking aspen and its silvery leaves. She sighed, as though something hurt.

Jack put an arm around her waist and pulled her back against him and away from the edge.

"I don't think I can go back to Portland," she said, her voice dreamy and a little sad, "and leave that beautiful tree. I think I'll have to get a little apartment for Francie and me in North Conway so I can come and see it anytime I want to."

Jack sighed, too, falling into her fantasy. "Then I'll have to stay, too."

She turned her head on his shoulder to look up into his eyes. "Are you also attached to the tree?"

"No, to you," he replied. Then he leaned down to kiss her slowly, sweetly. "If you stay, I stay."

"What about the bank?"

He shrugged. "Drew will be in charge. What about Nurse-care?"

"They existed before I joined them. If we can make Emily stay, too, I can continue to look after her."

Jack laughed softly. "But I won't be able to continue to pay you, because I'll be selling 'leaf-peeper' brochures to tourists on fall weekends."

"Leaf-peeper?"

"That's what they call the weekends in late October and early November when the leaves are at their most beautiful. The area's packed with tourists, then."

Genny nodded and settled back against him. "I'll have to support you, then. Okay. Well, first thing we'll do is put the girls on the road as a song-and-dance team. They should be supporting us in a year."

"Good. I like it."

"We'll have to live frugally, though. You'll have to sell your classic Jag, and we'll send to Portland for my Nova."

"Francie told me the police have stopped you twice because of the muffler."

Genny pulled out of his arms to frown at him. "She did? What else has she told you?"

He hooked an arm around her neck and walked on with her.

"That you're looking for a man who likes the opera and who'll give you daisies and some other kind of flower she couldn't remember."

"Tiger lilies," Genny supplied.

"Hmm." He stared ahead thoughtfully. "Now the man who'd stop at a florist and request that combination would probably be rare indeed. Is that particular requirement negotiable?"

"Oh, I'm afraid not," Genny said gravely. She looked up at him. "But forewarned is forearmed, isn't it?"

"If one happens to live in Asia where tiger lilies grow. In the wilds of New Hampshire being forewarned is no advantage."

Genny slumped her shoulders dramatically. "All right, the tiger lilies are negotiable."

"Good. Because I do enjoy opera, though I've had little chance to attend thus far. And I'd have probably put roses with the daisies, but I'd have thought of them."

Genny smiled. "Really? Why?"

He stopped her at a narrow point in the trail in the shade of a swamp maple, graceful, hand-shaped leaves dappling patterns on her face. She looked into his eyes, her own filled with humor and affection and pleasure in their stolen hours. Life had planed many edges on him. He felt every one of them soften.

"White petals," he whispered, stroking her bare upper arms and touching his lips to hers, "and a heart of gold."

Breath left her in a rush as his mouth closed over hers. She wrapped her arms around his neck and held, letting her lips tell him everything for which there seemed to be no words.

In an instant the moment was shattered by the rowdy laughter and antics of a group of scouts in their early teens. A score of them raced past on the narrow trail, pushing and playfully taunting one another with feinted shoves toward the drop to the trail below.

Instinctively Jack pushed Genny against the tree, pinning her behind him to protect her from the mishap.

Genny knew only that at a moment when she'd been completely unprepared, she found herself pinned between Jack's broad back and the unyielding trunk of a tree whose leaves clustered tightly overhead, blocking out the light—blocking out her air.

There were cries of alarm, orders shouted. For a moment of

disorientation she was a child again in the rubble of the hospital, hearing faraway shouts and cries and the sound of her own sobbing. In a nightmare kaleidoscope she saw her mother's face, her mother's hand, lifeless under hers, and a blackness that stretched on forever.

She heard herself scream in a high, shrill tone that horrified even her. Jack swung around, his eyes reflecting surprise. She looked beyond him to see several young boys staring at her, looking as terrified by her reaction as she felt.

Embarrassment, disappointment in herself, swept over her, but they were less important to her than air and freedom. She ran down the trail, through the knot of boys at the bottom who'd stopped to see what the commotion was about, and past families just starting up the trail. She didn't stop until she reached the parking lot where she leaned against Andrew's sun-warmed Cadillac and gulped her precious air.

Jack joined her a few moments later, a paper cup of icy soft drink in each hand. He handed her one and leaned against the front fender, several inches away from her.

"I'm sorry," he said gently. "I forgot again. My instinct was to keep you from getting tossed over the edge in the boys' rowdy tussle. I—"

Genny stopped him with a shake of her head and a glance from tear-filled smoky eyes. "A perfectly normal, chivalrous reaction. I'm just not a normal woman."

Jack didn't like her tone. It negated all the progress they'd made in the past few weeks. "*You're* normal," he corrected. "You just have a problem that requires conditioned response, and I keep forgetting."

"No." The single word had an air of finality, and Jack waited uncomfortably for her to explain. "You can't be expected to react a certain way because I need you to. That isn't fair. This—" she glanced at him, then looked into her cup with a sigh "—it isn't going to work, Jack."

"I don't want to hear that," he said mildly.

"It's the truth."

"It's surrender."

"It's common sense." She pinned him with a firm look, determined, he could see, to make him understand what she felt.

He looked back at her steadily, just as determined that she was wrong.

"Imagine something...physical...came of our relationship," she said, her tone theoretical.

"That's easy," he said. "I've done nothing else but for weeks."

She ignored that except to give him an impatient sigh, then went on. "How do you think you'd feel when I'd have to struggle out of your arms every time you forgot and held me too tightly? Every time you unconsciously teased me with a hug, inadvertently pinned me in a corner—"

"You only react that way," he reminded quietly, "when you're taken by surprise. And even then, you're the one we should be worried about, not me."

"I'll be hurting your feelings all the time."

"You're hurting my feelings now," he said with a frown, "by suggesting I can't deal with it."

"Will you listen to me!" she shouted, slapping her drink on the hood of the car with a splash, then straightening, her eyes angry.

He blinked at her show of temper but didn't move. "All right," he said. "But say something that makes sense."

A young couple wandered onto the parking lot, laughing as they wrestled for a set of keys. Genny focused on them a moment, then snatched her drink from the hood of the car, took Jack's out of his hand and walked two aisles over to the nearest trash bin and dropped them in.

Jack folded his arms and watched her, thinking absently how amazing it was that one small woman could cause him more anxiety than all the world's stock markets combined.

She came back to the car, opened the back door and gestured him inside.

He raised an eyebrow. "The backseat of the car?" he asked suggestively. "Now you're talking."

She slammed the door on him, walked around and got in the other side. She quickly opened her window, then leaned back into the opposite corner, leaving the empty cushion between them.

She opened her mouth as though to speak, then closed it and

shook her head. She closed her eyes, but not before a tear spilled over.

"Genny," Jack said gently, reaching across the seat.

She pulled her hand away and folded her arms. She didn't want to talk about this. She hated even thinking about it and hadn't for years. But he was determined to play knight-errant, and she wanted him to know what he was up against.

"Since subtlety just doesn't work with you," she said, "I'll be blunt." She hesitated for a heartbeat, wincing against the words, her bottom lip giving one little tremor. "I can't make love."

He wasn't sure what he'd expected to hear, but that wasn't it. He repeated it to himself, trying to make sense of it. He didn't. "Excuse me?"

"You asked me to say something that made sense," she said, closing her mind to the snarl of memories that admission uncurled. "I tried to put this out of my mind the first time you kissed me, but it just came back to throttle me. Jack..." She drew a breath and said again, clearly, "I cannot make love."

He realized she meant precisely what she said. Still confused, he asked with mild impatience, "The stork brought Francie, then?"

Genny put a hand to her forehead and drew another, deeper breath, reminding herself that, considering what she'd told him, that wasn't so absurd a question.

"I was made love *to*," she said, closing her eyes against the memory of her wedding night. "Francie was conceived. But...I'm sure it wasn't lovemaking like you've ever known it. I—" she shook her head, the memory intruding despite her efforts to hold it at bay "—it was all my fault...I..."

Jack saw her face contort, saw the tension in her hands and stretched his to the middle cushion before she could pull away. Genny looked at it, then up at him, some of her grimness lightening.

"How can you keep doing that?" she asked, her voice quiet with wonder.

"Holding your hand?"

"Making concessions."

He smiled. "That's how all agreements are reached. Countries and corporations do it. You did it with the tiger lilies."

She smiled despite herself. She turned to sit straight, lean her head against the back of the seat and lace her fingers in Jack's.

"It's not a pretty story," she warned.

He turned as she'd done, staring at the back of the seat ahead. "Does it beat mine?"

That reminder allowed her to start. Jack had been plagued all his life by his illegitimate beginning. It had taken something from him he could never recover. But he never held back from her because of it. She took a deep breath and began.

"I was seventeen and Bill was eighteen. We were in the same public-speaking class together. We got married right out of high school." She sighed, startled even now by their youthful ignorance. "He was just a kid who thought he was in love. I had learned to deal with my claustrophobia so well that almost no one knew I had the problem, except Bill, and then he'd only seen it manifested in small ways." She opened her eyes to stare at the ceiling of the car. "I married him because I wanted so much to have someone who belonged to me." She turned in Jack's direction to give him a wry smile. "I didn't understand then how selfish that is." She turned back, unable to maintain eye contact for the rest of the story.

"Anyway, since my mother died, I'd felt...adrift, I guess. Very solitary. My father still loved me in his way but without my mother he couldn't relate to me. And my problem was just a reminder of what he'd lost. My aunt was kind and loving, but I wanted to start my own life—free of the past." She laughed softly but without humor. "I actually thought one could do that."

Jack glanced at her with a sympathetic smile. "I can relate. Personal history is sticky stuff."

"Isn't that the truth?" Genny met his smile, then her expression clouded and she fell silent.

Jack held her hand and waited.

"It's a clinical fact," Genny said finally in a flat, husky tone, "that a woman who is severely claustrophobic can't be made love to. The pressure of a large, strong body over hers is like being closed in a closet..." She hesitated, the memory overwhelming, breath stalling in her lungs.

"Easy now," Jack said gently. He opened his window, maintaining his hold on her hand.

"I thought," she went on, afraid if she hesitated further she wouldn't be able to, "marriage would make me feel protected and secure. But he was young and eager and at that moment more interested in his gratification than mine. He got grabby and a little frantic, and I got nervous and..." She expelled a little gasp of dismay, and put a hand to her eyes to blot out the mental picture. "It was all my fault. I started to gasp for air and cry at the same time. I tried to pull away from him, but by then he was a little panicky himself and getting impatient with me. He wouldn't let me go. He knelt astride me and forced the issue. I screamed the whole time."

Jack turned to her, pulling her knuckles to his lips, holding them there a moment as he imagined her panic and humiliation. He didn't know how to offer comfort. He waited until she expelled a breath, then asked quietly, "Did you try again?"

"Every night for a week with the same result," she said dully. "He went back to his parents, his emotional manhood almost destroyed. Our marriage was annulled a week later."

"Have you made love since?"

"Once." She sighed heavily. "Same reaction."

Jack pulled her around to face him, taking her other hand also. His eyes were warm and sympathetic.

"Same position?" he asked.

She opened her mouth to respond but no sound came out. The question startled her. "Yes," she replied warily.

"Well, Genny..." He smiled, reaching a hand up to touch her face. "The obvious answer is to reverse positions. Didn't your husband think of that?"

Genny stared at him, part of her unable to believe they were sitting in the back of a parked car discussing sexual positions. Another part of her was thinking that had occurred to her, but abstaining had been so much easier than ever trying to explain that to someone—or risking proving the theory wrong.

She shook her head. "We were so young. I think he was too hurt to be creative, or to consider alternatives." She looked down at her hands, admitting reluctantly, "The other man was a doctor."

Jack frowned. "It's hard to believe it didn't occur to him."

"I thought...we had feelings for each other and that it might work that time. Apparently all he wanted was an uncomplicated evening. I just gave it up."

"I'll wager it would make all the difference," Jack said quietly.

She didn't know what to say to that. It might and it might not. It was easier to never know than to risk being wrong.

"Shall we?" he asked.

Everything stopped inside her—breath, heartbeat, brain. She was getting a strong affirmative from somewhere, but fear was too strong.

"Wager, I mean," Jack explained, one hand going gently to her hair.

She leaned into his hand, hating herself for her cowardice. "How can a banker possibly be a betting man?" she asked.

His eyes met hers and held them, refusing to be distracted by her tactic. He combed the hair back from her temple with the tips of his fingers.

"It's something Cavendish taught me," he said. "Betting's iffy, but you can't win if you never put your money down."

Sensation rose along Genny's scalp, his small touch awakening receptors all along her body. She wondered with desperation if he could be right. If he wasn't, she would hurt him as well as herself.

"I..." Her voice came out high and ragged. She swallowed and tried again. "I'm not ready yet, Jack."

He smiled. "But you'll let me know?"

A warm rush of laughter filled Genny. Jack was the kindest man she'd ever known, but he was also audacious. She leaned forward to kiss him gently. "I will, I promise."

THE FAMILY WAS GATHERED on the patio, seated around the girls who seemed to be holding center-stage.

"What's going on?" Genny asked Jack.

He pulled the car to a stop behind Drew's Mercedes. "A rehearsal, maybe?"

As they stepped out of the car, the strains of the tune the girls were singing rang clearly in the driveway.

"He's been with us over thirty years, but now's into shifting gears, retirement is calling him, an RV will be hauling him— aroooouuund."

Lisette and Francie with Dani in the middle, bedecked in costumes and jewels, previewed their song and dance routine for George's dinner. The chorus met with uproarious laughter. On the sidelines, Trey and Robert exchanged a high five, congratulating themselves on their brilliant direction.

The girls turned sideways in a carefully choreographed move, shaking their fingers at the absent subject of their song. "Think about this, George— We know you're going to rue it—and so will we because we're used—to letting George do it!"

They carried the last note out of tune but with enthusiasm as everyone applauded, the morning's upsets apparently put aside for the moment.

The girls took a deep bow, then Dani swept a hand toward the boys, who took cheers and more applause.

"What did you think, Mom?" Francie ran to Jack and Genny, her eyes bright, her cheeks flushed. "Andrew and George went for a walk so we had a rehearsal. Were we good?"

Genny hugged her. "You were brilliant! You, too, Lisette."

Jack's youngest flung herself into his arms, her graceful stage persona abandoned. "Did you think we were good, Dad?"

"You were magnificent." Jack hugged her to him and kissed her hair. "Ziegfeld would have hired you in a minute."

Lisette frowned at him. "Who?"

"Ziegfeld. He was a theatrical producer in the 1920s. He staged beautiful women in elaborate musical revues."

Lisette's eyes widened. "And you knew him?"

Genny laughed. Jack slanted her a threatening glance, then turned back to his daughter. "When was I born?" he asked patiently.

"1951," she replied dutifully.

"If he was a producer in the twenties, how would I have known him?"

Lisette shrugged. "I don't know. You do lots of things I can't figure out."

Dani squeezed into the group. "Or he could have lived to be old and told you stories about when he was young like you do with us—over and over and over."

Jack frowned down at her. "How'd you like your clothes allowance cut?"

She leaned her head on his shoulder. "Please, Daddy. It's so low already I borrow half of what I wear from my friends. So, what do you think? Are we ready to start touring with this show?''

Jack waved as his father and George materialized out of the woods, talking and laughing as they strolled in their direction. Jack tweaked Dani's nose. "You may start touring with some orphanage dance troupe if you're not careful."

Dani patted Jack's arm, a gaudy green ring flashing on her middle finger. "You couldn't live without me and you know it. Who'd keep you up on things so that you didn't leave the house thinking M.C. Hammer was a carpentry tool? But if you'd like to make other living arrangements for Lees, that's okay."

Jack heard only half of what she'd said. He'd taken a second look at Dani's ring and thought he recognized an emerald—a large one—surrounded by diamonds. He raised her hand in his and took a closer look. It couldn't be, he told himself. Where would Dani find a real emerald? But there was no mistaking that green fire.

"Where did you get this Dani?" he asked, pulling her around to let the sun beat on the stone. She wore a diamond necklace and large diamond earrings. Real ones. "In the cabin," she replied. "Lees and Francie found them. Grandpa left them for them to play with."

"Left what?" Andrew asked as he approached.

"These." Lisette held an opulent ruby necklace away from her throat. "And these." She flicked a finger at long, matching earrings.

Andrew stared, frowning. His eyes widened as he pulled the child toward him. The patio fell to complete silence as he studied the cuff bracelet on Lisette's wrist, then removed it, blinking. He handed it to Jack. "Is it a trick of the light, or are those real?"

Jack held up Dani's ringed fingers. "Just what I was wondering. Where the hell did this stuff come from?"

"I've got some, too." Francie came forward, displaying an ornate brooch and a choker necklace. "It changes colors."

"Opals," Genny breathed, looking closely at her daughter's baubles for the first time. Never having had expensive jewelry, she hadn't given the gaudy things the girls wore a second thought. She'd presumed they'd come from Lisette's stash of dress-up things.

"I say they're real," Emily declared. "What do you think, Andrew?"

The family had clustered around, the boys crowding in for a closer look. Andrew took the ruby bracelet and held it up, frowning. "I think so," he said finally.

Sheila put covetous hands on the necklace at Dani's throat. "I know so," she confirmed reverently. "Fourteen carat gold, and those diamonds are E to F in color, at least. Highest quality. Probably VVS 1."

When everyone looked at her in surprise, she said defensively, "Well, you'd need a ten-power loupe to know for sure. But I have an instinct about these things."

"Is it finders keepers?" Francie asked hopefully.

"Those belong to someone," Genny explained as a smattering of laughter broke the silence.

"But who?" Jack asked. "Are they your mother's Dad?"

Andrew shook his head. "I don't remember them. Drew?"

Drew shook his head. "They weren't mentioned in her will," he said. "Grandma was more interested in investing in stocks than in jewelry."

Jack felt a moment's resentment that he hadn't known that. "And why would she have hidden them there?"

Sheila folded her arms and suggested quietly. "Perhaps you should question Cavendish and Mrs. Pratt?"

There were many groans from the assembly, and Emily snapped, "That's ridiculous!"

"Just yesterday," Sheila went on dauntlessly, "Cavendish visited that butler friend of his at the Crosley Mansion. These could be Mrs. Crosley's jewels."

"Sheila, that's unfounded and completely—"

Sheila interrupted before Jack could finish. "You know how he is about Mrs. Pratt. And she's always fretting about her widowed daughter. Maybe they found a way to help her. And incidentally, where are they now?"

"On an afternoon walk," Andrew replied. "With my blessing."

Sheila smiled suggestively. "What do you bet they don't come back? What do you bet they're checking the cabin at this very moment? Once they conclude their stash has been found, we'll never see them again."

Emily suggested quietly, significantly, "Maybe the thief is someone we'd all consider above suspicion. Someone who loves pretty things."

Sheila's eyes rounded. "Are you suggesting..."

"It makes about as much sense as implying that Cavendish or Mrs. Pratt did," Drew said.

"Why don't I call the police?" Andrew offered. "Maybe there's been a jewelry store robbery. The thief could still be around, wondering what's happened to his stuff."

"They look like antiques to me," Genny thought aloud, studying the fussy, filigreed settings. "The clasps are old, too."

Sheila raised an eyebrow. "You know a lot about old jewelry for a nurse."

Genny wondered if her daughter's development would be adversely affected if she were to see her mother beat up one of her employer's relatives. The temptation was so strong, she might have taken the chance if she hadn't had to occupy herself with preventing Francie from doing it herself.

"Mom knows a lot about everything because she's smart!" Francie shouted as Jack caught her in mid lunge. "And *you* knew all that E F stuff!"

"Whoa," he said, setting her down beside him and holding her there. "Aunt Sheila was just about to apologize for that, wasn't she?"

"I just think—"

"That's where you always get in trouble, darling," Drew said mildly. "Apologize. That was uncalled for."

Sheila glared at Drew then turned angry, embarrassed eyes on Genny. "I'm sorry," she said grudgingly.

Genny nodded, pulling Francie protectively into her arm.

"Why don't you put the jewels away, Dad," Jack suggested, "until you have a chance to check the insurance inventory." He turned to Lisette. "Where exactly did you find the jewelry, Lees?"

"It was in a leather bag in that water jug on the sink thing that doesn't have any water."

"The dry sink. Where's the leather bag?"

"In my room."

"Will you get it, please?"

Lisette ran off and returned in a minute with a fairly large but nondescript suede bag. The leather was old and cracked, but had no monogramming or distinguishing marks. Still in the bottom of the bag was a pin fashioned out of a spray of diamonds, and an ornate topaz ring.

Shaking his head over the mystery, Jack held the bag open and put the girls' find inside, then handed it to his father.

"Couldn't we just fence the stuff and split the take?" Trey asked. "And make a pact to keeps our mouths shut and never spill what's happened even if we're tortured?"

"Creative but impractical," Drew said with a grin, ruffling his son's hair. "Somebody's bound to be looking for these. We wouldn't want to be caught with them when the trail leads here."

"And Robbie would rat on you in a minute," Lisette prophesied.

Robert nodded candidly. "That's true."

"I'll lock these away," Andrew said. "My accountant has the inventory, and he's away for the weekend, but I'll check it out first thing Monday morning. If they're not on the list, we'll contact the police. George, Drew. Come with me as witnesses."

As they all went into the house, the back door could be heard opening and closing. The sound of Cavendish's rich laughter was followed by the seldom-heard sound of Mrs. Pratt's high, girlish giggle.

"Want to check out who that is, Sheila?" Emily asked. "Maybe turn out their pockets?"

Sheila angled her chin and stormed toward the French doors. The children ran upstairs to change out of their costumes. Emily followed the girls with a roll of her eyes at Genny over Sheila's behavior.

Jack rested an elbow on Genny's shoulder and said softly, "Tell me the truth. You rolled a rich dowager, copped her jewels, and stashed them so you and I could run away together."

"Actually—" she gave him a teasing grin that almost knocked his feet out from under him "—I was planning to run away with George."

He gasped indignantly. "Why George?"

"He has cute knees."

"*I* have cute knees." He leaned closer and asked in her ear, "Want to follow me upstairs and refresh your memory?"

She sighed with a dramatic regret. "I'm afraid I have to work on my quilt. Perhaps another time."

He nipped her ear lobe. "Time is the enemy, Genny. We'll talk about this tonight."

"You should spend your time solving the mystery of the jewels," she scolded.

He took her chin between his thumb and forefinger and planted a slow kiss on her startled mouth. His green eyes went over her face with such deliberation that a ripple of sensation went up her spine. "My pearl of great price," he said. "Tonight."

Chapter Twelve

"My eyes are beginning to cross," Dani said, leaning away from the quilting frame to study her stitches. She grimaced. "Looks like my stitches did, too."

"That's the beauty of a quilt," Genny reminded her. "Any imperfections only make it more unique. It's a collection of color and mood and design rather than one single work. It looks better if you can see differences in style and texture."

Lisette, kneeling beside Genny while she worked on a bottom square, pointed to the blue square near the middle that Robert had worked on and said, "That's Robbie's. Even it looks neat."

"And Uncle Drew did that one."

One rainy afternoon Genny had watched Drew sit between his nieces and trim a red square with a heart pattern in surgically precise cross-stitches.

"Why the heart square, Uncle Drew?" Lisette had asked him. "I thought you'd want to do that gold one."

"Love's more important than gold," he'd explained with a smile. "It takes a while to realize that."

"Do you think Aunt Sheila ever will?"

"Lees!" Dani had scolded while Genny closed her eyes and waited.

Mercifully Drew had laughed softly. "It takes longer for some people. But anybody's who's paying attention realizes it sooner or later."

Genny's eyes went to the square Sheila had contributed, a large checked piece on which she'd made delicate daisies in the dark squares, complete with French-knot centers, and leaves on the white squares. The work showed a skill that surprised Genny.

"I didn't know you did needlework," she'd said.

Sheila had shrugged. "I learned it from a friend's mother. Mine said it was servant's work and threw my piece away."

That encounter had given her a new perspective on Sheila. It made it easier to see how her priorities had gone wrong.

Lisette stood up to stretch. "Where's Francie? I thought she was coming back with cocoa?"

Dani yawned as she put her needle and floss in Genny's sewing basket. "I think I'll pass on cocoa and go right to bed. Good night, Genny." Dani gave Genny a hug, then pointed a threatening finger at her sister. "Don't wake me up when you come to bed."

"Want me to bring you some cocoa?" Lisette offered Genny.

"No, thanks." Genny kissed the top of her head and sent her on her way. "I'm going to find Francie and get her to bed. Good night, sweetie."

After a quick glance into the playroom, the library, and their bedroom proved futile, Genny went outside, fighting down a little pinch of alarm. The night was moonlit and warm, but the grounds were shadowy and quiet. There was no one in the pool or on the lounge chairs around it.

"Francie!" she called, her voice betraying her alarm.

"Here."

She spun toward the deck at the unexpected response of a male voice. She ran up the steps and found Jack lounging in an Adirondack chair, Francie sound asleep in his lap. Bull and Bear flanked the legs of the chair.

She stood looking down at them, longing gripping her heart in a fist. This was what she'd wanted all those years ago when she'd married right out of high school. The sweetness and security of family. This was what Francie wanted when she launched her search for a father. The sheer size and strength with which a man made a child feel secure—something a woman simply couldn't offer.

"I'm sorry," she said. "I couldn't imagine where she was. She left our little quilting bee for cocoa and never came back."

He indicated his empty cup on the table with his free hand. The other arm was wrapped around Francie. "She must have seen me out here from the kitchen and brought me a cup. We got to talking and she fell asleep.'' His smile flashed in the shadows. ''Seems you reneged on the deal you made with her.''

Genny sank onto the arm of a nearby chair, frowning. ''What deal?''

''The daddy deal,'' he replied. ''You told me she was on the lookout for a father, but you didn't give me all the requirements.''

''I—''

''He was supposed to love the opera,'' he went on, ignoring her attempt to interrupt, ''buy you daisies and tiger lilies and a new muffler for the car, *and* be able to carry you up a long flight of stairs. *And* look good in a tux.''

Genny folded her arms. ''I told you about the daisies and the tiger lilies.''

''You did, but I don't know how I can be expected to compete when I don't have the entire list of qualifications. I'm told I'm pretty passable in a tux, but you might have never discovered that if Francie hadn't told me.''

''An important point you've both ignored,'' she said, smiling at him in the shadows, ''is that I have to be in agreement with the daddy candidate.''

Jack shifted Francie so that she rested on just one knee. She allowed the adjustment without waking. Then he pulled Genny down onto the other.

''Jack...'' She tried to protest, but he shushed her, indicating the sleeping child. ''Now, look up there.''

Hooking an arm around his neck for balance, Genny leaned back to look up at the sky. It was a star-dazzled swatch of black silk that stretched into infinity. Directly overhead was a perfect opal moon.

Jack's arm tightened around her waist. ''I love you, Genny,'' he said. ''Can you really sit here under Vaughan Monroe's moon and tell me you don't love me?''

Disarmed by his honesty and his charm, Genny kissed his cheek. Then she leaned her forearm on his shoulder and looked into his eyes. ''I do love you, Jack. That's why I must be particularly careful not to hurt you.''

He frowned. ''Do I look fragile to you?''

"Jack," she said with a helpless little gesture, "we're all fragile inside, where it doesn't show."

She could hurt him; he knew that. But he had the sense that loving her would be worth the risk. She already lived in his thoughts, in his dreams, and she was beginning to take shape in his plans as well. He needed her in his arms, in his bed, in his life.

"I'm not afraid," he said.

She swept Francie's hair from her face with her free hand. Her eyes were as dark as the night. "I know. That's why I have to protect you."

He groaned softly in frustration, prepared to offer another argument. But Genny cut him off. "Francie should be in bed," she said, standing, trying to take her from him again.

He brushed her hand away. "I'll carry her in for you." He stood easily with his burden and followed Genny inside.

Jack placed Francie gently in her nest of blankets beside Lisette in the playroom. Francie stirred, opened her eyes, gave him a hug, then curled into the pillow Genny put under her head.

As Jack checked Dani and Lisette, Genny looked at Francie, the sleepy smile she'd given Jack still lingering on her lips. She'd found so much here, was so lighthearted and happy. She'd always been a cheerful child, but Dani and Lisette's friendship had helped her blossom. Genny smiled over her like some brilliant gardener who'd nurtured the seed and now saw a bright and beautiful bud.

"Stop beaming," Jack whispered. "My girls are pretty great, too, you know."

Smiling, she followed him into the hallway. "I know," she said quietly. "I love both of them."

She realized suddenly the ammunition she'd given him with that admission.

But he said nothing. He simply tilted her chin up and kissed her slowly, lingeringly, as though determined to show her in delicious detail what she denied herself by her reluctance to allow their relationship to proceed.

She felt his touch even after he drew away.

"The cabin has that wonderful old bed," he whispered. "Let's go, Genny."

She wanted to go with him more than she wanted anything.

But the last thing she wanted was to hurt him. She touched his cheek, pleading for understanding. "Jack, I can't."

He caught her hand and squeezed it. "You can."

"No," she insisted. "Believe me. I know. It won't work."

There was understanding mingled with disappointment and that curious, ever-present trust that seemed to define him. He touched her cheek, and ran his thumb along her cheekbone.

"The time's going to come, Genny," he said softly. "I'll wait there until you meet me."

"Jack, I won't," she said firmly.

He smiled teasingly. "Then you'll have to accept the responsibility for the confusion that results when some future archaeologist finds the bones of a twentieth-century man in a nineteenth-century cabin.

Genny dismissed the guilt with an answering smile. "They'll just think you were a tourist."

The gentle mood was suddenly shattered by the slam of the glass doors onto the patio and the intrusion of loud voices.

"You don't know what you're talking about, Andrew Fleming!" Emily's voice shouted. Her footsteps could be heard across the sun-porch floor.

Stronger, slower footsteps followed her. "I know I want to marry you," Andrew said calmly.

Genny and Jack hung back silently as Emily and Andrew walked past the playroom to the kitchen. Afraid she couldn't get past the kitchen to the stairs without detection, Genny shrugged helplessly at Jack.

He nodded, putting a finger to his lips and holding her beside him.

"That's absurd!" Emily's voice was accompanied by the sound of cupboards opening and closing and crockery clinking. "You don't even know what I...what I—"

"Look like?" Andrew supplied. "I know. That's such an issue with you, isn't it?"

"It's important," Emily said defensively.

"Emily—" Andrew's voice sounded weary "—it's only important to you. I can't believe you could have reached your age and still have an ingenue's concept of what a man wants in a woman."

Something slammed on the counter. "You mean you wouldn't want sex?" Emily's tone was ironic.

"No," Andrew replied. "I wouldn't want sex." He emphasized her word. "I'd want to make love to you long and often."

"Andrew..." Emily gasped frustratedly. "I have only one breast. I can...I can live with the fact a little easier now, but I can't see you spending the rest of your life with a woman who'll repulse you in bed."

"God!" Something else slammed—something bigger and louder than before. Genny started and Jack pulled her closer, exhaling, obviously as uncomfortable as she was. "I was repulsed in bed by a woman who was physically perfect and spiritually stagnant. She had two flawless breasts and a soul so black I couldn't make myself touch her for fear of being infected. Emily—" Andrew sounded like a desperate man, striving for reason. "—why don't you show me?"

Genny put both hands over her mouth, afraid she would burst into tears. Jack closed his eyes. A long silence pulsed. The refrigerator hummed, the hall clock struck the half hour, the kettle whistled. It was silenced instantly. "I can't," Emily said, her voice breaking.

"You're afraid I'll be shocked?" Andrew asked. "Or you're afraid I won't?"

"What does that mean?"

"It means that I know these are our golden years, time of freedom and opportunity. That doesn't appeal to me because I have yet to have my life the way I've always wanted it. The only other woman I've loved besides you I couldn't have. But you can have whatever you want now. You're used to having stardom, to having things your way. Maybe you don't want to marry me because you simply don't want to entangle your life with someone else's and suffer all the little pressures that puts on you. And you can blame your breast for it, claiming you're being noble, when really you're thinking of yourself."

"Andrew..." There were tears in Emily's voice. "I *do* love you."

"Then, don't do this to us. Show me."

"I...can't."

Loud footsteps paced across the kitchen, then could be heard going up the stairs.

Genny wrapped her arms around Jack, something about what they'd overhead making her need to cling to him. Emily could be heard sobbing in the kitchen. Genny finally pulled away. "I'd better see what I can do for her," she whispered.

Jack kissed her cheek. "You know where I'll be, Genny," he said softly.

"Jack..."

He was gone before she could tell him again she wouldn't come to the cabin.

She found Emily leaning against the counter, staring into space as tears streamed down her face. She put an arm around her shoulders and pushed her gently through the kitchen toward the stairs.

"Oh, Genny," Emily wept softly. "I...I..."

"I know." Genny flipped the hall light off and they climbed out of the downstairs darkness into the dim light on the second floor. "I was putting Francie to bed and overheard. I'm sorry."

"Why am I such a coward?" Emily asked as Genny closed her bedroom door behind them and settled her on the edge of her bed.

She shouldn't scold Emily tonight for her feelings of inadequacy. In view of her own cowardice, it would be a case of the pot and the kettle. Fortunately, however, Emily didn't know that.

She sat beside her. "Because life is difficult and painful, and you're just trying to protect yourself."

Emily shook her head. "If I saw horror in his eyes when he looked at me, I don't think I could stand it."

"I can't imagine that of Andrew," Genny said. "He loves the woman you are, who isn't changed by a mastectomy."

Emily put a hand over her eyes and uttered one deep harsh sob. "I can't, either. But he'd pretend it didn't matter, even if it did. It wouldn't fool me."

Genny gave her shoulders a squeeze. "And you can pretend you can live without him, but *you* aren't fooling him—or me." She went to the dresser and pulled out a silky fuchsia nightgown. "I think you should take the chance. If you're willing to live without him anyway, what's the difference whether you do it knowing you made him turn away, or wondering if he might not have?"

Emily yanked the gown from her with a knowing pout. "You set me up for that."

Genny gave her a quick, heartfelt hug. She hadn't realized how much Emily had come to mean to her until she'd stood in the darkened playroom and heard her back away from the rest of her life.

"Sleep on it," Genny said. "And remember your friends in the support group. There isn't a coward in the bunch. Good night."

"You total fraud," Genny mumbled to herself as she crossed the hall and went into her own empty room.

"I SUPPOSE YOU SLEPT like a baby while I kept a candle burning for you all night long." Jack sat in the midst of a pile of cushions on the sun-porch floor, sipping coffee while Genny whipstitched a binding onto the edges of the quilt.

She glanced up with a grin. "Uh-huh."

He rolled his eyes. "Fiend," he accused.

In truth, she'd stared at the ceiling most of the night, torn between her own self-protection and the nagging echo of the advice she'd given Emily. She'd gotten up for a glass of water at four a.m. and looked out her window to see Jack emerge from the woods, shoulders hunched against the early-morning chill. Her heart had ached for the faith he'd had in her that she'd been unable to justify.

Jack fingered one corner of the quilt. "I suppose you've forgotten," he said, "that if I hadn't been such a good sport, you'd have never gotten the stuff to put this quilt together. What're you going to do with it, anyway?"

She smiled at him, letting her affection for him show. In the bright sunlight, loving him seemed less threatening than it had in the dark tunnel of night.

"Give it to Andrew and Emily as a wedding present," she replied.

Jack read love in her eyes and grew more confused. He hadn't been entirely surprised when she hadn't come to the cabin last night. But when she'd greeted him with a warm smile this morning, he hadn't been sure what to make of it. Had she given up on them, or not?

He watched her miter the binding around a corner of the quilt with great skill, and decided he might never understand her. Somehow, that didn't seem to matter.

"After last night?" he asked. "Do you know something I don't know?"

She concentrated on her task. "Yes. Any woman worthy of the name isn't going to let a man like your father get away."

"Good morning." As though conjured out of their discussion, Andrew strode onto the sun porch in white cotton pants and navy knit shirt. He looked robust and vital—and thoroughly unhappy. He tapped a finger against a manila envelope under his arm. "On my way to the post office with these reports."

"You ought to get a fax out here," Jack said.

Andrew grimaced. "Then I'd be as accessible to the world as it is to me. Anybody need anything?"

"I do." Emily appeared in the doorway, a large straw purse over the shoulder of a red-and-white cotton skirt set. A careful application of makeup didn't quite conceal what had probably been a sleepless night. She looked from face to face with forced brightness. "Good morning, all."

Andrew studied her shadowed eyes worriedly. "What is it? I'll bring it back for you."

She smiled. "I was looking forward to a drive and maybe coffee and a doughnut. I'll even treat." She took his arm and led the way to the door.

Andrew went docilely, looking completely confused.

Genny caught Jack's eye and winked when their backs were turned, then called an innocent goodbye when they stopped at the door to wave.

"Amazing," Jack said, shaking his head. Then he focused on Genny. She knew what was on his mind—it was on hers, too.

"Has it occurred to you," he asked quietly, "that there's an interesting parallel here?"

Before she could answer, the room swarmed with children looking for an arbitrator to settle a dispute over the program planned for George.

Jack accepted the intrusion as just another setback in his pursuit of Genny. So near and yet so far was becoming, he thought, the story of his life—in more ways than one.

"Cavendish wants you, Unc," Trey said as the girls explained a complicated choreography problem to Genny. "I think it's the phone."

"Right." Jack took the boy's offer of a hand up, then playfully yanked him down and stood.

"Good going, Uncle Jack," Robbie approved.

"Jack!"

Genny's voice stopped him at the door. He turned, an eyebrow raised in question. Her eyes were deep and dark and had a message for him alone.

"Do you have another candle?" she asked.

The question drove the air from his lungs. He took a moment to answer. "I have enough candles," he said, ignoring the interested glances of the children, "to light us from here to eternity."

She smiled. "Good. But you only need one."

JACK MET GENNY at the entrance to the woods. The house was still, and everyone in it apparently asleep. A silver moon shone, and a light breeze bathed them in the scent of roses and the musky smell of the birches.

He crushed her against him, remembering belatedly that he shouldn't, then noting with a private smile in the darkness that, for this moment at least, care was unnecessary. Genny seemed free of the burden.

"I thought you'd like company through the woods," he said.

She gave him a squeeze of gratitude as she regarded the dark tunnel of trees with less than enthusiasm. She forced herself to think about what lay beyond—the cabin, Jack's figurative candle, life for the woman trapped inside her.

Holding her hand, Jack led the way through at a brisk pace. Genny concentrated on a small point of light in the distance that grew larger as they broke out of the trees and ran the last few feet to the cabin. His candle wasn't figurative after all, she saw with a rush of affection. A tall white taper lighted the window.

Wordlessly he led her up the steps. The night breeze wove through the open door and moonlight poured in, picking out the plump, narrow bed. Jack blew out the candle.

Genny felt a prickle of trepidation. She looked up at Jack,

smoky eyes turning silver in the light of the moon. "I love you, Jack," she whispered. "If I...if I do anything to..."

He kissed her gently. "Just be calm and trust me," he said. "If you get to feel panicky, it's just me in a cabin with an open door. Neither one of us is going to lock you in."

"Okay." Clearing her mind of the past, of everything in the world but Jack and this moment, she allowed him to lead her to the bed.

"Want me to leave the draperies open?" he asked.

She shook her head.

He swung the draperies closed, then pulled her with him onto the down mattress. They sat knee to knee, looking into each other's eyes. Genny saw herself reflected against a velvety darkness. Jack saw eagerness, concern, hope and a trusting love that underlined the tenderness he felt for her.

He leaned forward to kiss her lips, gently then tauntingly—suggesting, offering, promising.

Genny opened her mouth under his, understanding, accepting, trying however hesitantly to return the promise.

But her mind betrayed her, reacting instinctively to a forgotten but still-familiar stimulus. It crowded with images of her wedding night and the ugly nights that had followed. Her breathing became shallow and she sat back on her heels.

"Jack, I'm...I'm getting panicky," she admitted, wanting desperately to run, but wanting even more desperately to stay. Confused and frightened, she looked around frantically, as though a solution might present itself. She drew back when Jack reached out to touch her.

"It's all right," he said, his voice like a stroke in the darkness. "You're not afraid of me. You're afraid of becoming afraid."

She put a hand to her eyes. "I don't want to scream. I don't want to make a scene. I don't want to..."

Gently he lowered her hand. "The door is open," he reminded. "Your way out is clear. And you know I'm not going to hold you down." He smiled, a tenderly wicked look that tripped her pulse. "I told you how many candles I have. If not tonight, then tomorrow. Or the day after that."

Genny drew even breaths and made herself think about that. It would be different this time; she knew that. The unknown remained, however. Would *she* be different?

She remembered what she'd told Emily, and tried to apply it to herself. If she had to live without him, she may as well know it was because she'd horrified him, rather than because she hadn't had the courage to find out how he would react.

She expelled a ragged breath and knelt up again, reaching for Jack. "I love you," she said. "I do."

"Oh, Genny." Jack kissed her ear. "I love you," he whispered huskily, then trailed a path along the cord in her neck, across her silky throat and down, as far as the barrier of the neckline of her robe.

He leaned her back against the pillows and cradled her in his arms. She felt sheltered as he stroked her slowly, comfortingly.

Her nerves quieted as she concentrated on his touch. Genny put a tentative hand to Jack's broad, warm chest. When he remained quiet under her touch, she moved over the solid lines of his shoulders and down his muscled arms.

Jack tugged at the pearl buttons of her robe. Instinctively she caught his wrist, afraid her nakedness would dispel the lovely peace and her little burst of confidence.

He smiled. "Me first? Okay." He lay back, arms extended in an attitude of surrender. He closed his eyes.

Both amused and touched, Genny unfastened the buttons of his shirt. She opened it and tugged it off one shoulder. Jack opened his eyes and sat up to allow her to remove it. His chest was beautifully, perfectly muscled, and she molded the curve of a firm shoulder with her hand. Then cautiously but inexorably, as though driven, she leaned forward and planted a kiss there.

Jack decided this just might kill him—needing and wanting her, and holding himself in check so that she could catch up, or decide if, indeed, she even wanted to. He wasn't sure what he'd do if she didn't. One kiss on his shoulder and he could easily forget all his promises to her and to himself.

Then she lay beside him, assuming the open-armed pose he had taken, and he felt his spine go limp. Taking his cue, he slowly unfastened the pearl buttons.

He saw the outline of her breasts under the light cotton of her nightgown, their beaded nipples disturbing the soft folds of the fabric.

Genny watched his eyes and went weak with the utter tenderness she saw there. She felt the woman inside her that had been denied for so long give a cautious stretch and edge aside the fear.

She reached up for Jack and wrapped her arms around him, relishing the roughness of his cheek against the softness of hers, his muscled shoulders too wide for her arms to span, his warm lips along her throat.

Jack felt her clinging to him and wrapped his arms around her, hoping she was ready to cope with his embrace because he didn't think he could last another moment without holding her against him. From the skittish woman of a moment ago she seemed suddenly all softness and warmth.

Genny began to forget that panic might intrude at any moment. Her wariness dissipated. She felt eager and strangely anxious.

Jack brought a hand up between them. "I'm going to touch you," he warned in a whisper.

She waited, bracing herself, knowing this would be the test.

Through the filmy fabric of her gown, he closed a hand lightly over a breast.

Genny closed her eyes, expelling a small breath of delight at the exquisite sensation. It was new—completely unfamiliar. She'd never come this far before without panic blurring the experience.

He leaned forward to kiss her again, the skilled invasion of his tongue into her mouth coupled with the stroking of his thumbs across the tips of her breasts causing a quickening of her pulse and a paradoxical languor.

When he tugged at the fabric of her nightgown she rose onto her knees to free the hem. She waited for panic to rise and overtake her, but except for a feeble tremor she suspected was the result of heightened nerves, she remained in control. She noted that fact in amazement.

Now, willpower could no longer contain what Jack felt. Her small body burnished by moonlight, Genny looked like a figment of his dreams, spun-gold hair, limpid eyes, small, high breasts and slender hips and thighs inclined toward him, waiting for his touch.

"Genny!" he whispered, leaning into the pillows on an elbow and pulling her down beside him. He shed his shorts and briefs and tossed them with her things.

"Are you cold?" he asked. "I'll pull up the coverlet."

"I'm comfortable," she fibbed. Body to body with him, her heartbeat and her lungs were beginning to riot. He combed his fingers through her hair, feeling her pounding heart against his own.

"Jack," she whispered worriedly.

"Trust me," he cautioned softly, sweeping a hand down her ribs and over the swell of her hip. He hitched her leg over his and his fingers invaded, completely immobilizing her.

Surely now, she thought. Any moment. She'd rise up and scream. This was always where she...where she...what? She couldn't remember. Her mind lost its focus on the past because all it could absorb was what was happening now.

She closed her eyes on Jack's touch—to concentrate on it, to imprint it in her mind, to feel it in her soul where she knew it would live forever. She said his name with a desperation he recognized as his own.

He lay back and pulled her gently astride him. Genny felt one brief instant of fear. If she hadn't been able to cope conventionally...

Jack felt so in tune with her, so connected to her, that even in the grip of his own emotion, he felt hers. "Forget everything that's gone before," he said, gently bracketing her waist and lifting her. "This is *us* Genny. Us."

He entered her with an ease that surprised both of them. Genny felt him inside her with a kind of wonder—vitally strong, infinitely tender, real. Every dream she'd ever had about living normally stood on the brink of fulfillment.

"Jack," she said again, the awe she felt in her whisper and in her eyes.

Grasping her hips, he began to move her slowly. "I'm with you, Gen," he said, moving in harmony with her, feeling her take the rhythm on her own.

He swept his hands up her ribs, enclosing her breasts, feeling their beaded tips against his palm. She moaned softly and he saw her eyes close, saw a little frown of concentration form on her brow.

Tension built and tightened inside Genny. She was aware of every particle of her being, every breath in her body, every beat of her heart. She'd heard that women approached "the little death" in a mindless state, open only to sensation.

It occurred to her as she felt the tension in her strain even tighter that she felt as though her mind were opened and not closed—as though everything that had ever confused her now seemed clear. Love was stronger than doubt or confusion or potential danger. Love was stronger than the demon that had controlled her for so long.

Jack grasped her arms, made a small upward movement of his hips, and her tension snapped. He threaded his fingers in hers and held as she leaned backward, her body convulsed by its own pleasure and by his.

She felt her body open and close, open and close, like the subject of time-lapse photography, except that she felt every instant—not a second was lost. Pleasure rose and built until her entire being pulsed with it.

And at the heart of it was Jack. All around it was Jack.

Jack heard the sound of his name lovingly whispered as Genny collapsed against him. Still immersed in his own pleasure, he heard it like something out of a dream. It called to him as nothing in his life ever had. It brought him out of himself and took possession of him.

He wrapped his arms around a quaking Genny and accepted that he was no longer a free man.

Genny felt like someone else, as though she'd been reassembled with some new material that felt and understood everything. She had more intelligence, more heart, no darkness. Love illuminated the night like moonlight.

She lay against Jack, awash in their oneness. His warmth was hers, her tremor was his, their heartbeats and their whispers entwined.

Jack pulled up the coverlet, wove his fingers into her hair and held her to him as though he'd perish if she moved. He forgot she might find it confining. But so did she.

"WE REALLY CAN'T DO THIS all night," Genny protested halfheartedly. It was midnight and they lay like a pair of spoons, his arm and his leg holding her to him. She felt miraculously free and deliciously lazy.

"Sure we can." Jack snuggled closer as a cooler breeze

snaked into the cabin. "Should have brought another blanket, though."

"If we were warmer, we wouldn't have to be this close," she said.

He held her even tighter. "We'll always have to be this close. If I let you go, it'd be like cutting off my oxygen."

She laughed softly at the idea. "It would be difficult to get anything done this way."

"We'll delegate."

"How do you delegate appointments at the dentist and getting a haircut?"

He nuzzled under her hairline and kissed the back of her neck. "I'll become a hippy, and I'd love you even if you had dentures."

Genny laughed and turned until she could wrap her arms around him. "Got an answer for everything, haven't you, Fleming?"

"That's why I get the big bucks."

The small noise silenced both of them. The night had been filled with sounds—the gentle stirring of the breeze, the scratching, cooing sounds of nocturnal life in the woods, the quiet sounds of their own conversation. But the quiet shuffle had the distinct sound of human footsteps.

Genny looked at Jack, her eyes widening at the prospect of being caught. She opened her mouth to ask him what they should do, but he covered it with his hand, miming a shushing sound.

He lay back and pulled her with him. The danger, she realized belatedly, was more than the possibility of being discovered with Jack in the cabin's bed. No one ever came to the cabin but the girls, and they were sound asleep. It occurred to her with a sense of real fear that it was a distinct possibility they were about to be visited by the jewel thief.

Genny's heart pounded as quiet footsteps moved across the floor, their owner completely concealed from her and Jack by the curtain that surrounded the bed. There was the sound of scraping, as though the table were being pulled across the floor. Then a dim light appeared through the draperies, like that from a pocket flashlight. Genny shrank against Jack, afraid of casting a shadow on the curtains.

There was a mournful creak, a small crumpling sound, then another creak. The table was pulled back into place.

The footsteps hurried away, the cabin door closed. Jack ran through the draperies to the window.

"Can you see?" Genny asked tensely.

Jack strained his eyes through the old rippled glass as a shadowy figure walked away. It stopped just before the trees in a listening attitude, bathed for a moment in moonlight.

Jack stared.

"Who was it?" Genny appeared beside him, pulling on her nightgown, trying to peer through the window.

He shook his head, not sure what to make of what he'd seen. "Sheila," he replied.

Chapter Thirteen

Jack and Genny stared at each other in silence. The footsteps had receded. The breeze and the small sounds in the woods filled the night to make the footsteps, the creaking of the cabin door, and Sheila's mysterious presence, seem as though they'd never happened.

"Are you sure?" Genny demanded in a whisper.

"Genny, I know my own sister-in-law."

"But you don't like her."

He rolled his eyes. "That doesn't make her difficult to recognize." He pushed her toward the bed. "Come on. Get your things."

"What was that creaking sound?" Genny asked as she groped for her slippers.

"The trapdoor over the tunnel. It's under the table."

Jack slipped on his espadrilles while Genny pulled on her robe and scuffs. Incredibly—the sound of footsteps came from outside the cabin.

Jack pushed Genny into the bed. There were more than two footsteps this time and the sound of whispered conversation. The footsteps came into the cabin and Genny huddled against Jack as words became distinguishable.

"We shouldn't be doing this!" a woman's voice whispered.

"Will you for once do as I say!" a man's hushed tone demanded.

Genny opened her mouth in surprise, recognizing Cavendish and Mrs. Pratt's voices. Jack stifled her gasp with his hands, listening.

"But, you should—"

"Be quiet woman and hold the light!"

There was the creaking of the trapdoor, a grunt as though someone was straining to reach something in the hole. Then the door closed, the table was pulled over it again, and footsteps hurried from the room.

When they'd receded, Genny pulled Jack's hand from her mouth. "What is going on?" she whispered.

He frowned as he stared at the curtain that separated them from the completely inexplicable events of the past few minutes. Then he looked down at Genny, his attention arrested by the sight of her with moonlight in her hair.

His expression softened and, despite the curious circumstances, Genny felt her heart melt.

"I have no idea," he answered softly. "All I know is that life used to make sense. Then I made love to you, and now the world seems to be on its ear. How do *you* explain it?"

She shrugged, piecing together the odd fragments of what they'd observed. "It's easy. Cavendish, Mrs. Pratt and Sheila pulled a heist and they just met at the cabin to divvy the profits, unaware the jewels had been discovered."

"Sorry, Watson. Sheila was with us on the patio when we discovered the jewels were real. She knew they wouldn't be in the cabin."

"All right, Holmes," she said. "What's your explanation?"

"As I said," he replied, "I made love to you and everything went weird."

Genny reminded dryly, "The jewels were stolen before you made love to me."

"Not technically," he corrected. "I'd already made love to you in my mind."

"Really?" she whispered. "How was it?"

He pulled her off the bed and to the door, pausing to plant a firm kiss on her lips. "Cerebral love just doesn't compare to physical love. Now, hush. God knows who else might show up."

They approached the dark house quietly, Jack leading the way around to the kitchen, presuming that if Cavendish and Mrs. Pratt hadn't gone to bed, they might be talking in the kitchen. The arc of a flashlight's beam against the window proved him right.

Planting Genny against the wall with a firm gesture for quiet,

Jack sidled up to the window and peered inside. Two silhouettes hovered over the kitchen table while something on it glittered in the glow of the flashlight. He couldn't believe his eyes.

"Are they there?" Genny whispered.

He flattened himself against the wall, drew a breath to clear his head, and nodded, completely bewildered. "Cavendish and Mrs. Pratt are. Complete with diamond necklace."

"What?"

"I'm sure there's an explanation," he said, "but I'll be damned if I can figure it out. Come on."

Jack crept up to the kitchen door and pushed it open, pulling Genny in with him. The meager light was immediately doused and they were met with complete silence.

"I know you're in here, Cavendish," Jack said quietly. "Put a light on and tell me what in the hell is going on."

After a moment the room was bathed in light and a very sheep-ish-looking butler and a very nervous Mrs. Pratt stepped out of a corner toward the table.

Cavendish squared his shoulders, straightened his tie, cleared his throat, and looked Jack in the eye as he dropped the diamond necklace on the table. "We didn't steal it," he said.

"I know that," Jack said, mildly impatient, "but what are you doing with it?"

Cavendish glanced at Mrs. Pratt, who gave him a condemning look as she pulled out a kitchen chair and sank into it. "I told you this would happen, Roger. Didn't I tell you? Didn't I?"

Cavendish sighed and ran a hand over his face. "At least a dozen times, Louise." He smiled hesitantly at Jack. "May I sit, sir?"

"Of course." Jack pulled a chair out for Genny, then his own.

Cavendish took the chair at a right angle to Mrs. Pratt's. He sighed again and frowned at the necklace sparkling in the middle of the table, strangely out of place.

"I took Louise for a walk to talk," Cavendish said calmly.

"At midnight?" Jack asked.

"We'd been up late preparing food for the party."

"Right. Go on."

Cavendish cast a scolding glance at his companion. "Our dis-cussions sometimes tend to get—loud. I had things to say to her I wanted no one else to overhear."

"I resisted," Mrs. Pratt interjected.

Cavendish turned to her. "Louise, you probably came into this world resisting. Will you ever stop thinking like a victim and start thinking like a woman?"

Mrs. Pratt gave him a look that changed from anger to pain, then to withdrawal. Cavendish shook his head and went on.

"When we heard running footsteps on the trail behind us, we hid in the trees, afraid we were about to encounter whoever had stolen the jewels." He made a small sound of disbelief. "But it was Miss Sheila with a small flashlight and a paper bag." Cavendish frowned, as though still doubtful of what he'd seen. "When we saw her head for the cabin, I decided we should follow her. I mean, why on earth would she be going there at that hour? I watched through the window and saw her move the table and toss the bag into the tunnel." He indicated the necklace in the middle of the table. "That's what it contained. Sir, the thief is Miss Sheila."

Jack shook his head. "I don't think so, Dish."

"I know it's hard for you to believe, sir, but—"

"I believe you. We saw her, too." Jack picked up the necklace, let it dangle between his hands. It caught the overhead light and shone like a handful of stars. He remembered the avarice in her eyes when she'd studied the necklace on Dani's slender throat. He smiled at Cavendish. "I think Sheila might have 'liberated' this piece from my father's safe, but I don't think she stole the jewels in the first place."

"Did she know the safe's combination?" Genny asked.

Jack nodded. "She's kept her jewelry there on past visits. I think it was just another designer something she wanted. She probably thought she could swipe a bauble from the pile, and when the jewels finally were identified or turned over to the police, a missing piece could be blamed on whoever stole it in the first place."

"What now?" Cavendish asked.

Jack pocketed the necklace. "I'll put it back before the owner turns up and Sheila ends up in the slammer."

"You won't mention our—ahem..." Cavendish pointed to himself and Mrs. Pratt, apparently at a lost for words.

"I'm not in a position to, Dish," Jack said with a wry smile. "Genny and I were enjoying our own assignation this evening."

Cavendish seemed to note Genny's apparel for the first time and made a production of standing and pushing in his chair. "Oh, my. Yes. Well." He cleared his throat. "If that will be all, I'll get to bed. It'll be morning before you know it."

"Good night, Cavendish," Jack said.

Cavendish nodded in Jack and Genny's direction, bowed formally to Mrs. Pratt and turned to leave the room.

"Roger!" Mrs. Pratt stood, her voice a little desperate.

Cavendish stopped in the doorway and turned to her. She took several steps toward him then stopped, folding her arms. She shifted her weight uncomfortably. "Will...you be down to help me with breakfast?"

He studied her a moment, obviously surprised by the question. "If you like," he finally replied.

"I would," she said. "Good night, Roger."

He smiled slowly, then sobered, apparently remembering where he was and that there were witnesses. "Seven sharp, then," he said briskly. "Good night, Louise."

Mrs. Pratt watched him leave, seeming rooted to the spot for a moment. Then she turned to Jack and Genny, called a cheerful good-night and disappeared into the darkness of the hallway.

Jack stood, drew Genny with him, then hooking an arm around her shoulders, led her toward the stairs.

"My room or yours?" he whispered.

"You to yours and me to mine," she replied quietly. "Discretion, Mr. Fleming."

He laughed softly. "I think there are so many romances going on in this house, no one notices what anyone else is up to."

"Except the children, who never miss a thing."

In the upstairs hallway, they rounded the corner and almost collided with Drew. He was knotting the belt of a brown velour robe, looking tired and rumpled.

He frowned at them in the weak light from the hallway nightlight. "What are you doing up at this hour?" he asked.

Jack raised an eyebrow. "You've been married too long, Drew. We're enjoying a midnight assignation. What are you doing?"

Drew smiled in weary self-deprecation. Genny found the look disarming. She really liked Jack's brother, she thought.

"Looking for my wife. Is she downstairs?"

There'd been a time, Jack thought, when he'd have taken pleasure in telling him what Cavendish and Mrs. Pratt had seen and what he, personally, suspected. But that time had passed. He wasn't sure how or why, but all he wanted to do was keep what he knew to himself.

With the necklace heavy in his pocket, he shrugged. "Don't think so. We haven't seen her." He looked down at Genny for corroboration.

She shook her head. "Maybe she's checking on the boys."

Drew looked from one to the other in vague suspicion, then nodded. "Thanks. I'll try that. Good night."

Genny turned in the dark doorway of her room, and smiled up at Jack. "Why didn't you tell him?" she asked.

"Because Sheila did a stupid, impulsive thing she probably regrets already," he replied, keeping his voice down. "And there seemed little point in causing him pain or concern when it isn't necessary."

"Mm." Genny put her arms around his waist. "Not because you care."

He wrapped his arms loosely around her. "Because for all our differences, he's as honest as the day is long, and I didn't see why—"

"That's caring," she interrupted.

He framed her face firmly in his hands and leaned down to kiss her, gently at first, then with a growing hunger he wondered if he'd ever be able to satisfy. He finally raised his head. "*That's* caring. Are you going to invite me in, or consign me to my lonely bed?"

"Your lonely bed, I'm afraid." She looked as deprived as he felt. "See you at breakfast."

"I can't eat," he protested in a whisper, reaching for her. "I'm in love."

She put hand firmly in the middle of his chest. "You can drink coffee."

"That's sensitive of you, Gen."

Genny took his shirtfront in a fist and pulled him toward her. She looked up into his deep green eyes and asked in a whisper, "Do you want to see sensitive?"

Her smoky eyes were alight with humor and the passion she was trying hard to hold at bay. Seeing it there comforted him.

"Oh, please," he replied.

She stood on tiptoe as she pulled him down, opening her mouth on his, kissing him with all the fervor of love newly discovered. She nipped his lip as she pulled away.

"*That's* sensitive," she whispered. "Good night."

Genny stepped back into her room and closed the door. Jack resisted the urge to break through it and carry that kiss to its inevitable conclusion.

But she was probably right. What was needed here was time apart, he thought as he went slowly down the hall. Time to think. Time to rest and renew. Clear, creative planning had always been his forte.

He was almost at the end of the hall before he realized his room was in the other direction.

JACK FOLLOWED THE SOUND of giggles onto the sun porch and found Genny and the girls at work on the quilt while the boys played a board game and kibbitzed on the sidelines. The room glowed with early-morning light.

"Good morning," he called from the doorway.

The girls waved and threw kisses. Genny gave him a smile filled with intimate memories. Something electric crossed the distance between them and connected them as surely as if he had touched her.

Unable to do anything about it under the watchful eyes of the girls, he blew her a kiss and headed for the kitchen, needing his coffee.

He'd seen his father and Emily walk off into the woods hand in hand earlier, then heard the roar of a powerful motor as it raced down the drive to the road.

"Drew gone to town?" Jack asked Cavendish as he poured himself a cup of coffee.

The butler and Mrs. Pratt sat at the table eating breakfast. Both stood, apparently prepared to cook his.

He pointed them back to the table. "No, thanks. Not hungry. I heard his car leave."

"That would have been Miss Sheila," Cavendish said.

Jack pretended not to notice that the butler's hand covered the housekeeper's.

"Mr. Drew," Cavendish went on, "is repairing the lamppost she knocked down when she left. I tried to tell him I'd take care of it, but he insisted."

Jack went to the window and looked out to see Drew in jeans and a T-shirt, resetting the post. The large brass-trimmed lantern made it top-heavy, and Jack thought he lip-read a few choice profanities as Drew struggled with it.

Without stopping to analyze the impulse, Jack poured a second cup of coffee and carried both out the back door.

"Morning," he said, holding out the cup.

Drew looked at the cup, then at him, his dark eyes registering surprise, suspicion and caution all at once. He finally eased the post to the ground and accepted the coffee.

"Thanks," he said. He indicated the post with an inclination of his head. "Wide car, narrow gate, wife with no depth perception."

Jack nodded sympathetically. "I'll be teaching Dani to drive in the fall. Scares the hell out of me."

Drew grinned. "They deserve the right to vote, but I think we should have thought twice about the license to drive."

He moved to the steps leading down from the garden and sat halfway up. "Can you sit for a minute?" he asked.

Jack tried not to betray how much the question startled him— or how much it pleased him. He sat one step up from the bottom, leaning his elbows on an upper stair.

"Sheila left in a flap this morning," Drew said.

Jack presumed she'd gone to the cabin, found the necklace missing and was more upset by the possibility of discovery than by the absence of the jewels. He glanced at the post, determined to reveal nothing.

"Looks that way," he said.

"I found her in the garden last night."

"Oh?"

"Did she...say something to you?"

Jack turned to look up at him, surprised by the question. "No. Why?"

Drew looked at him steadily. "Because usually the only thing that upsets Sheila is being thwarted, and you stand in the way of what she wants."

That was honest. Jack felt as though he were twenty-one again and they were about to duke it out behind the gym after his graduation. "What *she* wants?" he challenged.

Drew nodded, his eyes drifting to the woods. "Position, prestige, a house in the seven-figure range." He looked at Jack again, that startling honesty in his eyes that always unsettled him. "All I've ever wanted was to be the son Dad loves best."

Jack made a scornful sound and looked away. "Then relax. You've got it."

"No." Drew stretched his legs out to a lower step. "I'm the one born on the right side of the covers. But I think he truly loves us equally. Makes me feel small for disliking you."

"Go easy on yourself. I'm not wild about you, either."

They were silent for a moment. They could hear the children laughing on the sun porch and the distant whoosh of highway traffic.

"You braced for tonight?" Drew asked. "I'll bet Dad makes the announcement after he applauds old George."

Jack stiffened at the cruel needling. It seemed to hurt more at the moment, probably because after Drew's earlier honesty it came as a surprise.

He replied calmly. "We both know he has only one choice," he said.

"Yes." Drew's voice was cool, and Jack braced himself for more verbal abuse. "The smart son—the one he's proudest of. I hope you'll remember to throw me a crumb."

Jack turned, ready to do battle, thinking Drew was being facetious. Then he looked into his face and saw all the insecurity, frustration and unresolved anger he always felt. Before he could express his surprise, Drew loped up the steps and was gone.

Jack stared after him, unable to believe what he'd heard.

GENNY TOOK STITCHES and listened to the children's chatter in a kind of daze. She was in love with Jack, and Jack loved her. For the first time in her life, her past didn't matter. She felt as though she were finally crawling out of the hospital debris. The future was suddenly as bright as the sun porch.

"Mom, is it okay if Lees borrows my heart necklace for tonight?" She and Lisette were sitting on the floor with the boys, the quilt abandoned for the board game. "Andrew put all the fun stuff in the safe."

Robert looked up from rolling the dice. "I wonder why nobody's come looking for the jewelry. Dad checked this morning's paper and there wasn't anything in it about stolen jewelry."

"Because somebody in the house did it," Trey observed matter-of-factly, "And no one else knows."

"Who?" Lisette challenged.

He shrugged. "I don't know."

"Maybe Dad," Robbie joked. "'Cause he always says Mom's gonna put us in the poorhouse."

Francie frowned. "What's the poorhouse?"

"A place where you go when you don't have any money."

"Will you make your move," Trey asked his brother impatiently. "You're just putting it off because you know you're losing."

Robert jerked a thumb in Francie's direction. "I'm losing because my partner's dweeby."

Francie pounced on him, the element of surprise allowing her to pin him to the linoleum. "Take that back!" she demanded laughing.

Genny smiled. The children had become friends, and though they quarreled continuously it was more for the sake of the action than because of any real grudge. She peeled Francie off of Robert. "Why don't you go get the necklace for Lisette," she suggested, "and I'll see if Mrs. Pratt's cinnamon rolls are out of the oven yet."

"I'll get you for that!" Robert threatened as the girls skipped away.

"Taken down by a girl," Trey taunted. "Wait till I tell the guys at school."

Robert did not appear alarmed. "Go ahead. I'll tell them you spent most of the summer quilting."

Mrs. Pratt was pulling a tray of fat, sizzling rolls out of the oven when Genny walked into the kitchen. Cavendish, in a white apron, stirred a bowl of icing.

"Just about ready," Mrs. Pratt said, tossing aside her oven mitt. "Those wild Indians hungry?"

Genny nodded. "So am I. I'm going to have to Jazzercise six

times a week to work off what your cooking has put on me this month."

"And you fight it so valiantly," Jack teased, pocketing his keys and closing the back door behind him.

Genny made a face at him, then noticed the paper-wrapped bouquet of flowers in his arms. Daisies and tiger lilies.

"Excuse us, please," he said with a nod of his head to Cavendish and Mrs. Pratt. He caught Genny's hand and pulled her into the hallway behind the stairs. It was shadowy and cool and filled with the aroma from the kitchen and the spicy fragrance of the bouquet.

Jack handed it to her, his eyes soft with love.

Genny gave them a gentle hug. "But where did you get them?"

"Read the card."

She opened the small envelope tucked into the paper and found the answer. "So you'll never have to compromise on anything," it read, "I had these flown in from New York. Love, Jack."

She looked up at him, her eyes bright with an answering love. The flowers clutched in her arm, she reached for him with the other.

"It's a morning-after present," he said, enveloping her in his embrace. "Or, more precisely, and ever-after present. Will you marry me?"

Genny flung herself into his arms, laughter and tears caught in her throat. The flowers crushed between them filled the dark, narrow corridor with a perfume both earthy and exotic. "Yes!" she whispered. "Oh, yes!"

She clung to him, afraid to believe this was real, that the night before had been real, that the future suddenly opening for her was real.

But it was. Jack was solid in her arms, and his embrace was so strong it would have hurt had the touch been anyone else's.

"Before we go home so everyone will be here?"

She didn't hesitate. "Yes."

"Mom! Mommy!" Francie's voice shouted from upstairs. "I can't find it!"

Genny stroked the back of Jack's neck and smiled into his eyes. "Duty calls. Francie's going to be one happy little girl."

"One of three," he said, giving her a quick kiss. "Go on. I'll test the cinnamon rolls and wait for you."

Genny rolled her eyes. "Replaced by a cinnamon roll. Can this be the real thing?"

Jack pulled her back as she drew away, crushing the flowers between them. His eyes were dark and earnest. "Don't doubt it for an instant," he said. "Love doesn't come any more real than what I feel."

She put a hand to his face, her own eyes locked with his. "Unless it's what *I* feel."

"Mo-om!"

"Go." Jack pushed her gently toward the sound of Francie's voice. "We'll talk later."

Genny hurried up the stairs, buoyed by love, bubbling over with her news.

Francie had most of the contents of her side of the dresser scattered across the floor. "I can't find it!" she said.

"Honey, it's in that tote bag you carried on the plane," Genny said, giving her shoulders a squeeze. "In that inside pocket. You probably just forgot we'd put it there."

"You look happy," Francie observed, sitting back on her heels.

"I am!" Genny confirmed. "I'll tell you about it in a minute."

Genny walked into the closet, expecting to find the bag on the shelf where she'd put it. When it wasn't there, she conceded that that had been optimistic—she shared the closet with Francie.

Getting down on her hands and knees, she crawled under the clothes hanging from the rod and rooted through the pile of Francie's things tossed in the corner—the windbreaker it was always too warm to wear, the shoes she preferred to do without...

The closet door closed behind her with a firm, forceful bang. Shrouded in darkness, feeling the thick press of clothes above her and the closet wall directly in front of her face, Genny didn't have time to put her brains to work before her body reacted to its instinctive fear.

She scrambled to her feet, tangled in the clothes. With a scream, she fought her way out of them and came up against the door.

"Let me out!" she screamed.

"You don't push Robert Fleming and get away with it!" a

voice shouted from beyond the door. There was an exaggeratedly wicked laugh. "I've locked you in and you'll have to stay there forever until your skin falls off and your eyeballs fall out!"

Genny heard herself screaming, felt her precious air foolishly diminished by it. A corner of her brain knew Robbie thought he had trapped Francie and was gaining retribution for their tussle earlier. Either he couldn't hear her, or he wasn't listening, too excited by the success of his vendetta. The screaming in the closet would mean nothing to him; the children never played without screaming.

Genny tried to engage her brain, but didn't seem able to. She was now rasping for air and seeing colors and patterns in the dark she knew weren't there. Fear, like a pair of strong, bony hands, cinched around her throat.

"Mom!"

The door burst open and air rushed in. Genny felt it on her face, against her body damp with perspiration, but she couldn't breathe it in.

Through a haze she saw Francie's frightened face, Robbie's horror-stricken expression, Lisette with both hands over her mouth.

"Come on, Mom," Francie said gently, trying to tug her out of the closet. Genny fell to her knees, hearing Francie's and Lisette's cries of alarm.

Then strong hands pulled her to her feet. Jack lifted her against his hip and carried her to the open French doors.

"Breathe!" he ordered. "Come on, you're out in the open now. Breathe, Genny."

The first draft of air felt barbed and hot. It hurt all the way down.

"That's it," Jack encouraged. "Another one. Deeper, this time."

Genny took a breath, then another.

Jack rubbed her back, fighting the urge to hold her. She felt so fragile under his hand. Her color was ghostly, her eyes still terrified.

"I was just...I thought she was Francie..." Robert stammered, almost as pale as Genny. "I didn't...know..."

"I was in the bathroom," Francie explained tearfully.

"It's okay," Jack said to Robert. "It was just an accident. Genny has a fear of closed-in places and you scared her."

Robert looked close to tears. "Genny, I'm sorry."

Genny managed to focus on him, coming back to awareness because of the guilt he felt when he'd really done nothing wrong.

"It's okay," she said, taking another deep breath. "It wasn't your fault."

Francie put an arm around her waist. "Are you okay, Mom?"

Sanity returned as Genny began to breathe evenly—bringing with it a truth she refused to face. Then she looked into Jack's anxious face, Francie's worried eyes, Lisette's and Dani's frightened expressions, and the concern of everyone else in the house who'd crowded into the room. Jack and his family could have no sunny future if she was in their lives.

Drew came to put a comforting arm around Robert. "Genny, I'm sorry," he said. "I'm sure Rob…"

Genny shook her head, her breathing stabilizing, her heart sinking. "No need to apologize. It was harmless play that wouldn't have upset anyone else." She gave Robert a quick hug and a forced smile. "Go on, now. I'm fine, and those cinnamon rolls must be ready."

Everyone stood another moment, as though reluctant to believe her.

"Come along," Cavendish finally said briskly. "Let's give her air." He caught Jack's eye. "I'll bring up a cup of tea."

"You're sure you're okay, Mom?" Francie asked.

Genny held her close for a moment and dispensed another artificial smile. "I'm fine. You and Lees and Dani go ahead, and later I'll French braid your hair for tonight like I promised."

Francie turned gravely to Jack. "Will you stay with her?"

"You bet." Jack walked her to the door, then closed it behind her.

Genny sank down to the carpet in front of the open French doors, tears streaming silently down her face. Her dreams of only moments ago had been shattered by a hard dose of reality. She couldn't enter into marriage like an ordinary woman. She wasn't ordinary. She freaked out unpredictably and frightened little children. She made men look at her in helpless concern.

Jack sat down beside her, but didn't touch her. The tears worried him, but he tried to tell himself they meant nothing except that she just wasn't free of the episode.

"Think about honeymooning on a ship," he said, his voice quietly spinning out the image. "Not one of those big jobs with all those tiny cabins, but a sailing ship that takes only twenty passengers. The ocean extends to the horizon and the air is pristine and perfumed."

Genny looked at him with a longing so strong it ripped at his heart. Then she looked away and shook her head. "I've changed my mind," she said.

Jack had always thought himself panic-proof. That statement proved him wrong. He forced himself to think. "You've decided not to love me?" he asked. Make her look that in the face, he thought. Make her see she didn't mean it.

She turned to him, her eyes tired and filled with pain. "No. I'll always love you." The words quivered and she swallowed. "But I won't marry you. I have to live with this, but you and the girls don't."

"You don't think we can?"

"I don't think you should have to."

"I see." He leaned back against the door frame and struggled against the need to shout. "Maybe you'd like to give me Francie so she doesn't have to put up with it, either."

She glanced at him suspiciously, apparently unsure of his point.

"Well, if you're going to martyr yourself over this," he said, "you may as well go all the way."

Anger ignited in her eyes. He found that hopeful.

"Do you want your children to have a mother who frightens them?" she demanded.

"They had one who left them without a second thought," he replied. "That creates a fear you probably can't even imagine. Your mother died and left you alone in the dark, but you didn't grow up having to live with the knowledge that she did it on purpose."

She put a hand to her eyes, unable to look at the desperation in his.

"What if last night was a fluke?" she demanded. "I mean, I thought...I thought..."

Suddenly he understood. Empathy filled him, but he wouldn't

let it sway him. "You thought you'd licked it," he asked gently, "and it came back to kick you in the face?"

She started to sob. He reached a hand to her knee, afraid to move too close. He tried to reach her with his voice. "Genny, you took a giant step. Don't give up now. Francie's one of the most well-balanced kids I know. Your problem hasn't hurt her, and it won't hurt my girls. They need you. They love you."

She shook her head, resisting his coaxing.

"Or maybe that's what's bothering you," he suggested brutally. Reason and coaxing hadn't worked. "Marriage is the quintessential tight spot, isn't it? You explained it to the girls on our way to the airport. Maybe you're developing an emotional claustrophobia. After all these years of being responsible to no one, maybe you don't want to upset the balance with a husband and *three* children."

She glowered at him, her face blotchy and swollen. "Maybe I don't want one who thinks so little of me."

He looked at her levelly. "Maybe you need one," he said, "who thinks enough of you to make you come out of the dark. Or do you plan to spend the rest of your life under that damn desk with the rubble of the past over your head?"

"I don't know!" she shouted, angry with him, angry with herself. "Maybe!"

He got to his feet before he gave in to the impulse to shake her. "If you make up your mind," he said, "let me know."

She rose up beside him, furious. "Are you that much better than I?" she asked. "You need to belong, to be accepted, to finally feel first-class. Getting the appointment will do that for you for all outward appearances, but inside you'll always be under as much rubble as I am until *you* believe in *you*. When you come to terms with that, it won't matter if Andrew puts Drew in the president's seat, or if you and I are married or not. You'll be a whole person."

He turned to give her one last long look. "At least there's hope for me," he said. He stormed from the room, his progress impeded just beyond the door by Dani, Lisette and Francie gathered there, obviously caught in the act of eavesdropping. Their wide-eyed expressions were horror-filled, accusatory, devastated. He hesitated a moment, then walked around them, for the first time in his paternal life unable to consider their emotional comfort before his own.

GENNY LAY ON HER BED, the flowers clutched in her arms, when she heard a light rap on her door. She ignored it, but the visitor rapped again.

Genny dragged herself to her feet, set the flowers aside and went to the door. She opened it only slightly, prepared to tell whoever it was to go away. She wasn't prepared to face Emily and Andrew, arm in arm, beaming. Surprised, she opened the door further, and Emily took that opportunity to let herself in. With an uncomfortable and apologetic smile, Andrew followed.

"We want you to be the first to know!" Emily announced gaily. "We're getting married."

As Emily wrapped her arms around Genny, Andrew said with an indulgent shake of his head, "Actually I think you're about the fourth to know. There was the waitress where we had coffee, the teller at the bank, the—"

Emily cast him a threatening glance. "You came along to be helpful, remember?"

"I was *coerced* into coming along," Andrew corrected with another apologetic glance at Genny, "to provide moral support while you poked your nose in where it's likely to be bitten off. But don't let me stop you."

With an indignant hand on her hip, Emily said, "I could still change my mind, you know."

Andrew gave her a look that was amused and charming and sure, and reminded Genny startlingly of Jack. "No. You can't," he said.

Emily turned to Genny and groaned. "The worst of it is, he's right. Genny—" she folded her arms, apparently ready to discuss what she'd come for "—the girls tell me you've declined Jack's proposal because of the closet incident. That's absurd."

Andrew leaned a hip on Genny's desk and shook his head. "Don't hedge, Em. Tell her what you think."

Emily took Andrew's arm and pulled him toward Genny. "Tell her. Tell her what you told me when I showed you my scars."

Andrew looked first reluctant, then resigned. He hooked an

arm around Emily's shoulders and pulled her close. "All I saw when I looked at Emily," he said with utter sincerity, "was beautiful Emily."

Emily wrapped both arms around his waist and a tear slid unheeded down her cheek.

"Of course." Genny put an arm around each of them. "You're beautiful because you're a bright, funny, sexy lady. And because he loves you, whatever scars you have are part of what you are."

The dreamy quality in Emily's eyes darkened into sternness. "Well put. Now, why can't you see that about yourself?"

Genny let her hands fall, ambushed. "Emily...it's not the same."

Emily grasped Genny's arms and turned her to face her. "The girls told me what happened. And the little darlings listened at the door after everyone left, expecting to hear a proposal. Instead they heard you reject them."

"I didn't reject them," Genny denied. She looked from Emily to Andrew. "Your granddaughters have already lost one mother, and Francie's wanted a father for so long. What if I married Jack and I couldn't cope? How many times can children see someone they care about screaming and gasping for air? If it didn't work out, the girls would be devastated."

Emily took her hand, studying it a moment before she spoke as though groping for the right words. She looked up at Genny, her eyes apologetic. "I don't think your claustrophobia is involved here, I think you're just scared."

"Em—"

"I know. Marriage is its own little prison. But what could be more restrictive than motherhood, and you cope with that just fine. Every day you meet the needs of patients whose very lives often depend on you, and you deal with that." She smiled gently. "You're doing the same thing I did. You're curling up around your wounds so no one can see them, and you're comfortable. Life is lonely and missing a lot of things you'd like to have, but it's kind of safe. Jack's life isn't. So you think the fear you feel at the thought of marriage to him is caused by your claustrophobia, because that defines fear for you." Emily shrugged a shoulder. "But falling in love is frightening on its own. You bullied me into taking the chance. Can't you?"

Genny shook her head. "Our situations are different, Em. I'm glad you and Andrew have worked things out. You can't hurt anyone else if you fail. I can make five people miserable. Now, I'd really like to nap before dinner."

Andrew took the point of Genny's chin in his fingers and looked into her eyes. She saw so much there that reminded her of Jack—sweetness, humor, a shading of grief that nothing would ever rub away.

"You are incapable of making my son miserable," he said. "You might make him angry, crazy, exasperated, but you would never hurt him unless you leave him. Any man who's given his heart to a cold, traitorous woman knows what to look for the next time—if he's lucky enough to have one. We look for warmth in the eyes, spontaneity of touch, laughter, loyalty, trust. I found it." He gave Emily a look that made her blush, then turned back to Genny. "And Jack found it. Before you walk away from him, make sure which of the two of you you're protecting." He leaned down to kiss her cheek. "Get some rest. There're only two hours until the party."

Chapter Fourteen

Genny zipped Francie into a mint-green, full-skirted dress then turned her around, combing her full curly bangs with her fingers. "You look beautiful," she said with false enthusiasm.

Francie, who hadn't looked into Genny's eyes since they'd begun preparing for dinner, continued to stare at the floor. "Thank you," she said stiffly.

Genny went back into the bathroom to comb her hair. Francie followed, standing in the doorway. She folded her arms and leaned her right foot to the side, twisting it back and forth nervously.

"Jack thinks *you're* beautiful," she said.

Genny stared into the mirror, fluffing the ends of her hair. "I think he's very handsome."

"The other night," Francie went on, her voice tightening with emotion, "he told me if he could pick another little girl for his family..." She drew a breath and Genny could hear the pain in it. "It would be me."

Genny had to fight for composure. In three days they'd be leaving New Hampshire, and she'd probably never see Jack again. Or the girls, or Emily. She'd have only the quilt they'd all made together to remind her of a month in August in a birch forest in New Hampshire when she'd had everything any woman could want.

She wanted to cry because all the sparkle had gone out of her daughter, because there would be no fairy-tale end to their summer story.

She put her arms around her and held her close. "Honey, I

can't marry Jack, no matter how much you'd like it to happen. He lives a very different life than we do, and we wouldn't be very comfortable in it.''

Genny drew back to see if her words were having any effect. They were, but not what she'd hoped. Francie was looking at her as though she were speaking a foreign language.

''But we've all had so much fun together,'' she said.

Genny nodded. ''I know, Francie, but this was vacation. The other eleven months of the years he works in a big office in downtown Portland, he sees lots of important people, goes to lots of parties, travels...''

It wasn't working. It was obvious Francie could find little problem with big offices, parties and traveling.

''It's the closetphobia stuff, isn't it?'' Francie asked.

Genny sighed. It was difficult to skirt an issue with her daughter. ''Yes, partly.''

''But I've seen him hug you and you didn't get scared. Families don't scare a person, Mom. They help each other, and they like to be together all the time.''

''That works for people who are normal, Francie,'' Genny said quietly, trying desperately to make her understand. ''I'm not.''

Francie remained unconvinced. ''The whole time we've been here, we've all been like a family. You did all the stuff for Dani and Lisette that you do for me and you never seemed scared of it.''

Emily's voice surfaced in Genny's mind. ''Take a good look at yourself. Giving all of that is frightening. Accepting all of that is a responsibility...

Genny glanced at her watch and discovered it was two minutes until seven. She framed Francie's face in her hands and kissed her nose. ''Darling, I know this is hard for you, but you have to trust that I know what I'm doing. When we get home and life gets back to normal, you'll feel better about everything, okay?''

Tears pooled in Francie's eyes, but she sniffed them back. ''You mean you're not going to make the promise so you won't ever break it?''

When Genny couldn't think of an answer worthy of the question, Francie simply nodded. ''I'm going down now, okay?''

''Okay.'' Genny watched her go with her shoulders slumped, her eyes downcast. She squared her own shoulders and tried not to hear what Francie was thinking. The words filled her mind anyway. "That's chicken."

"WHAT'S GOING TO HAPPEN if Grandpa gives the job to Uncle Drew?" Dani asked. She sat on the edge of Jack's low dresser running his tie through her fingers.

He glanced away from the mirror in the act of buttoning his shirt, surprise visible in his eyes.

Dani smiled. "You've got to quit thinking of me as a little kid, Dad. I know what's going on even when you don't tell me."

"Really?" He pinched her chin then snatched his tie from her and turned back to the mirror. "I thought I might become a rock star."

Dani laughed.

"What?" he demanded teasingly. "You could get your concert tickets wholesale, I—"

"Wholesale!" Dani protested. "Why not free?"

Jack shook his head, seesawing the tie back and forth under his collar. "That's not good business."

Dani edged closer and looked into his averted eyes. "You don't have to worry about that so much if you're not in banking anymore. Will you be able to get another job?"

"I think so," he said. A headhunter from Bank of the Union had offered him twice his current salary only months ago. He cast her a sidelong grin. "Nothing will affect your clothes allowance, I promise."

"That isn't why I asked," she said, her tone suddenly sober and mature. "I know how much you enjoy working. I was just worried if you don't have that, and...and you don't have..."

His tie knotted, Jack turned to her, looking into her beautiful face. She was beginning to look so much like her mother it startled him sometimes. But for all her physical resemblance, she was lighted by an inner sweetness Sarajane had never had. In that she reminded him of his own mother.

He knew the name on the tip of her tongue but it would hurt too much to say it. "I'll still have you, won't I?" he asked.

She nodded and swallowed with obvious difficulty. "But Lees is thinking about running away, and Grandma's going to stay with Grandpa."

Jack took a side step to put his arms around her. Lisette hadn't spoken to him since the girls had overheard his quarrel with Genny, and he would miss Emily terribly. In a few short hours a beautiful summer had taken a dark and stormy turn.

"It could end up being just you and me," Dani said into his shoulder.

He hugged her tightly. "If Lees did run away, she wouldn't be able to afford a television, so she'd be home the first Wednesday night to watch Doogie what's-his-name. And I'm happy Grandma's happy."

She twined her arms around his neck. "So far, except for her, everyone who's in love is miserable. Cavendish and Mrs. Pratt yell at each other all the time, and you and Genny..." She sighed, her lip quivering, and leaned her head against his shoulder. "I wish she'd said she'd stay with us, Daddy."

His heart broke with her words—for her, for Lisette who refused to understand, for Genny who consigned herself to loneliness, and for himself. He had no idea how he was going to live without her. He thought grimly that since she'd rejected him this afternoon, his father's decision had paled in importance.

"I know." He stroked Dani's back and kissed her hair. "But she can't, and that's what we have to live with. Everything will be all right. I don't want you to worry."

"Right." She drew away, swiping a hand across her eyes. "As long as you're sure about my clothes allowance."

"Absolutely."

"Okay." She smiled and leapt off the dresser. "What time do you have to meet Grandpa and Uncle Drew in the library?"

He glanced at his watch. "Five minutes ago."

She kissed his cheek. "Good luck, Dad." She hurried to the door and stopped to turn to him. "I love you," she said.

He decided life had its compensations. "I love you, too, babe."

IT WORRIED HIM that he felt calm. He hurried down the corridor to his father's office, knowing that this meeting would decide his future. His future. He repeated the words to himself, trying to force the impact. It simply wasn't there.

Whatever happened wouldn't affect how he felt about his father, and he suddenly had a far less active dislike for his brother. He suspected it might even change to something more positive given time and the right circumstances. But he'd still have to leave if Drew was appointed. He couldn't expect Drew to feel the same.

He turned down the dimly lighted corridor, lost in thought. He was surprised to look up and find the object of this thoughts leaning against the wall near the library door, smoking a cigarette.

"Dad busy?" Jack asked.

Drew looked at him a moment, opened his mouth as though to say something, then shook his head. "I don't know. Haven't had the guts to knock, yet." He took several steps back to the pedestal ashtray and extinguished his cigarette. "But I guess I've wasted enough time."

Jack reached up to rap on the door, then hesitated. He turned to Drew and offered his hand, unafraid of having it ignored. Loving and losing, he thought, made it easier to take chances.

Drew looked at it one interminable moment, then took it in a firm grip. "Good luck, Jack," he said.

Jack rapped on the door and waited. There was no reply. He frowned at Drew and tried again. Greenwich mean time could be set by his father's punctuality. When there was still no reply, he pushed the door open and stepped inside. What he saw stopped him cold. Behind him, he heard Drew's whispered epithet.

"Come in, gentlemen," George Spears said. "Close the door."

Andrew stood behind his desk, pale but composed. George stood beside it, a small, stainless steel revolver pointed at his companion. He moved to the side and gestured Jack and Drew into the room with the gun.

George, dressed in a suit and tie for his celebratory dinner, looked nervous. "Andrew," he said reasonably, though his voice was high, "don't make this hard for me. I'll ask you one more time. What have you done with the jewels?"

Andrew raised a hand toward the open, empty safe. "That's where I put them, George. You witnessed it, remember? I've no idea what's happened to them since then."

"You moved them."

"No. I didn't."

"*You* stole the jewelry?" Drew asked in disbelief.

Jack suddenly remembered George trying to get a cab at the airport, looking panicky when he finally located him, clutching his luggage and briefcase as though his life depended on it, jogging early in the morning the day after he'd arrived.

George looked less proud of the fact than regretful. He turned back to Andrew, his voice quiet and tired. "It wasn't supposed to turn out like this but, yes. Now, where are they?"

"But how? Where did they come from?"

"They were abandoned property," George said patiently. "They belonged to Millicent Yardley. Her family's been with us for two generations, and I've personally helped with her banking for years. Her mind began to fail last year. She had no family, no friends."

He sighed. "Not unlike myself. Of course, even when she had a sound mind, she was careless about her affairs. She kept receipts in a shoebox, cash in her mattress, and antique jewelry in a cookie jar in the kitchen. She trusted me."

Andrew pulled his chair out and George started anxiously.

"I'm going to sit down," Andrew said quietly. "That's all right, isn't it? You will allow me that after thirty-three years together?"

"Andy, I'm sorry." George's voice was filled with guilt. "I don't expect you to understand. You had Laurie, and you have two sons any man would be proud of. I have no one."

"Do you think jewels will compensate for that?" Andrew asked softly.

George smiled as though the question were naive. "Of course not. But I've made the acquaintance of a young lady who would compensate any man for anything. Unfortunately she has a taste for good food, fast cars and exotic locales. If I'm to keep her interested..." He left the obvious unsaid.

"I had a wife like that," Jack said. "You won't keep her interested. She'll wipe you out and be gone in a year with some other guy."

George shrugged a shoulder. "So I'll have a year. After a lifetime of loneliness, that's a lot."

"Surely this Yardley woman's family will discover the jewels missing," Drew said.

George shook his head. "She died without any next of kin. I suggested she keep her jewels in a safety-deposit box with sincere intentions of protecting her possessions. When she died, it occurred to me that no one knew what was in the box but me. And I personally handle the bank's dormant accounts."

"You have to make a list of them and turn the property over to the State Land Board," Drew said.

George shrugged again. "I simply left one account off the list. It was an easy matter to open the box late one night and remove the contents. When I was kidnapped to come here for the party, I had to have a safe place to put the jewels. I came across the cabin while I was jogging and thought no one would ever find them there. Obviously I was wrong." He sighed, suddenly growing anxious. "Now please, the young lady is waiting for me at Logan airport. Where are the jewels?"

"In my room," Jack replied.

Andrew and Drew turned to him in surprise.

He didn't want to explain why. "I thought they'd be safer," he said.

George swung the gun toward the door. "Then let's go get them."

Jack shook his head. "I don't think so, George."

George looked first suspicious, then alarmed. He stiffened, working the gun nervously in his hand. Jack tried not to notice.

"What do you mean?" George demanded.

Jack turned to Drew. "This man taught us most of what we know about banking," he said, trying desperately to transmit a message with his eyes. "I don't think we can let him do this."

"What do you mean?" George shouted again.

Drew nodded. Jack was surprised to read understanding in his eyes.

Drew turned to George. "He means we're going to take that gun away from you."

George cocked it and took a nervous step backward.

"Boys…" Andrew half rose out of his chair.

"I'll get one of you," George threatened, taking another backward step.

Drew laughed softly. "That'll solve Dad's problem of naming a successor."

Curiously that struck Jack funny, too. "There's an up side to everything. You just have to know where to look for it."

Jack was close enough now to see the perspiration on George's brow. He grabbed at George, who backed away, pointing but not using the gun. Drew pushed George's arm up and Jack pinned the other behind his back. Jack waited for the discharge of the bullet, but nothing happened.

He straightened, frowning at Drew, who rolled the cylinder to show that it was empty.

"Wasn't loaded," Drew said with a grin. "But heroic of us all the same, don't you think?"

ON HER WAY DOWN to dinner, Genny heard the shouts and thumps in Andrew's office. Any consideration that whatever was going on was none of her business was superceded by concern for Andrew.

She pushed the door open to see him fall into his chair as Jack and Drew grappled with George. "What are they doing?" she demanded, walking into the room.

Andrew glanced her way, his face pale and grim. "Close the door, Genny," he said.

She obeyed, pausing to lean against it in an attempt to make sense of what was happening. She blinked as Drew placed a gun on Andrew's desk. Jack eased a pale and panting George into a chair.

"Is what we found all of the jewelry?" Andrew asked.

George was silent a moment, catching his breath. Then he nodded.

Andrew studied him a moment, then slammed his hand on the desk. "Damn it, George! You've stolen from a customer. I can't *not* report that!"

George nodded again. "I know."

Genny stepped closer, unnoticed. George had stolen the jewels? She tried to imagine the scenario and couldn't.

"Why can't you?" Jack asked quietly.

"Because I'm retiring," Andrew shouted. "That's why not. If word got out that we covered this up with one of you as president, your career would be ruined."

Drew sat on the edge of Andrew's desk. "For George," he said, "I'd take the chance." He looked up at Jack.

"Of course," Jack said.

Andrew looked from one son to the other as though he couldn't believe what he was hearing. "That would be taking a foolish chance."

"Did you break into the box?" Jack asked George.

"No," George frowned. "I had both keys. Look, I don't want—"

"Then one of us can go back with him, Dad, put it all back, and as far as we're concerned this never happened."

"I—" George tried to stand but Jack pushed him down.

"Having to explain a retirement income to the lady with the expensive tastes will be like ten to twenty in the federal pen, I'm sure."

"I think we should give this a little more thought." The sound of Sheila's voice turned everyone's attention to the door. She wore a snug red dress and a wide smile.

Genny had no idea how long she'd been standing there, except that it must have been long enough to hear the plan they'd conceived.

Drew got slowly to his feet.

"It occurs to me that this gives us a bargaining position, Drew," she said, stopping in front of Andrew's desk. "You get the position, or I start making phone calls to the governor's office and the appropriate person in the Federal Reserve System."

Drew paled, Andrew's mouth fell open, and Jack's jaw firmed, but no one spoke as Sheila's threat reverberated in the closed room.

Genny waited for Jack to destroy the power in her threat by telling what he knew. But he said nothing, simply sat on the arm of George's chair and waited.

Genny refused to let him lose what he'd wanted all his life because of a selfish woman's machinations.

"Drew is your legitimate heir, Andrew," Sheila pressed. "Jack is your—"

Genny took a step toward her, but was halted by Drew's quiet order. "*Don't* say it, Sheila."

"Drew..."

"You're a thief," he said, walking around the desk to confront her. "I don't think you should be calling other people names. I know about the diamond necklace. I coerced the story out of Cavendish." Drew took a deep breath and turned to Andrew. "Give the presidency to Jack, he's the better qualified. I doubt that anyone with the bank is concerned about the fact that you weren't married to his mother. I know how much love and comfort you got from her, and how little my mother gave you. Legality be damned. He's more your son than I am. Excuse us, please." He took the now-sobbing Sheila's wrist and led her from the room.

As everyone stared after them, Jack felt a lifetime of confusion resolve itself. What existed in life was what was important, not the circumstances that brought it around. His father loved him, and his father loved Drew. It didn't matter that one son was legitimate and the other not. It mattered only that he loved them both. In love they were equal, and it was only love that counted.

A moment ago, with George's gun aimed at Jack's chest, Drew would have had the perfect opportunity to secure his own position. But he'd chosen to back Jack up instead. He didn't think he could ask more of a brother than that.

Andrew leaned across his desk toward George. "My grandchildren have planned a special entertainment for you, and you're going to enjoy it."

George nodded, looking a little as though he found himself on an alien planet. "Andy, I—"

"Then you are flying back to Portland with Jack and replacing every last bauble. I know you're no thief, but to think an intelligent man like yourself would do something so foolish to hold on to a lady—" Andrew stopped, suddenly aware his history left him in no position to criticize.

"Excuse us," Jack said, taking Genny's arm. "Shall I tell Mrs. Pratt to hold dinner?"

Andrew nodded. "Please."

"I can't believe it," Genny said in the hallway, their strained relationship forgotten in the drama of the moment. "He's such a sweetheart. Why would he do such a thing?"

"You heard him," Jack replied. "He was in love, or thought he was. After a lifetime of loneliness, he found someone he wanted to spend the rest of his days with. He did what he thought he had to do to keep her. I can relate. I wish I had so handy a solution. Excuse me.''

Genny headed for the patio, unable to watch him walk away. It was too prophetic.

STILL HIGH AND STILL FAT, the moon beckoned Genny to the cabin. She turned her back on it and walked along the patio, telling herself firmly there would be little point in torturing herself. She couldn't have Jack. Reliving their night together would serve little purpose.

She drew in deep gulps of air, trying to hold back a sudden, incapacitating desperation. A lifetime without Jack would be an eternity now that she knew what it was like to lie in his arms.

At first she thought the tears she heard were her own. Then she saw Sheila sitting in the shadows on the garden wall. She sounded despondent.

Genny felt anger for the other woman's shallowness, for the ease with which she would have hurt Jack to help her husband's position. Then Genny remembered her own swift rise in defense of Jack, the accusation of ''thief'' that had been on the tip of her tongue. Had Drew not interrupted, she'd have revealed herself what Jack had taken pains to keep hidden.

That made it a little more difficult to walk away from Sheila— that and the fact that she was too much nurse to abandon anyone in such obvious pain.

She sat beside her on the wall. ''Can I get you something?'' she asked quietly.

Sheila sobbed into her handkerchief, then shook her head and looked at Genny. The snob was gone. This was a real woman dealing with real pain.

''Can you get my husband back?'' she asked ironically. ''He's leaving me.'' She shook her head, and her face crumpled. ''I don't think I can live without him.''

''Without him?'' Genny couldn't help asking. ''Or without his money and position?''

Sheila took a moment to compose herself. ''I'm sure that's how it looks to you,'' she said, dabbing at her eyes. She stared into the dark distance, her tear-filled eyes losing their focus as she drew a ragged sigh.

"We weren't a love match, you know. We'd met at school and had a good time together. Both of us wanted wealth and power—I because I'd been brought up to think people who didn't have it were insignificant, and Drew because his entire aim in life was to do Jack one better. His mother told him from the time he was a child that he would have to be better than Jack for his father to notice him." A solitary tear fell down her already-damp cheek. She shook her head. "Pathetic, weren't we?

"Drew was very honest with me. He told me he wanted to marry me because Jack had just married Sarajane. Since his brother was projecting the image of a family man, he wanted to do the same." Her voice deepened, as though the memory of Jack's wife inspired dark thoughts. "Sarajane was more beautiful than I, and more ruthless. But I had all the social connections. Drew and I made a deal. I'd keep my ear to the gossip and hold our social position, and in exchange Drew would see that I got all the material things I wanted.

Sheila closed her eyes and more tears fell. "Trouble was, I fell in love with him. When my love for him grew and his didn't, I asked for more and more, hoping it would compensate—and secretly, I think, hoping it would jar him enough to make him take a second look at me. It didn't.

"I come from a family of infighters, Genny." Sheila folded her arms and shook her head, her brow pleating as though over an unpleasant memory. "Tonight I did what I thought would gain Drew the company, but he's changed on me. I guess...he didn't want it that way. I've outlived my usefulness."

Genny remembered the sadness she'd seen in Drew's eyes when he looked at Sheila. She suggested gently, "Maybe as a social tactician, but are you sure he no longer needs you as a wife?"

"He's leaving me," Sheila reminded her.

"Because all you've let him see is what the two of you wanted in the beginning. Getting, taking, having. He's grown, Sheila, and he probably thinks you haven't."

She shook her head, her mouth quivering dangerously again. "I don't know if I have or not. I just know I love him and I want to stay with him even if he has to work in a hardware store."

"Then go tell him that."

Sheila looked at her doubtfully, then shook her head. "He'll never believe me."

"I do," Genny said.

Sheila looked at her again, her eyes brimming with tears and a very fragile hope. "Thank you," she whispered.

JACK NEEDED A FEW minutes alone. A plan was developing in his brain for the future of First Westward Bank, and he wanted to give it a moment of quiet thought, to analyze whether he was being hysterical or stupidly sentimental.

He walked into the library, hoping to spend a precious ten minutes in his father's chair and contemplate Drew's reaction to what he had in mind.

Drew, it seemed, had entertained the same notion for reasons of his own. He reclined in Andrew's chair, contemplating the silver pen set on the desk.

Jack waited to feel resentment at the sight of his half brother in his father's chair. He didn't. But he hesitated inside the door, not certain he'd be welcome.

"Come in," Drew said, raising his eyes from the desk. "I was just leaving."

Jack took the chair facing the desk. "Not on my account, I hope."

Drew looked him in the eye and smiled thinly. "Not directly, no. I've just decided to make some changes in my life, and I have a lot of work to do."

"Changes?"

Drew pulled the cactus Jack and Jenny had bought Andrew closer. "My marriage, my career, my...priorities."

Jack didn't know what to say about Drew's marriage, and he wasn't sure how to approach the subject of his career. While he considered it, Drew went on.

"This is what you always were to me, Jack." He touched the pad of his finger to the long, sharp quills on the cactus. "A thorn in my side, an irritant. Not because you'd ever done anything to me directly, but because I just didn't want you there, being brilliant, looking confident and controlled, having a mother who was all the things mine wasn't. God, I was jealous of you."

Jack shook his head, still finding Drew's envy difficult to believe. "I was jealous of *you*. Maybe we were both short-sighted—so afraid we wouldn't get what we wanted that we missed what we had."

Drew met his gaze and searched it. "I'm sorry about what Sheila did."

Jack dismissed it with an inclination of his head. "You stopped her. You came through for me twice today, Drew. And once in front of a gun. Thank you."

"It wasn't loaded."

"You didn't know that."

Drew grinned. "Couldn't let him kill you. I'd hate to win the presidency by default."

Jack plunged in before he lost his nerve. "Then why don't we do what Dad's wanted all along?"

Drew frowned in puzzlement. Apparently, knowing how Jack felt about it, Andrew had never proposed a copresidency to his older son.

"We'll share the job, see how it works out. If it doesn't, I'll step aside and it's all yours."

Drew was silent for one startled moment. "You think that'd work?"

Jack shrugged. "I don't know. But I'm willing to try it."

Drew leaned back into the chair, obviously needing a moment to absorb what Jack suggested. He pulled at his tie and unbuttoned the top button of his shirt. "You and me?"

"We can pull this off, Drew."

Drew got to his feet and offered his hand. "Then let's do it."

Jack stood, knowing they were about to embark on more than a business partnership. They shook hands. Then it occurred to Jack that he owed his brother something else.

"Now we have that change in your life taken care of," he said. "Let's move on to your marriage."

Drew gave him a frown of annoyance that was only partly genuine. "You're not taking over this brother thing, you know. I'm still the oldest."

Jack nodded. "I just want to point out something you might have missed."

"What's that?"

"Sheila loves you."

Drew jammed his hands in his pockets and turned away to the window. "She loves the money, Jack, not me."

Jack perched on the edge of the desk. "I don't think so. Undoubtedly she likes what comes her way when you succeed, but I think she wants the success for you and for the boys."

Drew turned to Jack. "She was about to call you a bastard."

For the first time in his life that he could remember, Jack was able to smile over it. "I am." Then something else broadened his smile. "Genny was ready to call her a thief, though I'd taken great pains to keep the necklace thing quiet. Each was ready to kick and scratch to get us what they thought we wanted."

Drew considered that concept with a frown.

"I just think," Jack said reasonably, "you should give it some thought before you do anything you'll regret. Talk to her. Tell her how you feel. Ask her how she feels and you might be surprised."

Drew raised an eyebrow. "A pretty nurse comes along and suddenly you're the expert on relationships?"

Jack's smile slipped just a little. "Actually, to this point, it's not looking very good. But I'm not ready to give up. I don't think you should, either."

The library door opened and Andrew took a step inside, grumbling to himself about being too old for all this emotional upheaval. He stopped at the sight of Jack and Drew in conversation in his office.

"There you are." He looked from one to the other, frowning. "I've been looking for you. We need to talk."

Jack shook his head. "Not anymore. We've settled everything."

Andrew looked from one to the other again, this time his expression wary. "Really?"

Drew put an arm around his shoulders. "Yes. We've decided to share the presidency, throw in with the savings and loans and buy three tickets to Mexico. Are you in?"

Andrew grinned cautiously. "We'll end up sharing space in that federal pen you talked about."

Jack laughed. "No problem. We'll have the place turning a profit in no time. They'll have to let us out to deal with the IRS."

"Well, if you two have worked it out..."

"Trust us," Drew said.

Andrew smiled from one to the other. "I do."

The library door opened and Cavendish's head appeared around it, his brow knitted in a frown. "I'm sorry," he said. "But I was looking for the children. I can't find them anywhere."

"Aren't they supposed to perform any minute?" Drew asked.

Cavendish nodded. "But they've disappeared."

"Genny might know," Jack suggested.

"Well, she and Miss Sheila...that is—" Cavendish shifted uncomfortably "—they were talking and someone was crying and I didn't want to interrupt." He frowned. "But I'm beginning to get concerned."

Jack and Drew came instantly alert.

"Where are they?" Jack asked.

"Sitting on the garden wall."

Jack started for the door, Drew right behind him. They met Genny and Sheila, arm in arm, at the bottom of the stairs. Sheila's face was red and puffy from crying. Genny's was pale, her eyes empty.

Jack looked from one woman to the other, not certain what to say.

"Are you...all right?" he asked.

Genny turned to Sheila, who stared at Drew. She took a step away from her. "Speak up, Sheila," she prodded gently. "Now's the time."

Sheila tore her eyes from Drew with great effort and turned to Jack. She was composed and quiet. "I'm sorry, Jack," she said, her voice high and tight. "I've always been afraid of you because I wanted Drew to succeed Andrew, because I thought that was what he wanted and you were the only one standing in the way. You were always so smart and so controlled, and I always resented that because so much of the time I'm so scared."

"Scared?" Drew asked. "Of what?"

Sheila turned to him, her eyes darkening. "You married me to help you get what you wanted. I was afraid if you didn't get it, you wouldn't need me anymore."

Drew shook his head in surprise. "Sheila, we've come a long way from the two kids who made that deal. I thought you knew that."

"You never told me," Sheila accused.

"You're always shopping or busy with the kids."

"I thought a handsome family would advance your career."

Drew closed his eyes a moment and shook his head. When he opened them his expression had softened. "My career is very healthy. Jack and I have agreed to share the presidency. But could we forget my career for the moment and concentrate on us?"

Sheila took a hesitant step toward him. "I'd like to."

He studied her one long moment then opened his arms.

Genny heaved a sigh of relief when Sheila ran into them.

Jack took Genny's arm and pulled her to the other side of the stairs. "The nurse cures an ailing romance?" he asked with a look that condemned as well as praised.

She refused to accept the implied rebuke. "Sharing the presidency? Seems you've done a little doctoring yourself."

He nodded. "But it was on your prescription. You told me until I believed in me, it wouldn't matter what position I held, I wouldn't be a whole person. So I had enough faith in myself to risk rejection and ask Drew to be my partner—and my brother."

Genny swallowed a pointed lump in her throat. "Well done," she said softly.

"Thank you." Jack leaned a shoulder against the side of the railing. "But you were wrong about something else."

"Oh?"

"You said when I became a whole person, it wouldn't matter whether or not you and I were married."

"Jack—"

"It matters, Genny."

Genny's heart swelled with pain. "Jack, please understand. I can't—"

The sudden commotion through the front door turned all of them toward the noise. Three grubby children came running into the foyer. Francie, sobbing, launched herself at Jack. Trey and Robert ran to Drew and Sheila, both talking at once.

For a moment, the only word what made sense in all the confusion was the name "Lisette."

"Stop!" Jack ordered, raising his right hand to quiet everyone. Francie tugged on his left. He pulled at her wrist as he leaned over her, trying to calm her. "I can't understand you, Francie. Take a breath."

She tried to comply, but it came out like a sob.

"Lees is stuck!" she cried. "We went into the tunnel under the cabin to hide from you and Genny. Dani said we shouldn't but we wanted to be sisters!" Francie sobbed, her face and her hair smeared with dirt and tears. "We thought if you couldn't find us, you wouldn't be able to go home and we wouldn't have to go back to our apartment. But..." She shook her head, sobs and panic overtaking her.

"They went too far in," Trey reported calmly, though his voice shook. "Lees can't get out. I crawled in to try to get her, but she's caught on something and my arms aren't long enough to reach around her. Dani sent us for help."

Jack and Genny left at a run, Drew following with a shout over his shoulder, "Bring flashlights. Get Dad and Cavendish!"

GENNY FOLLOWED JACK through the darkness, drawn by his running footsteps and the thought of bright, sassy Lisette trapped in the frightening darkness.

When Jack's long legs ate up the ground faster than Genny could follow, Drew ran abreast of her, took her hand and pulled her with him.

Jack heard the sound of hysterical sobbing before he even cleared the cabin steps. The sound ground at his gut. Banking in the eighties had conditioned him to think and plan under pressure, then carry on with the threat of enormous losses riding on his shoulder, and to ignore success and simply move on to the next crisis. But the sound of his daughter's cries would reduce him to mush if he didn't pull himself together.

He burst through the door to find Dani standing in the the tunnel opening, in the sickly pool of light from a pocket key chain.

"Daddy!" She looked up at him, her face dirty and ghostly in the dim light. He reached down to lift her out. The room fell to utter darkness as the light in her hand went behind his neck. "We can't get her out, Daddy. And she's so scared."

Lisette's screams came loud and lustily from under the cabin. Though her obvious terror upset him, he took comfort in the fact that she was still considerably healthy, judging by the noise she created.

"All right. Give me the light." He made his voice calm to calm himself. Dani forced it into the palm of his hand. Hers felt small and cold and trembled violently.

He flashed the light into the hole to the entrance of the tunnel and felt his heart sink. It was small, smaller than the width of his shoulders.

"Lees!" he shouted.

"Daddy!" Her cry was filled with terror and trust. "Daddy, come and get me!"

"Hold on, baby." He leapt down into the hole to his shoulders and flashed the dim light into the tunnel. Lisette was farther in than the frail light could penetrate. But it illuminated the area enough to tell him that a grown man couldn't fit into it. Years of erosion had reduced the tunnel to the size of a culvert.

Lisette's sobs clouded his thinking. They could pull up the floor, but the rough planking was solidly in place and heavy. Could he find a backhoe at this hour?

"How far in is she?"

Drew's voice penetrated Jack's thoughts as he knelt on the rim of the hole.

"A good eighty feet," Jack replied.

"Tunnel's too small for you or me."

"I know." The only other solution Jack could think of was out of the question. They'd have to call for help. He didn't want to consider how long it might take.

GENNY LOOKED DOWN at Jack and the small dark opening of the tunnel, and felt everything inside her constrict.

No, she told herself. I can't do it. It would be wonderfully heroic of me if I could, but I can't. I can't. I'd end up screaming and ranting, probably frighten Lisette even more, and the tunnel would collapse from the vibration. No. I can't.

"Daddy!" Lisette wailed, her voice sounding disembodied, lost. "Daddy!"

Genny had a startling, chilling sense of déjà vu. Except that in the eternal darkness after the earthquake her own voice had called, "Mommy! Mommy!" Nausea rolled over and over in her stomach, pushed its way into her throat.

She swallowed and faced the irrefutable fact that she had no alternative. They could call for help, but how long would that take? She knew what it was like to be stuck in a dark hole, every second a terrifying eternity.

The front door burst open and the small cabin was suddenly filled with people, almost everyone carrying a flashlight. Cavendish pushed his way to the front.

"I'm going in, sir," he said, handing his light to Genny. "Out of there, gentlemen, give me some room."

Jack reached up for a light Sheila handed him, pushing Cavendish back with his other hand. "Sorry, Cavendish. You're a forty-eight tall and the hole's about a thirty-two short."

Genny sat down on the rim of the hole, letting her legs dangle into it. "I, on the other hand," she said, "am an eight, petite. Would you give me a hand, please?" She leaned forward, reaching for Jack's shoulders.

He saw her clearly in the foglike glow created by the flashlights. Despite the small smile for his benefit, she was terrified. He saw the darkness deep in her eyes fighting its way forward.

She'd worked so hard to keep it in its place, out of her way. He couldn't let her do it.

He put his hands at her waist. When she tried to lean into him he held her in place. "No," he said. "We're going to call 911 and get someone out here—"

"Who'll be as big as you are," she predicted calmly, "and still unable to fit into the tunnel. They'll have to send more help, which will take time."

As though to reaffirm the desperate need for action, Lisette's panicky cry split the tension in the cabin. "Daddy! Where are you?" The buried, disembodied sobs that were so difficult to listen to filled the room. Drew winced, Sheila held a weeping Emily and Trey, and Robert flanked Dani, awkwardly offering comfort. George had an arm around Andrew's shoulders, and Cavendish held Mrs. Pratt.

Jack wanted to scream. He wanted to rip up the floor with his bare hands. He wanted another way out. But there wasn't one. It was Genny, or the hours it might take to get heavy equipment there.

Genny wound her arms around his neck and pulled him close. "Let me do this, Jack," she said softly, her voice quivering. She swallowed. "*Help* me do this."

He leaned away to look into her face. "*Can* you do it?"

"Yes," she fibbed bravely. "If I can hear the sound of your voice while I'm in there. Help me down."

With more reluctance than he'd ever felt in his life, Jack swung her down beside him.

Genny got down on her knees in the sandy loam and looked into the hole. She could fit with a little room to wriggle around in—enough to make a normal person comfortable. But she wasn't normal. She knew the moment she crawled into the tunnel it would close around her so that she would feel it like a physical thing, squeezing her heart, her diaphragm, her lungs.

Sweat broke out on her forehead, and her hands began to shake.

"That's it," Jack said firmly. "You're not—"

But she wasn't listening to him. She was flashing her light in the tunnel, leaning into it to see.

"Lisette!" she called. Her voice was strong if a little high. "It's Genny. I'm coming!"

"Genny!" Lisette wept. "Hurry!"

On his knees beside Genny, Jack looked at her helplessly. He was afraid to touch her. If she was about to walk deliberately into the claustrophobic episode of her life he didn't want to complicate it for her by bringing it on earlier. But he needed desperately to hold her, to tell her that his overwhelming love for her over the past month was nothing compared to what pulsed in him now.

Genny looked into his eyes, saw everything any woman could want there, and wrapped her arms around his neck. "Hold me," she said fiercely. "Just for a minute, hold me." His touch was no longer confinement but freedom to her. It didn't close her in but brought out the woman she'd always known she could be— brave, confident, strong. She needed that woman now. She needed her desperately.

As Jack crushed her to him, she absorbed his love and his strength. Over his shoulder, between the silhouettes of Cavendish's head and Mrs. Pratt's, she saw the moon in the upper right pane of the cabin's small window.

It called her, reminded her of their night in the bed just beyond the draperies, of Vaughn Monroe's rolling bass promising that love could outrun anything. It opened the sky for her.

Genny pulled away, kissed him quickly and started into the tunnel.

Chapter Fifteen

Genny inched forward on her elbows. The flashlight picked out the tubular structure of her prison, small insects moving beside her and overhead, small, hairlike roots of grass and weeds dangling down, brushing her shoulders, touching her face.

She shuddered and tried to think about an open field and she and Jack on their backs on a blanket looking at the sky. It stretched on forever and a breeze blew, reminding her of how free she was.

But she couldn't hold the thought for long. Lisette screamed for her, and one quick glance around brought reality back with a crash. She was in a tunnel six feet underground, and it would now take her as long to wriggle out backward as it would to go forward and find Lisette.

Her heart thudded with dread, and sweat rolled into her eyes and plastered her dress to her back.

"Genny!" Lisette cried.

From overhead, sounding as though they were miles away and trapped in a bottle, she heard the family singing. They were out of tune, but they were there. They sang one very creative arrangement of the first chorus of a current popular tune, then voice after voice peeled off when they reached the second verse no one seemed to know.

The instant of silence terrified Genny. She looked around, saw the feet of earth confining her and slapped a grubby hand over her mouth to stop herself from screaming. She was six years old again, and only a few feet away, her mother lay dead.

She was going to fail. She knew it. Not only would she not

reach Lisette, but she would die right here, wedged into the tunnel and make Lisette's rescue impossible.

"Genny!" It was Jack's voice, strong, near.

She wanted to answer but it would require so much air and she seemed to have so little. She turned the light off, hoping the darkness would lessen her feeling of capture.

"Genny, I love you!" he shouted. "I'm waiting for you, Genny."

"Mommy! Mommy, are you there?"

The child's voice was so clear. It was her own of twenty-two years ago, calling desperately in the darkness for the sound of her mother's voice—the mother who'd spoken to her only moments ago, but who now lay cold and still.

"Mommy, did you find Lees? Bring her back, Mom."

Lees. Lisette. Still somewhere ahead of her in the overwhelming darkness. The voice was Francie. She hadn't crossed over, Genny realized with a wry sense of fatality. She was still very much alive and trapped in her worst nightmare. But so was Lisette. And she couldn't let Francie's call go unanswered.

She gathered all her strength to draw a shallow breath and shouted back. "I'm here, Francie!"

"Mom, I'm scared," Francie cried. "Hurry up!"

In the darkness, Genny had to allow herself a feeble laugh. "Hurry up, Gen," she muttered to herself. "Get the lead out."

"Are you okay, Genny?" Jack asked.

That drew another wry laugh. Was she okay? As compared to Jonah in the belly of the whale? Maybe. He, at least, had the good fortune to be regurgitated. She would have to find her own way out of this earthly belly.

"Genny!" Jack's voice again, demanding, frightened.

"I'm okay!" she shouted back.

"Genny?" This voice was high and frail and directly ahead of her. "Why did the light go out?"

Genny flipped the flashlight on again, careful to look ahead and not up or to the side. Lisette was still several yards away.

"Better?" Genny asked.

"Yes." Lisette stretched a grubby hand toward her.

Genny inched her way toward it, her own hand outstretched the last few inches until their fingers laced together and Lisette screamed in relief.

"Genny!" Jack shouted.

"It's okay!" she called back. "I've reached her!"

Genny propelled herself forward with her other elbow until she and Lisette were hugging, the child sobbing as she clutched the shoulder of Genny's dress.

I haven't failed, Genny realized in amazement. I haven't succeeded yet, but I'm halfway there.

The musical repertoire from overhead changed to blues. It sounded as though Emily were in control.

"I'm stuck, Genny," Lisette wailed. "I think something's caught on my pocket."

Genny reached over the girl's slender back to her thin hips, groping for the pocket of her pants. She could feel nothing there. She reached back up and struck a strong, gnarly root, probably of one of the birches near the back of the cabin. It appeared to be caught in the belt loop of Lisette's jeans.

Laboriously in the tight quarters, Genny switched the light from one hand to the other and shined it over Lisette's head to the back of her jeans. The loop was simply hooked. She rested the light on Lisette's back, gave the root a strong pull and freed the loop.

A large clump of dirt loosened and fell on them with a plop. Both screamed as loose earth rained down on them for several seconds.

"Genny!" Lisette cried.

Genny fought herself and her circumstances for clear thought. If anything could have galvanized her into hurrying out the way she'd come, that did it.

She shimmied backward, and Lisette needed little encouragement to follow.

The way back was hard on Genny's bare legs. Her stockings were now shreds, and the backward movement kept the skirt of her dress up around her waist. Rocks and roots scraped and gouged her thighs and knees.

She stopped halfway back, her eyes spilling tears. It was taking an eternity, and she didn't know how long she could hold the panic at bay. Everything hurt. The muscles in her arms ached with the effort of pulling and pushing her body, her elbows and her knees were scraped raw. Her eyes and her lungs burned with dirt and tears.

"I'm sorry, Genny," Lisette whispered tearfully, holding on to her like a little leech. "We just wanted you to stay with Dad. I promise," she said on a sob, "if you become my mother, I'll never crawl into a tunnel again."

Genny kissed her grubby cheek. "I'll hold you to that. But first, we've got to get out of here."

The strains of "Racing With the Moon" drifted down into the tunnel.

Lisette shook her head in confusion. "Why are they singing, anyway?"

"To help me," Genny replied. She laughed breathlessly. "It isn't so dark in here when you can hear the music, is it?"

Lisette listened as someone hit a sour note. She smiled. "They're pretty awful, aren't they?"

Genny thought about Cavendish, who'd have come in for Lisette himself if the tunnel had accommodated his girth, or Mrs. Pratt who finally put her past aside to love him, of Andrew and Emily, both deserving of so much, of Drew and Sheila finding their way back to what had once been a hopeful relationship, of Trey and Robert, so bright and clever and needing a dose of nondesigner living, of beautiful Dani, full of life, and poor, kindly George who'd almost thrown away his future to assure that it wouldn't be lonely.

"They're pretty wonderful," Genny corrected. "Come on. Let's get back to them."

JACK, ON HIS KNEES in front of the tunnel entrance, thought he'd never seen a more beautiful sight than the soles of Genny's feet, followed by the wriggle of her pink-lace-covered posterior backing toward him.

He reached in to brace a hand under her waist and one under her thighs and slide her out of the hole. Lisette, face smudged with dirt and tears, appeared immediately and he grabbed her upper arms and pulled her out.

Screams and shouts and laughter filled the small cabin, but Jack didn't notice. On his knees in the hole with Genny in one arm and Lisette in the other, he held on to them with the fierceness engendered by almost having lost them. He forgot that Genny might welcome room to breathe, and that he'd intended to scold Lisette for such a foolish action. The way she clung to him made that seem unnecessary, anyway.

Then Dani and Francie squeezed into the hole, forcing their way into the tight circle.

Dani hugged her sister while Francie wrapped Genny in a death grip. Jack closed his eyes and offered up a thankful prayer. Nothing this world had to offer, he thought, could give him the joy he felt at this moment—nothing he could ask for himself could give him the sense of fulfillment he felt.

For the first time, Genny understood the freedom of love. It was a paradoxical fact that its powerful demands freed her of the enslaving tyrannies of fear. It forced one to rise above all that would hold him down so that he was free to offer, to give, to love. That truth settled over her like a comfortable blanket. She hadn't defeated her claustrophobia tonight, but she'd showed it who was boss.

Lisette already dry-eyed and telling Dani and Francie with more excitement than regret all that had transpired in the tunnel, Jack turned to Genny.

He kissed her tenderly. "Thank you," he whispered.

Her smile glowed as she nuzzled into his neck. "Sure," she said.

"Hey."

Jack looked up to find Drew on his knees on the rim of the hole.

"You turning into a troglodyte," Drew asked, "or you want to pass the girls up so we can all go home?" He tugged on Lisette's arm. "Come on, you little varmint. I'll carry you."

Cavendish and Emily led the way back with flashlights clearing Drew's path. Sheila followed with the boys, Dani and George.

In the cabin, Andrew pulled Genny out of the hole then reached down for Francie, then Jack. He closed the trapdoor with a slam and pulled the rug and table back in place. "That's it!" he said. "I hate to disturb the cabin, but I'm having that tunnel filled. God Almighty! This night's taken years off my life!"

That was a sentiment Jack could share. He swept Genny up in his arms and followed his father, who led off with the light. Francie and Mrs. Pratt followed behind.

Genny clung to Jack's neck, unable to think, only to feel.

Jack's grip on her was so tight it would have hurt had it not told
her how much he loved her—had she not lived a lifetime needing
just this kind of a welcome back from the darkness.

In the house, Emily and Dani took Lisette upstairs for a bath.
Jack, carrying Genny and trailed by Francie, hurried up the stairs
into Genny's room. Sheila put a stack of towels and a lacy white
negligee on the foot of the bed.

"Thank you, Sheila," Genny said.

"Sure," Sheila replied with a quick, genuine smile, then left
the room.

Jack placed Genny in the middle of the bed. "I'm going to
run you a bath," he said, leaning over her. "Don't move from
here."

She wasn't sure she could if she wanted to. Everything was
beginning to hurt.

"Okay," she said.

He frowned worriedly and stroked the bangs back from her
forehead. "You're sure you're all right?"

"Just stiff," she assured him. "I don't make a habit of crawling around in tunnels."

Jack pulled Francie onto the edge of the bed. "Keep your eye
on your mom, okay?"

Francie waited until Jack had disappeared into the bathroom
and turned the taps on. Then she turned to Genny, her eyes wide
as saucers. "Mom!" she whispered loudly. "He carried you up
the stairs!"

Genny smiled, touching Francie's face, knowing she could
give her what she wanted at last. "Yes, I know."

Francie caught her hand and held it in both of hers. "We won't
find a better dad, Mom. Please! Please!"

Genny sat up to hug her. "Okay, okay. You go check on Lees.
I need a little privacy."

"Are you gonna ask him to marry you?"

"Yes."

"Can I tell Lees?"

"You'd better wait until..."

But Francie was already at the bedroom door, turning to blow
her a kiss, then running off to tell Lisette she was about to ac-
quire a mother. Genny hoped it was true.

"Wait until what?" Jack walked into the room, the sleeves of his dirty dress shirt rolled up to his elbows. "Where's she going?"

He pulled Genny gently onto her feet and unzipped her torn and soiled dress.

"I asked her to leave," she said, moving obediently as he turned her around and stripped the tattered dress from her. "I wanted to talk to you alone."

About why she couldn't marry him, he guessed. He didn't want to think about that now. He wanted to just look at her, safe if a little bruised and dusty. He wanted to relish what she'd done for him—pretend for a few moments that she belonged to him and he had the right to put her in a warm tub and rub her down.

He stripped her slip and underwear off. "What about?" he asked with clinical detachment.

He lifted her in his arms and carried her into the bathroom—his jaw set, his manner distant.

Genny wondered for an awful moment if those were indications of how he truly felt. Then she remembered his embrace when she'd come out of the tunnel and knew he loved her. It was only then that it occurred to her that she hadn't told him she loved him, too.

Genny blew lightly into his ear. "I want to talk about tiger lilies," she said. "Mufflers." She nipped his ear lobe. "The opera."

He uttered a small gasp that she covered with her open mouth. After a moment she drew away. "Tuxedos," she whispered. With a sigh of utter and complete happiness, she snuggled into his shoulder, "and being carried up the stairs."

Jack leaned over to put her into a foot and a half of warm water. Her hands remained locked behind his neck, her eyes filled with love and joy and hope. He lost himself in them, almost afraid to believe she meant what they told him.

"The daddy deal," he whispered, feeling he had to caution her, "is going to put you in a tight spot. I'll love you like no man has ever loved a woman, but I'll never let you go."

She pulled him toward her. "Then draw up the contract. I have plans to broaden my horizons, and I'm taking you with me."

"Really?" Realizing he was about to land in the tub, fully

clothed, Jack stepped out of his shoes. "How far are we going?"
he asked with a laugh.

She gave him a firm tug until he was in the water with her,
slacks and all. He knelt astride her, blocking her escape. She felt
no confinement, only security.

So happy it hurt, Genny reached up for Jack's kiss and whispered, "Till we're racing with the moon."

Harlequin Romance

Delightful

Affectionate

Romantic

Emotional

Tender

Original

Daring

Riveting

Enchanting

Adventurous

Moving

Harlequin Romance—the
series that has it all!

HROM-G

LOOK FOR OUR FOUR FABULOUS MEN!

Each month some of today's bestselling authors bring
four new fabulous men to Harlequin American Romance.
Whether they're rebel ranchers, millionaire power brokers
or sexy single dads, they're all gallant princes—and
they're all ready to sweep you into lighthearted fantasies
and contemporary fairy tales where anything is possible
and where all your dreams come true!

You don't even have to make a wish...
Harlequin American Romance will grant your every desire!

Look for Harlequin American Romance
wherever Harlequin books are sold!

Harlequin® Historical

From rugged lawmen and
valiant knights to defiant heiresses
and spirited frontierswomen,
Harlequin Historicals will
capture your imagination with
their dramatic scope, passion
and adventure.

Harlequin Historicals…
they're too good to miss!

HARLEQUIN PRESENTS®

HARLEQUIN PRESENTS
men you won't be able to resist
falling in love with...

HARLEQUIN PRESENTS
women who have feelings
just like your own...

HARLEQUIN PRESENTS
powerful passion in
exotic international settings...

HARLEQUIN PRESENTS
intense, dramatic stories that will keep you
turning to the very last page...

HARLEQUIN PRESENTS
The world's bestselling romance series!

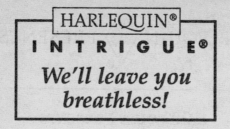

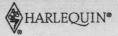

Not The Same Old Story!

Exciting, glamorous romance stories that take readers around the world.

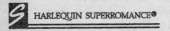
Sparkling, fresh and tender love stories that bring you pure romance.

Bold and adventurous— Temptation is strong women, bad boys, great sex!

HARLEQUIN SUPERROMANCE®
Provocative and realistic stories that celebrate life and love.

Contemporary fairy tales—where anything is possible and where dreams come true.

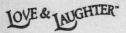
Heart-stopping, suspenseful adventures that combine the best of romance and mystery.

LOVE & LAUGHTER™
Humorous and romantic stories that capture the lighter side of love.